T. A. BARRON

THE SEVEN SONGS OF
MERLIN

BOOK TWO OF
THE LOST YEARS OF MERLIN

PHILOMEL BOOKS ◆ NEW YORK

Text copyright © 1997 by Thomas A. Barron
Frontispiece illustration copyright © 1997 by Mike Wimmer
Map illustration copyright © 1996 by Ian Schoenherr
All rights reserved. This book, or parts thereof, may not be reproduced in any form
without permission in writing from the publisher, Philomel Books, a division of
The Putnam & Grosset Group, 200 Madison Avenue, New York, NY 10016.
Philomel Books, Reg. U.S. Pat, & Tm. Off. Published simultaneously in Canada
Printed in the United States of America.
Book design by Gunta Alexander. Text set in Galliard
Library of Congress Cataloging-in-Publication Data
Barron, T. A. The seven songs of Merlin / by T. A. Barron.   p.   cm.
"Volume two of 'The lost years of Merlin'"
Summary: Having stumbled upon his hidden powers, the young wizard Merlin
voyages to the Otherworld in his quest to find himself and the way to the
realm of the spirit.   1. Merlin (Legendary character)—Juvenile fiction.
[1. Merlin (Legendary character)—Fiction.   2. Wizards—Fiction.   3. Fantasy.]
I. Title.   PZ7.B27567Sev   1997   [Fic]—dc21   97-9619   CIP   AC
ISBN 0-399-23019-X   10 9 8 7 6 5 4 3 2 1   First Impression

This book is dedicated to
Currie
who sings her life as if it were a verse
of the seventh Song

with special appreciation to
Ross
age two, who sees so well with his heart

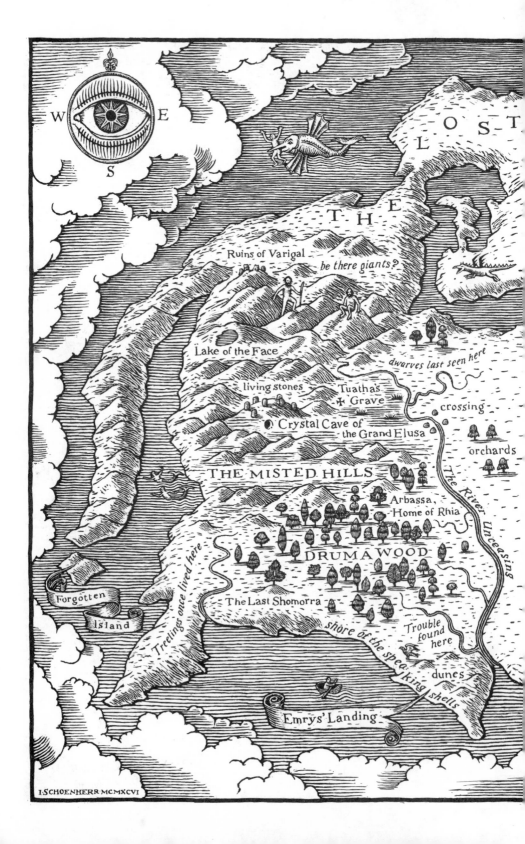

W · E
S

L O S T

T H E

Ruins of Varigal

be there giants?

Lake of the Face

dwarves last seen here

living stones

Tuatha's
Grave

crossing

Crystal Cave of
the Grand Elusa

orchards

THE MISTED HILLS

Arbassa,
Home of Rhia

Treelings once lived here

DRUMA WOOD

The River Unceasing

Forgotten

Island

The Last Shomorra

Trouble
found
here

shore of the speaking shells

dunes

Emrys' Landing

I·SCHOENHERR·MCMXCVI

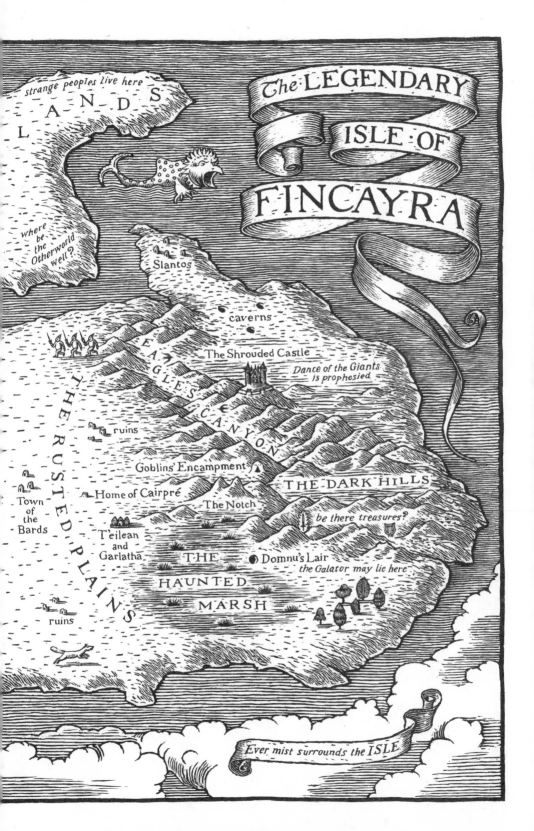

CONTENTS

PART THREE

AUTHOR'S NOTE

Sometimes, in the long hours before dawn, I lie awake, listening. To the boughs of cottonwood, stirring in the wind. To the great horned owl, hooting quietly. And, on rare occasions, to the voice of Merlin, whispering. Before I could even begin to hear Merlin's voice—let alone hear it clearly enough to tell the tale of his lost youth—I needed to learn a little. And to unlearn a lot. Most of all, I needed to listen with care, using more than just my ears. For this wizard is full of surprises.

The Lost Years of Merlin, volume one of this sequence, revealed the strange events that began his years lost from time. Why should those years have disappeared from the traditional lore, only to come to light now, centuries later? The answer may have something to do with the profound changes—and terrible pain—that Merlin himself experienced in that period. Yet those years proved to be exceptionally important ones for the person who would one day serve as the mentor to King Arthur.

The story of Merlin's lost years began when, as a boy at the very edge of death, he washed ashore on the rugged coast of Wales. The sea had robbed him of everything he had once known. Completely unaware that he would, one day, become the greatest wizard of all time, he lay tormented by the shadows of things he could not recall. For he had no memory. No home. And no name.

From Merlin's own words, we can feel the lasting trauma, and hidden hope, of that day:

> *If I close my eyes, and breathe to the rolling rhythm of the sea, I can still remember that long ago day. Harsh, cold, and lifeless it was, as empty of promise as my lungs were empty of air.*
>
> *Since that day, I have seen many others, more than I have the strength left to count. Yet that day glows as bright as the Galator itself, as bright as the day I found my own name, or the day I first cradled a baby who bore the name Arthur.*
>
> *Perhaps I remember it so clearly because the pain, like a scar on my soul, will not disappear. Or because it marked the ending of so much. Or, perhaps, because it marked a beginning as well as an ending: the beginning of my lost years.*

Now the young Merlin's story continues. He may have solved the riddle of the Dance of the Giants, but a dark knot of riddles lies just ahead. Whether he can successfully pull them apart, in time to complete his quest, remains to be seen. The challenge is enormous. While Merlin has stumbled upon his hidden powers, he has not nearly mastered them. While he has heard some of the wisdom of the Druids, the Greeks, and the Celts, he has only begun to understand it. And while he has discovered his own name, and a hint of his true destiny, he has yet to find the secret of his innermost self.

In short, he does not yet know what it means to be a wizard.

If he is to find the wizard in himself, the young Merlin, who has already lost so much, must lose something more. Along the way, he may gain a few things, as well. He may finally learn the truth about his friend Rhia. He may grasp the difference between sight and insight. He may even find, to his sorrow, that he holds both the dark and the light within himself—even as he finds, to his joy, that he also holds other qualities often called opposites: youth and age, male and female, mortal and immortal.

Legendary heroes sometimes ascend through the three levels of self, world, and Otherworld. First he or she must discover the hidden pathways within. Next the hero must triumph over the enemies of mortal life on Earth. Finally, he or she must confront the perils and possibilities of the spirit. In a sense, Merlin alters this traditional pattern by attempting to voyage to the Otherworld in this book, only the second volume of the sequence. But Merlin, as we have seen, is not very good at following the rules. The truth is that in this book, as in the others, Merlin finds himself exploring all three levels at once.

Yet it is the Otherworld, the realm of the spirit, that holds the key to this quest. It is a mysterious place, rarely visited by mortals, full of danger as well as inspiration. If Merlin can somehow master the Seven Songs of Wizardry, defeat the same forces that destroyed his own grandfather, and discover the secret of the Otherworld Well, he could indeed find his way to the spiritual realm. If he does, he may meet both the mysterious Dagda and the treacherous Rhita Gawr . . . and whatever might be left of his loyal friend Trouble.

And, in the process, he may find something more. As W. B. Yeats once wrote, humanity has always yearned to find some connection with the cosmic order, "to reunite the perception of the spirit, of the divine, with natural beauty." That is why the young Merlin, who first sensed his own powers of renewal by riding out a storm in the branches of a tree, struggles to make such a connection as he follows the winding path to wizardry.

This portion of Merlin's journey begins where the last one ended, on the legendary isle of Fincayra. The Celts believed it to be an island beneath the waves, a halfway point between this world and the Otherworld. An *omphalos*, the Greeks might say. But Fincayra's best description came from Elen, Merlin's mother, who called it simply an *in between place*. Like the mist, which is neither quite water nor quite air, Fincayra is neither quite mortal nor quite immortal. It is something in between.

Merlin, too, is something in between. He is not truly a man, yet not truly a god. He is not really old, yet not really young. Carl Jung would have found him a compelling character, for Merlin's mythic powers sprang from both the unconscious and the conscious, just as his wisdom flowed from both nature and culture.

It is no accident that the most ancient tales of Merlin give him a saintly mother and a demonic father, metaphors for the light and the dark sides within us all. And Merlin's greatest wisdom came not from expelling or eliminating his dark side, but rather from embracing it, owning it as part of himself. Ultimately, it is this sense of human frailty, along with human possibility, that makes Merlin the fitting mentor for King Arthur.

I remain deeply grateful to all those people named in the Author's Note of the first volume, most especially my wife and best friend, Currie, and my immensely wise editor, Patricia Lee Gauch. In addition, I would like to thank Lloyd Alexander, whose works continue to inspire us all; Susan Cullinan, who understands the wisdom of humor; and Sasha, our gentle Labrador, who often warms my feet as I write.

Once again, Merlin whispers. Let us listen, but with care. For this wizard, as we know, is full of surprises.

T. A. B.

I was taken out of my true self.
I was a spirit and knew…
the secrets of nature,
bird flight,
star wanderings,
and the way fish glide.

—Merlin,
    quoted in Geoffrey of Monmouth's
    twelfth-century book *VITA MERLINI*

PROLOGUE

How the centuries have flown . . . Faster, by far, than the brave hawk who once bore me on his back. Faster, indeed, than the arrow of pain that lodged in my heart on the day I lost my mother.

Still I can see the Great Council of Fincayra, gathering in the circle of standing stones, all that remained of the mighty castle after the Dance of the Giants. Not for many ages had a Great Council been called on that spot; not for many ages would one be called again. Several difficult questions awaited resolution by the delegates, including how to punish the fallen monarch, and whether or not to choose a successor. But the gravest question of all was what to do with the enchanted Treasures of Fincayra, especially the Flowering Harp.

I cannot forget how the meeting began. Nor, hard as I try, can I forget how it ended.

A cluster of shadows more dark than the night, the circle of stones stood erect on the ridge.

No stirring, no sound, disturbed the night air. A lone bat swooped toward the ruins, then veered away, perhaps out of fear that the Shrouded Castle might somehow rise again. But all that remained of its towers and battlements was the ring of standing stones, as silent as abandoned graves.

Slowly, a strange light began rippling over the stones. It was not the light of the sun, still hours from rising, but of the stars overhead. Bit by bit the stars grew steadily brighter. It seemed as if they were somehow drawing nearer, pressing closer to the circle, watching with a thousand thousand eyes aflame.

A broad-winged moth, as yellow as butter, alighted on one of the stones. Soon it was joined by a pale blue bird, and an ancient horned owl missing many feathers. Something slithered across a fallen pillar, keeping to the shadows. A pair of fauns, with the legs and hoofs of goats and the chests and faces of boys, gamboled into the clearing inside the circle. Next came the walking trees, ashes and oaks and hawthorns and pines, sweeping across the ridge like a dark green tide.

Seven Fincayran men and women, their eyes full of wonder, stepped into the circle alongside a band of red-bearded dwarves, a black stallion, several ravens, a pair of water nymphs raucously splash-ing each other in a pool beneath one of the stones, a speckled lizard, popinjays, peacocks, a unicorn whose coat shone as white as her horn, a family of green beetles who had brought their own leaf to sit on, a doe with her fawn, a huge snail, and a phoenix who stared at the crowd continuously without ever blinking.

As more delegates arrived, one of the Fincayrans, a shaggy-headed poet with a tall brow and dark, observant eyes, stood watching the scene unfold. In time, he stepped over to a tumbled pillar and sat down next to a robust girl dressed in a suit of woven vines. On her other side sat a boy, holding a twisted staff, who looked older than his thirteen years. His eyes, blacker than charcoal, seemed strangely distant. He had recently taken to calling himself Merlin.

Screeching and fluttering, buzzing and growling, hissing and bellowing filled the air. As the sun rose higher, painting the circle of stones with golden hues, the din rose higher as well. The cacophonous noise subsided only once, when an enormous white spider, more than twice as big as the stallion, entered the ring. As the other creatures hushed, they moved quickly aside, for while they might have felt honored to be joined by the legendary Grand Elusa, they also suspected that she might well have worked up an appetite on her journey from her crystal cave in the Misted Hills. She had no difficulty finding a seat.

As the Grand Elusa positioned herself on a heap of crushed rock, she scratched the hump on her back with one of her eight legs. Using another leg, she pulled a large, brown sack off her back and placed it by her side. Then she glanced around the circle, pausing for an instant to gaze at Merlin.

Still more came. A centaur, wearing a beard that fell almost down to his hooves, strode solemnly into the ring. A pair of foxes, tails held high, pranced in his wake, followed by a young wood elf with arms and legs nearly as wispy as her nut brown hair. A living stone, splotched with moss, rolled into the center, barely missing a slow-moving hedgehog. A swarm of energetic bees hovered close to the ground. Near the edge, a family of ogres viciously scratched and bit each other to pass the time.

And still more came, many Merlin could not identify. Some looked like bristling bushes with fiery eyes, others resembled twisted sticks or clumps of mud, and still others seemed invisible but for a vague shimmer of light they cast on the stones. He saw creatures with bizarre faces, dangerous faces, curious faces, or no faces at all. In less than an hour, the silent ring of stones had transformed into something more like a carnival.

The poet, Cairpré, did his best to answer Merlin's questions about the strange and wondrous creatures surrounding them. That, he explained, was a snow hen, who remained as elusive as a moonbeam. And that, a glyn-mater, who ate food only once every six hundred years—and then only the leaves of the tendradil flower. Some creatures he could not recognize were known by the leaf-draped girl, Rhia, from her years in Druma Wood. Yet there remained several that neither Cairpré nor Rhia could identify.

That came as no surprise. No one alive, except possibly the Grand Elusa, had ever seen all of the diverse residents of Fincayra. Soon after the Dance of the Giants had occurred, toppling the wicked king Stangmar and destroying his Shrouded Castle, the call had risen from many quarters to convene a Great Council. For the first time in living memory, all the mortal citizens of Fincayra, whether bird or beast or insect or something else entirely, were invited to send representatives to an assembly.

Almost every race had responded. The few missing ones included the warrior goblins and shifting wraiths, who had been driven back into the caves of the Dark Hills after the defeat of Stangmar; the treelings, who had disappeared from the land long ago; and the mer people, who inhabited the waters surrounding Fincayra but could not be found in time to be invited.

After studying the crowd, Cairpré observed sadly that the great canyon eagles, one of the oldest races on Fincayra, were also not present. In ancient times the stirring cry of a canyon eagle always marked the beginning of a Great Council. Not this time, however, since the forces of Stangmar had hunted the proud birds to extinction. That cry, Cairpré concluded, would never again echo among the hills of this land.

Merlin then glimpsed a pale, bulbous hag with no hair on her head and no mercy in her eyes. He shivered with recognition. Although she had taken many names across the ages, she was most often called Domnu, meaning Dark Fate. No sooner had he caught sight of her than she vanished into the throng. He knew she was avoiding him. He also knew why.

Suddenly a great rumbling, even louder than the noise of the assembly, shook the ridge. One of the standing stones wobbled precariously. The rumbling grew still louder, causing the stone to crash to the ground, almost crushing the doe and fawn. Merlin and Rhia looked at each other—not with fright, but with understanding. For they had heard the footsteps of giants before.

Two gargantuan figures, each as tall as the castle that had once stood on this spot, strode up to the circle. From far away in the mountains they had come, leaving the rebuilding of their ancestral city of Varigal long enough to join the Great Council. Merlin turned, hoping to find his friend Shim. But Shim was not among the new arrivals. The boy sighed, telling himself that Shim would probably have slept through the meeting anyway.

The first giant, a wild-haired female with bright green eyes and a crooked mouth, grunted and bent down to pick up the fallen stone. Although twenty horses would have strained to move it, she placed it back in position without any difficulty. Meanwhile, her companion, a ruddy-skinned fellow with arms as thick as oak trunks, placed his hands on his hips and surveyed the scene. After a long moment, he gave her a nod.

She nodded in return. Then, with another grunt, she lifted both of her hands into the air, seeming to grasp at the streaming clouds. Seeing this, Cairpré raised his bushy eyebrows in puzzlement.

High in the sky, a tiny black dot appeared. Out of the clouds it spiraled, as if caught in an invisible whirlpool. Lower and lower it came, until every eye of every creature in the circle was trained on it. A new hush blanketed the assembly. Even the irrepressible water nymphs fell silent.

The dot grew larger as it descended. Soon massive wings could be seen, then a broad tail, then sunlight glinting on a hooked beak. A sudden screech ripped the air, echoing from one ridge to another, until the land itself seemed to be answering the call. The call of a canyon eagle.

The powerful wings spread wide, stretching out like a sail. Then the wings angled backward, as enormous talons thrust toward the ground. Rabbits and foxes squealed at the sight, and many more beasts cringed. With a single majestic flap, the great canyon eagle settled on the shoulder of the wild-haired giant.

The Great Council of Fincayra had begun.

As the first order of business, the delegates agreed that no one should leave the meeting until all the questions had been decided. Also, at the request of the mice, each of the delegates promised not to eat anyone else during the course of the proceedings. Only the foxes objected to this idea, arguing that the question of what to do with the Flowering Harp alone could take several days to resolve. Even so, the rule was adopted. To ensure compliance, the Grand

Elusa herself kindly offered to enforce it. Though she never said just how she planned to do that, no one seemed inclined to ask her.

As its next act, the assembly declared the circle of stones itself a sacred monument. Clearing her throat with the subtlety of a rock slide, the wild-haired giant proposed that the ruins of the Shrouded Castle receive a new name: Dance of the Giants, or *Estonahenj* in the giants' own ancient tongue. The assembled delegates adopted the name unanimously, though a heavy silence fell over the circle. For while the Dance of the Giants signified Fincayra's hope for a brighter future, it was the kind of hope that springs only from the most profound sorrow.

In time, the discussion turned to the fate of Stangmar. While the wicked king had been overthrown, his life had been saved—by none other than Merlin, his only son. Although Merlin himself, being only part Fincayran, was not allowed to voice his own views at the assembly, the poet Cairpré offered to speak on his behalf. After hearing the boy's plea that his father's life, no matter how wretched, should be spared, the Great Council argued for hours. Finally, over the strong objections of the giants and the canyon eagle, the assembly decided that Stangmar should be imprisoned for the rest of his days in one of the inescapable caverns north of the Dark Hills.

Next came the question of who should rule Fincayra. The bees suggested that their own queen could rule everyone, but that notion found no support. So fresh was the agony of Stangmar's kingship that many delegates spoke passionately against having any leader at all. Not even a parliament of citizens would do, they argued, for in time power always corrupts. Cairpré, for his part, denounced such thinking as folly. He cited examples of anarchy that had brought ruin to other peoples, and warned that without any leadership at all Fincayra would again fall prey to that nefarious warlord of the Otherworld, Rhita Gawr. Yet most of the delegates dismissed his concerns. The Great Council voted overwhelmingly to do without any leadership whatsoever.

Then came the gravest question of all. What should be done with the Treasures of Fincayra?

As everyone watched in awe, the Grand Elusa opened the sack by her side and removed the Flowering Harp. Its oaken sound box, inlaid with ash and carved with floral designs, gleamed eerily. A green butterfly wafted over and alighted on its smallest string. With the swipe of one enormous leg, the Grand Elusa shooed the butterfly away, causing the string to tinkle gently. After pausing to listen, she then removed the rest of the Treasures: the sword Deepercut, the Caller of Dreams, the Orb of Fire, and six of the Seven Wise Tools (the seventh one, alas, had been lost in the collapse of the castle).

All eyes examined the Treasures. For a long interval, no one stirred. The stones themselves seemed to lean forward to get a closer look. The delegates knew that, long before the rise of Stangmar, these fabled Treasures had belonged to all Fincayrans, and were shared freely throughout the land. Yet that had left the Treasures vulnerable to thievery, as Stangmar had demonstrated. A spotted hare suggested that each Treasure ought to have a guardian, someone responsible for guarding it and seeing that it was used wisely. That way the Treasures could be shared, but still protected. Most of the representatives agreed. They urged the Grand Elusa to choose the guardians.

The great spider, however, declined. She declared that only someone much wiser could make such important selections. It would take a true wizard—someone like Tuatha, whose knowledge had been so vast, it was said, that he had even found a secret pathway to the Otherworld to consult with Dagda, greatest of all the spirits. But Tuatha had died years ago. In the end, after much urging, the Grand Elusa agreed to watch over the Treasures in her crystal cave, but only until the right guardians could be found.

While that solved the problem of the Treasures for the time being, it did not answer the question of the Flowering Harp. The surrounding countryside, afflicted by the Blight of Rhita Gawr, showed no sign of life, not even a sprig of green grass. The Dark Hills, especially, needed help, for the damage there had been the most severe. Only the magic of the Harp could revive the land.

Yet who should be the one to carry it? The Harp had not been played for many years, since Tuatha himself had used it to heal the forest destroyed by the dragon of the Lost Lands. While that forest had eventually returned to life, Tuatha had admitted that playing the Harp had required even more of his skill than lulling the enraged dragon into enchanted sleep. The Harp, he had warned, would only respond to the touch of someone with the heart of a wizard.

The oldest of the peacocks was the first to try. Spreading his radiant tail feathers to the widest, he strutted over to the Harp and lowered his head. With a swift stroke of his beak, he plucked one of the strings. A pure, resonant tone poured forth, lingering in the air. But nothing else happened. The Harp's magic lay dormant. Again the peacock tried, again with no result beyond a single note.

One by one, several other delegates came forward. The unicorn, her white coat glistening, slid her horn across the strings. A stirring chord resulted, but nothing more. Then came an immense brown bear, a dwarf whose beard fell below his knees, a sturdy-looking woman, and one of the water nymphs, all without success.

At last, a tan-colored toad hopped out of the shadows by Merlin's feet and over to the Grand Elusa. Stopping just beyond the great spider's reach, the toad rasped, "You may not be a wizarrrrd yourrrrself, but I rrrreally believe you have the hearrrrt of one. Would you carrrry the Harrrrp?"

The Grand Elusa merely shook her head. Lifting three of her legs, she pointed in the direction of Cairpré.

"Me?" sputtered the poet. "You can't be serious! I have no more the heart of a wizard than the head of a pig. *My knowledge so spare, my wisdom too rare.* I could never make the Harp respond." Stroking his chin, he turned to the boy by his side. "But I can think of someone else who might."

"The boy?" growled the brown bear skeptically, even as the boy himself shifted with unease.

"I don't know whether he has the heart of a wizard," Cairpré acknowledged, with a sidelong glance at Merlin. "I doubt even he knows."

The bear slammed his paw against the ground. "Then why do you propose him?"

The poet almost smiled. "Because I think there is more to him than meets the eye. He did, after all, destroy the Shrouded Castle. Let him try his hand with the Harp."

"I agree," declared a slender owl with a snap of her jaws. "He is the grandson of Tuatha."

"And the son of Stangmar," roared the bear. "Even if he can awaken its magic, he cannot be trusted."

Into the center of the circle stepped the wood elf, her nut brown hair rippling like a stream. She bowed slightly to Rhia, who returned the gesture. Then, in a lilting voice, she addressed the group. "The boy's father I know not, though I am told that, in his youth, he often played in Druma Wood. And, like the twisted tree that might have grown straight and tall, I cannot say whether the fault lay with him or with the elders who did not give him their support. Yet I did know the boy's mother. We called her Elen of the Sapphire Eyes. She healed me once, when I was aflame with fever. There was magic in her touch, more magic than even she understood. Perhaps her son has the same gift. I say we should let him try the Harp."

A wave of agreement flowed through the assembly. The bear paced back and forth, grumbling to himself, but finally did not object.

As Merlin rose from the pillar, Rhia wrapped her leaf-draped arm around his own. He glanced at her gratefully, then stepped slowly over to the Harp. As he carefully retrieved it, cradling the sound box in his arms, the assembled delegates fell silent once again. The boy drew a deep breath, raised his hand, and plucked one of the strings. A deep note hung in the air, vibrating, for a long moment.

Sensing nothing remarkable had happened, Merlin turned a disappointed face toward Rhia and Cairpré. The brown bear growled in satisfaction. All at once, the canyon eagle, still perched on the giant's shoulder, screeched. Others joined the cry, roaring and howling and thumping with enthusiasm. For there, curling over the toe of Merlin's own boot, was a single blade of grass, as green as a rain-washed sapling. He smiled and plucked the string again, causing several more blades of grass to spring forth.

When, at last, the commotion subsided, Cairpré strode over to Merlin and clasped his hand. "Well done, my boy, well done." Then he paused. "It is a grave responsibility, you know, healing the lands."

Merlin swallowed. "I know."

"Once you begin this task, you must not rest until it is finished. Even now, the forces of Rhita Gawr are making plans for a renewed assault. You may be certain of that! The Dark Hills, where many of the forces lie hidden in caves and crevasses, are the lands most scarred from Blight—and also most vulnerable to attack. Our best protection is to restore the hills quickly so that peaceful creatures may return there to live. That will discourage the invaders, and also ensure that the rest of Fincayra will have warning of any attack."

He tapped the oaken instrument gently. "So you must begin in the Dark Hills—and remain there until the job is done. Save the Rusted Plains, and the other lands yearning to live again, until later. The Dark Hills must be healed before Rhita Gawr returns, or we will have lost our only chance."

He chewed his lip thoughtfully. "And one thing more, my boy. Rhita Gawr, when he does return, will be looking for you. To show his gratitude for how much trouble you have caused him. So avoid doing anything that might attract his attention. Just stick to your work, healing the Dark Hills."

"But what if, after I've left here, I can't make the Harp work?"

"If the Harp simply does not respond to your touch, we will understand. But remember: If you can make it work but shirk your task, you will never be forgiven."

Merlin nodded slowly. As the delegates looked on, he started to slip the Harp's leather sling over his shoulder.

"Wait!"

It was the voice of the hag, Domnu. Advancing toward the boy, she opened wide her eyes, sending waves of wrinkles across the top of her scalp. Then she lifted her arm and pointed a knobby finger at him. "The half-human boy cannot carry the Harp. He must leave this island! For if he stays, Fincayra is doomed."

Nearly everyone cringed at her words, none more than Merlin himself. They carried strange power, cutting deeper than any sword.

Domnu shook her finger. "If he does not leave, and soon, all of us will perish." A chill wind passed through the circle, making even the giants shiver. "Have you all forgotten the prohibition, laid down by Dagda himself, against anyone with human blood remaining long on this island? Have you all forgotten that this boy was also born here, despite an even more ancient prohibition? If you let him carry the Harp, he will surely claim Fincayra as his rightful home. He probably has no intention of returning to the world beyond the mist. Heed my warning. This boy could upset the very balance between the worlds! He could bring the wrath of Dagda down upon us all. Even worse," she added with a leer, "he could be a tool of Rhita Gawr, like his father before him."

"I am not!" Merlin objected. "You just want me banished so you don't have to give me back the Galator."

Domnu's eyes flamed. "There, you see? He is speaking to the Great Council, even though he is not truly one of us. He has no respect for Fincayra's laws, just as he has no respect for the truth. The sooner he is exiled, the better."

Many heads nodded in the crowd, caught by the spell of her words. Merlin started to speak again, but someone else spoke first.

It was Rhia. Her gray-blue eyes alight, she faced the hairless hag. "I don't believe you. I just don't." Drawing a deep breath, she added, "And aren't you the one who has forgotten something? That prophecy, that very old prophecy, that only a child of human blood can defeat Rhita Gawr and those who serve him! What if that means Merlin? Would you still want us to send him away?"

Domnu opened her mouth, baring her blackened teeth, then shut it tight.

"The giiirl speeeaks the truuuth," thundered the deep voice of the Grand Elusa. Lifting her vast bulk with her eight legs, she peered straight at Domnu. "The boooy shooould staaay."

As if the spell had been broken, delegates of all descriptions thumped, growled, or flapped their agreement. Seeing this, Domnu grimaced. "I warned you," the hag grumbled. "That boy will be the ruin of us all."

Cairpré shook his head. "Time will tell."

Domnu glared at him. Then she turned and disappeared into the crowd—but not before shooting a glance at Merlin that made his stomach clench.

Rhia turned to Cairpré. "Aren't you going to help him put it on?"

The poet laughed, tossing his shaggy mane. "Of course." He lifted the Harp's leather sling over Merlin's head, resting it on the boy's shoulder. "You know this is a responsibility, my boy. All of us depend on you. Even so, may it also be a joy! With every strum of those strings, may you bring another field to flower."

He paused, gazing thoughtfully at Merlin. Lowering his voice, he added, "And may you heal yourself, even as you heal the land."

A roar of approval echoed around the sacred ring. With that, the Great Council of Fincayra disbanded.

PART ONE

I

RESCUER

Reaching the top of the rise, I hoisted the Flowering Harp a little higher on my shoulder. The first rays of dawn streaked across the sky, painting the clouds scarlet and crimson. Ruby light licked the farthest hills, igniting the few spindly trees that stood like forgotten hairs on the horizon. Yet despite the flaming trees, the hills themselves remained darkened, the same color as the brittle blades of grass under my leather boots—the color of dried blood.

Even so, as my feet crunched against the parched hillside, I began to smile. I barely noticed the chill wind that pierced my brown tunic and bit my cheeks. For I felt already warmed by my task. The task I had pursued now for more than three weeks. The task of reviving the land.

Just as the great wizard Tuatha, my father's father, had done long ago, I had borne the Harp across the remains of fields and forests. And, like Tuatha himself, I had coaxed those lands back to life—with surprising ease, I might add. The Harp responded more easily with each passing day. It seemed almost eager to do as I wished. As if it had been waiting for me since the days of Tuatha.

To be sure, even in the midst of my success I realized that I was no wizard. I knew only the barest rudiments of magic. I couldn't have lasted a day as an apprentice to someone like Tuatha. And yet . . . I was *something*. I had saved my friend Rhia from sure death at the hand of Stangmar. I had brought down his whole castle. On top of destroying the plans of his master, Rhita Gawr. It seemed only fitting that the Great Council had entrusted the Harp to me. And that the Harp should do my bidding.

As I approached a shadowy outcropping of rock, I noticed a dry gully that ran beneath it. Clearly, this gully had not seen a drop of water in years. Whatever soil had not already blown away looked as cracked and withered as a sunbaked carcass. But for a lone, scraggly tree wearing only a thin strip of bark on its trunk and bearing not even a single leaf, nothing lived here. No plants. No insects. No animals of any kind.

Smiling confidently, I rubbed the knotted top of my staff, feeling the deep grooves in the wood and smelling the spicy scent of hemlock. I laid it on the ground. Then I pulled the Harp's leather sling off my shoulder, careful not to tangle it with the cord of the satchel of herbs that my mother had given me in our last moments together. Holding the Harp in my left arm, I observed its intricately carved floral patterns, its inlaid strips of ash, its carefully spaced sound holes. The strings, made of goat gut, gleamed darkly in the early morning light. And the neck, joining the sound box to the pillar, curved as gracefully as the wing of a swan. Someday, I promised myself, I would learn how to make a harp such as this.

As another cold gust blew against me, I drew my fingers across the strings. A sudden burst of music poured forth, a lilting, magical music that lightened my heart like nothing I had heard since the singing of my mother so long ago. Although I had now carried the

Harp over dozens of these hills, I had not grown the least bit tired of its resonant song. I knew I never would.

A small sprig of fern lifted out of the ground and started to unfurl. Again I plucked the strings.

All at once, the hillside sprang to life. Brittle stems turned into flexible, green blades of grass. A rivulet of water started splashing down the gully, soaking the thirsty soil. Small blue flowers, sprinkled with droplets of dew, popped up along the banks. A new fragrance filled the air, something like lavender and thyme and cedar combined.

I drank in this melody of aromas, even as I listened to the Harp's own melody still pulsing in the air. Then my smile faded, as I recalled the fragrances of my mother's collection of herbs. How long it had been since I had smelled them! Since before I was born, Elen of the Sapphire Eyes had surrounded herself with dried petals, seeds, leaves, roots, shavings of bark, and whatever else she might use to heal the wounds of others. Sometimes, though, I suspected that she filled her life with such things just because she enjoyed the aromas. So did I— except for dill, which always made me sneeze.

Yet, far more than the aromas that she nurtured, I enjoyed my mother's company. She always tried to make me feel warm and safe. Even when the world did not let her succeed—which was all too often. She provided for me during all those brutal years in Gwynedd, called Wales by some, without ever asking for thanks. Even when she made herself aloof and distant in the hope of shielding me from my past, even when I nearly choked with rage at her refusal to answer my questions about my father, even when I struck back in my fear and confusion by refusing to call her by the one word she most wanted to hear—even then I loved her.

And now that I understood at last what she had done for me, I could not thank her. She was far, far away, beyond the mist, beyond the ocean, beyond the rugged coast of Gwynedd. I could not touch her. I could not call her that word: Mother.

A curlew chirped from the branch of the tree, pulling my thoughts back to the present. Such a glad, full-throated song! I plucked the harp strings once more.

Before my eyes, the tree itself burst to life. Buds formed, leaves sprouted, and bright-winged butterflies flew to the branches. Smooth, gray bark coated the entire trunk and limbs. The roots swelled, grasping the bank of the stream, now swiftly tumbling down the hillside.

A beech. I grinned, seeing its burly branches reaching skyward. The breeze rippled its silvery leaves. Something about the sight of a beech tree always filled me with feelings of peace, of quiet strength. And I had saved it. I had brought it back to life. As I had this entire hillside, like so many before. I felt the thrill of my own power. The Great Council had chosen well. Perhaps I did, indeed, have the heart of a wizard.

Then I noticed my own reflection in a puddle that had formed between the tree's roots near the bank. Caught short by my scarred cheeks and my black, sightless eyes, I stopped smiling. How had Rhia described my eyes, on the first day we met? *Like a pair of stars hidden by clouds.* I wished I could see with my eyes, my own eyes, again.

Seeing with my second sight was, of course, better than blindness. I could never forget that miraculous moment when I had discovered that I could actually see without my eyes. Yet second sight was no substitute for real eyesight. Colors faded, details blurred, darkness pressed all the closer. What I would give to heal my eyes! Burned and useless though they were, I always knew they were there. They reminded me constantly of everything I had lost.

And I had lost so very much! I was only thirteen, and already I had lost my mother, my father, and whatever homes I had known, as well as my own eyes. I could almost hear my mother, in her encouraging way, asking whether I had also gained anything. But what? The courage to live alone, perhaps. And the ability to save all the blighted lands of Fincayra.

I turned back to the beech tree. Already I had rescued a good portion of the Dark Hills, stretching from the ruins of the Shrouded Castle, now a sacred circle of stones, almost to the northern reaches of the Haunted Marsh. Over the next few weeks, I would bring life back to the rest. Then I could do the same for the Rusted Plains. Although it held more than its share of mysteries, Fincayra was not, after all, a very big place.

Setting down the Harp, I stepped nearer to the beech. Laying my hands on the smooth, silver bark, I spread my fingers wide, feeling the flow of life through the imposing trunk. Then, pursing my lips, I made a low, swishing sound. The tree shuddered, as if it were breaking free from invisible chains. Its branches quivered, making a swishing sound much like my own.

I nodded, pleased with my skills. Again I swished. Again the tree responded. This time, however, it did more than quiver. For I had given a command.

Bend. Bend down to the ground. I wanted to seat myself in its highest branches. Then I would command it to straighten again, lifting me skyward. For as long as I could remember, I had loved to perch in the tops of trees. Regardless of the weather. But I had always needed to climb there myself—until today.

Hesitantly, with considerable popping and creaking, the great beech began to bend lower. A section of bark ripped away from the trunk. I craned my neck, watching the highest branches descend. As the tree bent before me, I selected my seat, a notch not far from the top.

Suddenly I heard another swishing sound. The tree stopped bending. Slowly, it began to straighten itself again. Angrily, I repeated my command. The tree halted, then started bending toward me once more.

Again a swishing sound filled the air. The tree ceased bending and began to straighten.

My cheeks grew hot. How could this be? I dug my fingers into the trunk, ready to try again, when a clear, bell-like laughter reached my ears. I spun around to see a leaf-draped girl with gray-blue eyes and a mass of curly brown hair. Glistening vines wrapped around her entire body as if she were a tree herself. She watched me, still laughing, her hands on her belt of woven grass.

"Rhia! I should have guessed."

She tilted her head to one side. "Tired of speaking beech so soon? You're sounding like a Celt again."

"I'd still be speaking to the beech if you hadn't interrupted us."

Rhia shook her brown curls, enmeshed with leaves. "I didn't interrupt your speaking. Only your commanding."

Exasperated, I glanced up at the tree, which by now stood perfectly straight again, its silvery leaves tossing in the wind. "Leave me, will you?"

The curls shook again. "You need a guide. Otherwise, you might get lost." She looked with concern at the beech tree. "Or try something foolish."

I grimaced. "You're not my guide! I invited you to join me, re-member? And when I did, I didn't think you'd try to interfere."

"And when I started teaching you the language of trees, I didn't think you'd use it to hurt them."

"Hurt them? Can't you see what I'm doing?"

"Yes. And I don't like it." She stamped her foot on the ground, flattening the grass. "It's dangerous—and disrespectful—to make a tree bend like that. It might injure itself. Or even die. If you want to sit in a tree, then climb up there yourself."

"I know what I'm doing."

"Then you haven't learned anything in the last three weeks! Don't you remember the first rule of tree speech? *Listen before you speak.*"

"Just watch. I'll show you how much I've learned."

She strode up to me and squeezed my elbow with her strong hand. "You remind me of a little boy sometimes. So sure of yourself, with so little reason."

"Go away," I barked. "I saved this tree! Brought it back to life! I can make it bend if I want to."

Rhia frowned. "No, Merlin. You didn't save the tree." Releasing her grip, she pointed at the instrument lying on the grass. "The Flowering Harp saved the tree. You are just the one who gets to play it."

II

A FITTING
WELCOME

"Where has all the sweetness gone?"

I leaned back on the soft, fragrant grass of the gently sloping meadow, careful not to bump my head against the Harp. Even without the use of my eyes, my second sight could easily pick out the plump, pink berries in Rhia's hand. I knew that her question referred to the berries, which were not nearly sweet enough for her taste. But in the days since our confrontation at the beech tree, I had often asked the same question myself—about our friendship.

Though she appeared and disappeared at unpredictable times, Rhia never left me for long. She continued to accompany me over the ridges and valleys, sometimes in silence, sometimes in song. She continued to camp nearby, and share most of her meals with me. She even continued to call herself my guide, although it was perfectly obvious that I needed no guide.

Yet despite her continuing presence, an invisible wall divided us now. While in some ways we traveled together, we really traveled separately. She just didn't understand. And that continued to rankle me. The thrill of bringing the land back to life, of turning it green with buds and promise, I couldn't even begin to explain to her. Whenever I tried, she gave me one of her lectures on the Flowering Harp.

Or, worse, one of her looks that seemed to pierce right through me. As if she knew everything I was thinking and feeling, without even needing to ask. After all I had done for her! Were all girls as maddeningly difficult as she was?

I waved at the bush, its tangled branches heavy with pink berries. "If you don't like them, why do you keep eating them?"

She answered, still pulling berries off the branches. "There must be some sweeter ones here someplace. I *know* it."

"How do you know?"

She shrugged carelessly, even as she popped a handful into her mouth. "Mmmff. I just do."

"Did someone tell you?"

"A little voice inside me. A voice that understands berries."

"Be sensible, Rhia! This bush just isn't ripe yet. You'd be better off waiting to find another."

She ignored me, continuing to chew.

I tore a clump of grass and threw it down the slope. "What if you eat so many tart berries that you haven't any room left for sweet ones?"

She turned to me, her cheeks as packed with berries as a squirrel's would be with acorns. "Mmmff," she said with a swallow. "In that case, I guess it would have to be a day for tart berries, not sweet ones. But that little voice tells me there are some sweeter ones here. It's a matter of having trust in the berries."

"Trust in the berries! What in the world are you saying?"

"Just what I said. Sometimes it's best to treat life as if you're floating down a great river. To listen to the water and let it guide you, instead of trying to change the river's course."

"What do berries have to do with rivers?"

Her brown curls flopped as she shook her head. "I wonder . . . are all boys as difficult as you are?"

"Enough of this!" I pushed myself to my feet and slung the Flowering Harp over my back, wincing from the old pain between my shoulders. I started across the meadow, the base of my staff leaving a trail of tiny pits in the grass. Noticing a revived but still drooping hawthorn tree to my left, I reached over my shoulder and plucked a single string. The hawthorn instantly straightened and exploded with pink and white blossoms.

I glanced back at Rhia, hoping she might at least offer a word of praise, even something halfhearted. But she seemed completely occupied with fingering the branches of her berry bush. Turning to the rust-colored hill that rose from the edge of the meadow, I stepped briskly toward it. The crest of the hill was covered with shadowed rock outcroppings, the kind that could have concealed the caves of warrior goblins. Although I had seen many such places during my travels in the Dark Hills, I had yet to find any sign of goblins themselves. Perhaps Cairpré's worries had not been justified after all.

Suddenly I halted. Recognizing the pair of sharp knobs that rose from the crest, I toyed with my staff, twirling it in my hand, even as I toyed with a new idea. I veered westward, down the slope.

Rhia called out.

Planting my staff, I looked her way. "Yes?"

She waved a berry-stained hand toward the hill. "Aren't you going the wrong direction?"

"No. I have some friends to see."

Her brow furrowed. "What about your task? You are not supposed to rest until you've finished the Dark Hills."

"I'm not going to rest!" I kicked at the rich grass beneath my boots. "But no one said I had to avoid my friends along the way. Especially friends who might actually appreciate what I'm doing."

Even with my limited vision, I could not miss her reddening cheeks. "My friends have a garden. I am going to make it grow as never before."

Rhia's eyes narrowed. "If they are genuine friends, they'll be truthful with you. They'll tell you to go back and finish your task."

I stalked off. A stiff gust of wind blew in my face, making my sightless eyes water. But I pushed on down the slope, tunic flapping at my legs. *If they are genuine friends, they'll be truthful.* Rhia's words echoed in my mind. What, indeed, was a friend? I had thought Rhia was one, not long ago. And now she seemed more like a burr in my side. Do without friends! Maybe that was the answer. Friends were just too undependable, too demanding.

I bit my lip. The right kind of friend would be different, of course. Someone like my mother—totally loyal, always supportive. Yet she was one of a kind. There was no one like her on Fincayra. And yet . . . perhaps, with enough time, I might come to feel that way about others. Like the two people I was about to visit, T'eilean and Garlatha. With a single stroke of my harp strings, I would enrich both their garden and our friendship.

The wind relented for a moment. As I wiped my eyes with my sleeve, I heard Rhia's soft footsteps on the grass behind me. Despite my frustration with her, I felt somehow relieved. Not because I needed her company, of course. I simply wanted her to see all the thanks and admiration that I would soon be receiving from real friends.

I turned to face her. "So you decided to come along."

Somberly, she shook her head. "You still need a guide."

"I'm not going to get lost, if that's what you mean."

She merely frowned.

Without another word, I started down the slope, my heels digging into the turf. Rhia stayed close, as silent as a shadow. When we reached the plains, the remaining wind died away. Mist hovered in the muggy air, while the sun baked us. Now when I wiped my eyes it was because of the sting of perspiration.

Through a long afternoon we trekked in silence. Every so often, when the fields turned dry and brittle, I strummed a little, leaving behind us a wake of verdant grasses, splashing streams, and all manner of life renewed. Yet while the sun continued to warm our backs, it could not do the same for our moods.

Finally, I spied a familiar hillside, split by a deep cleft. Within it, seeming to sprout from the rocks and soil of the hill itself, sat a gray stone hut. It was bordered by a dilapidated wall and surrounded by a few trailing vines and thin fruit trees. Not much of a garden, really. Yet in the days before the fall of the Shrouded Castle, it had seemed like a genuine oasis in the middle of the Rusted Plains.

How surprised my old friends T'eilean and Garlatha would be when I brought endless bounty to their meager garden! They would be grateful beyond words. Maybe even Rhia would finally be impressed. On the other side of the wall, in the shade of some leafy boughs, I could make out two white heads. T'eilean and Garlatha. Side by side over a bed of bright yellow flowers, their heads bobbed slowly up and down, keeping time to some music only they could hear.

I smiled, thinking of the wondrous gift I had for them. When I had last seen them, on my way to the Shrouded Castle, I was nothing more than a ragged boy with only the faintest hope of living out the day. They had expected never to see me again. Nor had I expected to return. My pace quickened, as did Rhia's.

Before we were twenty paces from the crumbling wall, the two heads lifted as one, like hares in a morning meadow. T'eilean was the first to his feet. He offered a large, wrinkled hand to Garlatha, but she waved it away and rose without any help. They watched us approach, T'eilean stroking his unruly whiskers, Garlatha shading her eyes. I stepped over the wall, followed by Rhia. Despite the weight of the Harp on my shoulder, I stood as tall as I possibly could.

The wrinkles of Garlatha's face creased into a gentle smile. "You have returned."

"Yes," I replied, turning so they could see the Harp. "And I have brought you something."

T'eilean's brow creased. "You mean you have brought someone."

Rhia stepped forward. Her gray-blue eyes shone at the sight of the two aging gardeners standing before their simple hut. Without waiting to be introduced, she nodded in greeting.

"I am Rhia."

"And I am T'eilean. This is my wife of sixty-seven years, Garlatha."

The white-haired woman frowned and kicked at his shin, barely missing the mark. "Sixty-eight, you old fool."

"Sorry, my duck. Sixty-eight." He backed away a step before adding, "She is always right, you see."

Garlatha snorted. "Be glad you have guests, or I'd come after you with my trowel."

Her husband glanced at the trowel half buried in the flower bed, waving his arm in the air with the playfulness of a bear cub. "Right again. Without occasional guests to protect me, I doubt I would have survived this long."

Rhia suppressed a laugh.

Garlatha, her face softening, reached for T'eilean's hand. They stood together for a quiet moment, as gray as the stones of their hut. Leaves quivered gently all around them, as if in tribute to the devoted hands that had nurtured this garden for so many years.

"You remind me of two trees," observed Rhia. "Trees that have shared the same soil for so long they have grown together. Roots and all."

Garlatha, her eyes sparkling, glanced at her mate.

I decided to try again. "Speaking of things growing, I have brought you—"

"Yes!" exclaimed the old man, cutting me off. "You have brought your friend, Rhia." He turned toward her. "We welcome you, no less than we welcome the sunshine."

Garlatha tugged on the sleeve of my tunic. "What of your friend who came with you before, the one with the nose as big as a potato?"

"Shim is fine," I answered brusquely. "And now—"

"Though his nose," interrupted Rhia, "is even bigger than before."

Garlatha raised an eyebrow. "He did look full of surprises, that one."

With a dramatic tone, I cleared my throat. "And now I have a magnificent surprise for both of you."

Yet before I had even finished my sentence, the old woman was again speaking to Rhia. "Are you from Druma Wood? Your garb is woven in the way of the wood elves."

"The Druma is my home, and has been all my life."

Garlatha leaned closer. "Is it true what I have heard? That the rarest of all the trees, whose every branch yields a different kind of fruit, can still be found there?"

Rhia beamed. "What you have heard is true. The shomorra tree is indeed there. You might even say it's my garden."

"Such a garden you have, then, my child. Such a garden you have!"

My frustration growing, I pounded my staff on the soil. "I have a gift to bestow upon this very garden."

Neither of the elders seemed to hear me, as they continued to ask Rhia questions about Druma Wood. They seemed more interested in her than in me. Me, who had brought them something so precious!

Finally, T'eilean's muscular arm reached for a spiral-shaped fruit dangling from a branch overhead. With a graceful sweep of his hand, he plucked it. The pale purple color of the fruit glowed in his palm. "A larkon," he intoned. "The loveliest gift of the land to our humble home." He observed me quietly. "I remember that you enjoy the flavor."

At last, I thought. Even as I extended my hand to grasp the fruit, however, T'eilean swiveled and handed it to Rhia. "So I am sure that your friend will enjoy it just as much."

As I watched her take the fruit, my cheeks burned. Before I could say anything, though, he plucked another spiral fruit and offered it to me. "We are honored that you have returned."

"Honored?" I asked, my voice tinged with disbelief. I felt tempted to say more, but restrained myself.

T'eilean traded glances with Garlatha, then brought his gaze back

to me. "My boy, to welcome you as a guest in our home is the greatest honor we can bestow. It is what we did for you last time, and it
is what we do for you now."

"But now, T'eilean, I carry the Flowering Harp."

"Yes, yes, I have seen as much." The corners of his mouth drooped,
and for the first time he seemed to show the weight of his many years.
"My dear boy, the Flowering Harp is the most wondrous of all the
Treasures, blessed with the magic of the seed itself. Yet in our home,
we do not welcome guests for what they carry on their backs. We welcome them for what they carry elsewhere."

Riddles! From someone I had thought a friend. Scowling, I pushed
some straggly hairs off my face.

T'eilean drew a long breath before continuing. "As your hosts, we
owe you our hospitality. As well as our candor. If the weight of the
Harp lies upon your back, then so does the far greater weight of healing our lands before it is too late. Much depends on you, my boy.
Surely, you have precious little time for visits with simple folk like us."

My jaw clenched.

"Forgive me, but I am only trying to be truthful."

"Wait, Merlin," protested Rhia.

I did not hear the rest of her words, for I had already stepped over
the stone wall. Alone, I strode off across the plains, the strings of the
Harp jangling against my back.

III

WARM WIND

With nothing but the stars for my blanket, I spent that night curled up in the hollow of a stream bank. Rushes, moist with dew, lay under my head. With one hand, I could touch the splashing water that cascaded over the steps of stones carpeted with green moss. With the other, I could feel the Flowering Harp and my staff resting among the reeds.

I should have felt glad to be alone. Free of what the world called friends. Yet stroking the magical strings at this spot, bringing this stream to life, had given me no joy. Nor had watching the rushes and mosses spring from the dry soil. Nor had even spotting Pegasus in the midnight sky, though it had long been my favorite constellation, ever since the night my mother had first shown it to me.

This night, sleeping fitfully, I did not ride upon Pegasus' winged back as I had so many times before in my dreams. Instead, I found myself in a different dream. I sat upon a scarlet stone, watching my mother approach. Somehow, my eyes had healed. I could see again. Really see! Sunlight glinted on her golden hair, and a different kind of light played in her vibrant blue eyes. I could even see the tiny sprig of hemlock that she held in her hand.

Then, to my shock, I discovered that my front teeth were growing longer. Much longer. Bigger and bigger they grew, curling around like the tusks of a wild boar. Those daggerlike points were aiming straight for my eyes! As my teeth continued to lengthen, I flew into a panic. I screamed. My mother came running, but too late to help. I clawed at my face, trying to pull my teeth out bare-handed. I couldn't remove them. I couldn't stop them.

Slowly, inexorably, the teeth curled around until the tips reached my eyes. My own eyes! In just a few seconds they would be punctured. With a shriek of pain, I felt them rupture. I was blind again, utterly blind.

I awoke.

There was the stream, splashing beside me. There was Pegasus, sailing overhead. I lifted my head from the rushes. It was only a dream. Why then was my heart still pounding? Gingerly, I touched my cheeks, scarred from the fire that had blinded me in real life. They ached terribly from the new scratches I had just given them. Yet my heart ached even more. All this from a fire of my own making! To have lost my eyes was bad enough. To have done it to myself was still worse. For the first time in months, I wondered whether Dinatius, the other boy trapped in the fire that I had started, had survived. I could still hear his screams of agony, his whimpers of fear.

I put my face into the rushes and wept. As the stream flowed, so did my tears. In time, my sobbing subsided. Yet it seemed that the sound of sobbing continued, somewhere beyond the splashing of the stream. I lifted my head, listening closely.

More sobbing, punctuated by long, heaving moans. Patting my wet and sore cheeks with the sleeve of my tunic, I crept closer to the water's edge. Despite the darkness, my second sight traced the stream's path for some distance. Yet I couldn't find the source of the dismal sound. Maybe it was just my own echoing memory.

Leaning over the coursing water, I groped among the rushes with my hands. My knee kept sliding off the edge of the muddy bank, almost landing in the water. I continued to search, though I found nothing. Nothing at all. Yet the sobbing and moaning seemed to come from somewhere very near, almost in the stream itself.

In the stream itself. That was it! But how could that be?

I started to plunge my left hand into the water, then caught myself. The old pain throbbed between my shoulder blades. Could this be some sort of trick? One of Fincayra's hidden perils, like the shifting wraiths who take the form of something pleasant just long enough to lure you to your death? Rhia would know. But Rhia, I reminded myself bitterly, was no longer with me.

The moaning welled up again. Starlight sparkled on the dark surface of the stream, making it look like a river of crystals. Biting my lip, I thrust in my hand. A frigid wave washed over my wrist and forearm. My skin reeled from the shock of cold. Then my fingers touched something. Smooth. Round. Softer than stone. Fumbling to get a grip on the slippery object, I seized it and pulled it free from the water. It was a flask, not much bigger than my fist, made from a heavy bladder. Its leather cap had been sealed tight with a thick coating of wax. Bloated with air, the dripping flask glinted darkly.

I squeezed it. A loud wailing struck my ears. Then came sobs, heavy with heartache. Using the base of my wooden staff, I cut away the ring of wax. It came off only gradually, as if reluctant to loosen its grip. Finally it fell away. I tore open the cap. A rush of air blew across my cheeks. It felt warm and soothing, and smelled vaguely of cinnamon. As the flask collapsed, the gust of air flowed over my face and hair like a living breath.

"Thank you, person, thank you," came a wispy little voice from behind my head.

I dropped the flask and whirled around. But I saw nothing between me and the distant stars.

"Or should I say," whispered the voice again, "thank you, Emrys Merlin?"

I caught my breath. "How do you know my names?"

"Oh yes," the voice went on breezily, "I like the Merlin part so much better than dusty old Emrys."

Reaching up, I groped at the night air. "How do you know so much? Who are you? And where are you?"

A soft, breathy laughter rose out of the air before me. "I am Aylah, a wishlahaylagon." The laughter came again. "But most people simply call me a wind sister."

"Aylah," I repeated. "Wind sister." Again I reached skyward, and this time my fingertips passed through a warm current of air. "Now tell me how you know so much."

The smell of cinnamon grew stronger. Warm air swept slowly around me, fluttering my tunic. I felt embraced by a whirling circle of wind.

"I know as much as the air itself, Emrys Merlin. For I travel fast and far, never sleeping, never stopping."

Aylah's invisible cloak continued to spin slowly around me. "That is what a wind sister does, Emrys Merlin." A slight sob made her pause. "Unless she is captured, as I was."

"Who would do such a thing?"

"Someone evil, Emrys Merlin." The warm air spun away, leaving me with a sudden chill.

"Tell me."

"Someone evil, ahhh yes," breathed Aylah from near the bank where I had slept. "Her names are many, but most know her as Domnu."

I shivered, though not from the night air. "I know Domnu. I know her treachery. Yet I wouldn't exactly call her evil."

"She is surely not good, Emrys Merlin."

"She is neither good nor evil. She simply *is*. A little like fate."

"Dark Fate, you mean." Aylah's breeze blew across the strings of the Harp, tingling them lightly. "She is one of the few who are old and powerful enough to catch the wind. I don't know why, Emrys Merlin, I only know that she locked me away in that flask and cast me aside."

"I'm sorry for you."

A warm breath of air caressed my cheek. "If you hadn't helped me this night, Emrys Merlin, I believe I would have died."

My voice too a whisper, I asked, "Can the wind really die?"

"Oh yes, Emrys Merlin, it can." Once again she brushed my cheek. "The wind, like a person, can die from loneliness."

"You are not alone now."

"Nor are you, Emrys Merlin. Nor are you."

IV

TREASURES

The thrill of playing the Harp, which I had not felt since leaving the Dark Hills, filled me once again. Indeed, as I walked across the rolling plateaus of the Rusted Plains, the land seemed to erupt with new life even before I paused to pluck the oaken instrument. The driest grasses bent before me, as the most lifeless leaves arose from the ground, twirled, and danced in spirals at my feet. For Aylah moved beside me. Her gentle breeze often brushed against my arms, and her wispy laughter lifted every time I played the magical strings.

Even so, my steps sometimes grew heavy. Whenever I came across a stone hut, or a grove of fruit trees, I leaned against my staff, frowning at the memory of my encounter with T'eilean and Garlatha. I wished that I had never thought of visiting them and their garden. In addition, every time I glanced at the shadowed ridges to the east, I felt the gnawing sense that I was making a mistake by not returning to the hills to finish my work there. Yet . . . I just didn't feel ready to go back. Not yet. Let Rhia and the others fret a while longer.

Flushed with anger, I strummed the Harp. To my surprise, this time the brittle grass beneath my boots did not transform into lush, green blades. Instead, the entire meadow seemed to darken slightly, as if a cloud had covered the sun. Puzzled, I looked skyward. But I found no clouds.

Impatiently, I strummed again. But the grass only stiffened, darkened. I frowned at the instrument. What was wrong with it?

A warm wind billowed my tunic. "You are angry, Emrys Merlin."

I stiffened. "How do you know that?"

"I don't know things," breathed Aylah. "I feel them. And I feel your anger even now."

I strode faster, eager to leave this meadow behind. The darkened blades of grass jabbed at my boots like thousands of thorns.

"Why are you so angry, Emrys Merlin?"

Having moved beyond the darkened patch of grass, I stopped. I drew a deep breath and exhaled slowly. "I don't really know."

Aylah's airy form encircled me, filling my nostrils with the scent of cinnamon. "Could it be you are missing someone?"

I squeezed the shaft of my staff. "I am missing no one."

"Not even your mother?"

My knees nearly buckled, but I said nothing.

The wind sister swirled about me. "I never met her, Emrys Merlin, though I know many who did. She must have been a good friend."

I blinked the dew from my sightless eyes. "Yes. She was my good friend. Maybe my only friend."

Aylah's warm breath touched my cheek. "Tell me about her, would you please? I would like to hear."

Twisting my staff in the dry, rust-colored grass, I started walking again. "She loved the night sky, with all its stars and dreams and mysteries. She loved stories about ancient places like Olympus and

Apollo's Isle of Delos. She loved green, growing things, and all the creatures who soar or shamble or swim. And she loved me."

Although her spinning slowed, Aylah seemed closer to me than ever. Her winds embraced me.

"You're right," I admitted. "I do miss her. More than I ever believed possible." Haltingly, I took a breath. "If only I could be with her again, Aylah! Even for just an hour."

"I understand. Ahhh yes, I do."

It occurred to me that Aylah, despite her airy form, shared some qualities with my mother. She was warm, she was caring. And she did not try to give me advice.

Just then I noticed, not far ahead, a patch of low bushes with bluish bark and broad leaves. I knew from watching Rhia that they made good eating. Setting down the Flowering Harp and my staff, I went to the bushes and pulled up one by the roots, revealing a thick, blue tuber. After cleaning its skin with my tunic, I bit into the tangy flesh.

"Can I share this meal with you, somehow? I don't know what you eat, but whatever it is, I could try to find some for you."

The broad leaves of the bush fluttered as Aylah passed over them. "I eat only the faraway fragrances of lands I have not yet explored. I am made to wander, you see." Gently, she tousled my hair. "And now, I am afraid, it is time for us to part."

I stopped chewing. "Part? Why?"

The airy voice spoke into my ear. "Because I am the wind, Emrys Merlin, and I must fly. Always soaring, always circling, that is my way. I have many places to see, on Fincayra and the other worlds as well." For a moment, she seemed to hover near the Harp. "And you must fly, as well. For you still have work to do in the Dark Hills."

I frowned. "You too, Aylah? I thought at least you wouldn't try to tell me what to do."

"I am not telling you what to do, Emrys Merlin. I am only telling you that the winds bring tidings of disturbing things, evil things, in the Dark Hills. Rhita Gawr's allies are beginning to stir again. They grow bolder by the day. Before long the goblins will emerge from their caves, and with them the shifting wraiths. Then it will be too late for you to heal the lands."

My stomach knotted at her words. I recalled Cairpré's warning as he gave me the Harp. *The Dark Hills must be healed before Rhita Gawr returns, or we will have lost our only chance. Remember: If you shirk your task, you will never be forgiven.*

I surveyed the ridges on the horizon. Shadows of clouds stalked them. "If what you say is true, I must go back now. Won't you come with me? So we can travel together a while longer?"

"I have already stayed with you, Emrys Merlin, longer than I have ever been with a person who did not have wings of his own." She breathed against my neck. "And now I must fly."

Somberly, I tossed aside the tuber. "I've heard that Fincayrans once had wings of their own. Maybe it's just an old fable, but I wish it were true. I wish they had never lost them. Then I might have some myself, so I could fly with you."

I felt an eddy of wind across my shoulders. "Ahhh, Emrys Merlin, you know about that, do you? To have wings and then lose them. Such a tragedy that was! Even if many Fincayrans have forgotten how it happened, they cannot forget the lingering pain between their shoulders."

I stretched my arms stiffly, feeling the old pain. "Aylah, do you know how it happened? Even Cairpré, with all the many stories he has heard, doesn't know how the Fincayrans lost their wings. He told me once that he'd give away half of his library just to find out."

The warm wind encircled me now, spinning slowly. "I know the story, Emrys Merlin. Perhaps one day I might tell you. But not now."

"You're really leaving? It's always like this with me. It seems whatever I find, I lose."

"I hope you will find me again, Emrys Merlin."

A sudden gust of wind flapped the sleeves of my brown tunic. Then, just as swiftly, it was gone.

I stood there for a long while. Eventually, my stomach growled with hunger. I ignored it. Then, hearing it again, I bent down to retrieve the tuber I had discarded. I took another bite, thinking about Aylah, sister of the wind. At last, when I had finished it, I started walking—east, toward the Dark Hills.

All around me, the Rusted Plains rose and fell in great rolling waves. I shuffled along, dry grasses snapping beneath my feet. A soft wind blew against my back, cooling the heat of the sun, but it was not the wind that I wished for. And even more than Aylah's company, I missed the feeling of joy in my task that I had only just regained—and lost once again. The Harp felt heavy on my shoulder.

Sometimes, as I walked, I touched the pouch of healing herbs that my mother had given to me just before we said farewell, in that dank room of stone in Caer Myrddin. I missed her more than ever. And I also knew that she missed me. If she were here, she would not desert me as the others had done. Yet she was as far away as the farthest wind.

As the golden sun dropped lower in the sky, I neared a scraggly group of trees planted in six or seven rows. Although I could see no fruit among the branches of the orchard, a few white flowers gleamed, wafting a familiar scent in my direction. Apple blossoms. I took a deep, flavorful breath. Yet it did little to lift my spirits. Perhaps playing the Harp, feeling again the joy of bringing new life to the land, would help.

I cradled the instrument in my arms. Then I hesitated, remembering my strange experience in the darkened meadow. Merely a fluke, I assured myself. Slowly, I drew my fingers across the strings. All at once, a luminous paintbrush swept across the trees and the grassy fields surrounding them. Apples burst from the branches, swelling to hefty size. Trunks thickened, roots multiplied. The trees lifted skyward, waving their fruited branches proudly. My chest swelled. Whatever had happened at the darkened meadow was certainly not a problem now.

Suddenly a voice cried out. A bare-chested boy, about my own age, fell out of one of the trees. He landed in an irrigation ditch that ran beneath the branches. Another shout rang out. I ran to the spot.

Out of the ditch clambered the boy, with hair and skin as brown as the soil. Then, to my surprise, another figure emerged, looking like an older, broader version of the boy. He was a man of the soil. He was a man I recognized.

Neither he nor the boy noticed me as I stood in the shadow of the apple tree. The shirtless man straightened his broad back and then clasped the boy by the shoulders. "Are you hurt, son?"

The boy rubbed his bruised ribs. "No." He smiled shyly. "You made a good pillow."

The man eyed him with amusement. "You don't often fall out of branches."

"The branches don't often stand up and shake me out! And look, Papa! They're loaded down with apples."

The man gasped. Like the boy, he stared, jaw dangling, at the transformed trees. I too began to smile. This was the reaction that I had hoped to get from Rhia and the others—the reaction that I would have surely gotten from my mother. She had always delighted in the beauty and flavor of fresh apples.

"'Tis a miracle, son. 'Tis a gift from the great god Dagda himself."

I stepped out of the shadows. "No, Honn. It is a gift from me."

The man gave a start. He looked from me to the tree spreading above us, then back to me. At last he turned to his son. "It's him! The lad I told you about."

The boy's eyes widened. "The one who crushed the evil king? Who calls himself after a hawk?"

"Merlin," I declared, cuffing the boy on the shoulder. "Your father helped me once, when I badly needed it."

Honn ran a hand through his hair, flecked with dirt. "Good gracious, lad. Until I heard the tales of your success, I had given you up for dead thrice over."

Leaning on my twisted staff, I grinned. "With good reason. If it hadn't been for that handy blade you gave me, I surely would have been dead thrice over."

Rubbing his strong chin, Honn examined me for a moment. Below his bare chest he wore nothing but loose brown leggings. His hands, cracked and calloused though they were, looked as powerful as tree roots.

"I am glad the old dagger proved useful, my lad. Where is it now?"

"Somewhere in the ruins of the Shrouded Castle. It failed to slay a ghouliant, one of Stangmar's deathless soldiers. But it did buy me a few precious seconds."

"Of that I am glad." His gaze moved to the magical instrument. "I see that you found the Flowering Harp." He nudged the boy. "You see, my son, it was indeed a miracle! No mere mortal, not even one so talented as the young hawk here, could have done such a thing. It was the Harp, not the lad, that revived our orchard."

I cringed, then started to speak. Before I could say anything, however, Honn continued.

"To my mind, son, all the Treasures of Fincayra are the stuff of miracles, wrought by Dagda himself." In a quiet, almost reverent voice, he added, "There is even a plow, one of the Seven Wise Tools, that knows how to till its own field. Truly! It is said that any field it touches will yield the perfect harvest, neither too much nor too little."

The boy shook his head in amazement. Waving toward the rickety wooden plow that lay beside the ditch, he laughed. "No chance of mistaking it for that one, Father! My back hurts just to watch whenever you pull it."

Honn beamed. "Not so much as my own back hurts after you jump on me from a tree."

The pair laughed together. Honn wrapped a burly arm around his son's shoulder and turned to me, his face full of pride. "The truth is, I have a treasure of my own. My young friend here. And he's more precious to me than an ocean full of miracles."

I swallowed, running a finger over my mother's leather satchel. I could smell its sweet herbs even over the aroma of ripe apples. "What would you do, Honn, if you ever lost that treasure? That friend?"

His face became as hard as stone. "Why, I'd do everything in my mortal power to get it back."

"Even if it meant leaving your work unfinished?"

"No work could be more important than that."

I nodded grimly. *No work could be more important than that.*

Stepping over the ditch, I started walking. When I reached the edge of the orchard, I paused to face the Dark Hills, glowing like coals in the setting sun. The long, thin shadow of my staff seemed to point straight at the notched hill where I had turned aside from my task.

Slowly, I swung around to the north. I would return to those hills, and to my task, before long. And then I would revive every last blade of grass I could find. First, however, I needed to do something else. I needed to find my own mother again. And, like Honn, I would do everything in my mortal power to succeed.

V

THE JESTER

Late the following day, as strands of golden light wove gleaming threads through the grasses of the Rusted Plains, I stood on the crest of a rise. Below me sat a cluster of mud brick houses, arranged in a rough circle. Their thatched roofs glowed as bright as the surrounding plains. Long wooden planks stretched between their walls, connecting the houses like the arms of young children standing in a ring. The aroma of grain roasting on a wood fire tickled my nose.

I felt rising anticipation—and an undercurrent of dread. For this was Caer Neithan, the Town of the Bards. I knew that the poet Cairpré had promised to come here following the Great Council, to help repair the damage inflicted by Stangmar. And I also knew that if there was one person in all of Fincayra who could help me find my mother, it was Cairpré himself.

He would not be pleased to see me again, with so much of my work still unfinished. Yet he, too, had known Elen of the Sapphire Eyes, having tutored her years ago. I believed that he, too, longed for her return. Hadn't he once told me that he had learned more about the art of healing from her than she had ever learned from him? Maybe, just maybe, he might know some way to bring her through the curtain of mist surrounding this island. Then, reunited with her at last, I could finish my work in the Dark Hills with a glad heart.

I descended the slope, my staff striking the crusty soil in time to the Harp thumping against my back. Listening to the swelling sounds of the village, I could not forget the eerie silence that had shrouded it during my last visit. A silence that had been, in its way, louder than a thundering tempest.

Indeed, the Town of the Bards had only rarely known silence. No settlement in Fincayra possessed a richer history of story and song. For over the ages it had been home to many of this land's most inspired storytellers, and had witnessed many of their first performances. Even Cairpré himself, whose fame as a poet I had learned about only from others, had been born in one of those mud brick houses.

As I drew nearer to the village gates, which gleamed with golden light, more people started to emerge from their doors. Clad in long tunics of white cloth, they stood out sharply against the dry, caked mud of their homes, the dark planks of wood connecting the buildings, and the empty flower boxes clinging to most windowsills. I reached for the Harp, tempted to fill those flower boxes with something more than shadows. But I caught myself, deciding to wait before announcing my arrival.

More and more people emerged. They looked strikingly different from one another in skin color, age, hair, shape, and size. Yet they shared one common characteristic, in addition to their white tunics. All of them seemed hesitant, uncertain about something. Instead of congregating in the open circle in the middle of the houses, they kept to the outer edge. A few stood by their doorways, pacing anxiously, but most sat down on the wooden planks that ringed the open area. They seemed to be gathering for some purpose, but I couldn't shake the feeling that there was something grudging about their actions.

At that moment, a tall, gaunt fellow, wearing a brown cloak over his tunic, stepped into the center of the ring. Upon his head rested an odd, three-cornered hat that tilted precariously to one side like someone who had drunk too much wine. Dozens of gleaming metal spheres dangled from the hat's rim. The man began waving his long, spidery arms, flapping his loose sleeves, while bellowing some words I could not quite make out.

At once I understood the circular arrangement of the houses. The whole town was a theater! And I had arrived in time for some sort of performance.

As I reached the village gates, I halted. Unlike the last time I was here, no guard met me with a spear aimed at my chest. Instead, my greeting came from a newly carved sign attached to one of the gateposts. Shining in the late afternoon light, it read, *Caer Neithan, Town of the Bards, welcomes all who come in peace.* Below those words, I recognized one of Cairpré's own couplets: *Here song is ever in the air, while story climbs the spiral stair.*

No sooner had I stepped inside the gates when a slender, shaggy-haired man jumped up from one of the planks and strode over. His tangled brows, as unruly as brambles, hung over his dark eyes. I waited for him, leaning against my staff.

"Hello, Cairpré."

"Merlin," he whispered, spreading his arms as if he were about to clap his hands with joy. Then, glancing over his shoulder at the gaunt man who was reciting some passage, he apparently changed his mind about clapping. "Good to see you, my boy."

I nodded, realizing that he must have assumed that my work in the Dark Hills was done. It would not be easy to tell him the truth.

Again he glanced at the man reciting, and at the somber, almost tearful faces of the people in the audience. "I am only sorry you didn't arrive for a happier performance."

"Oh, that's all right," I whispered. "From all those sullen faces, it appears that fellow has a gift for making people feel sad. What is he reciting? Some sort of tragic poem?"

Cairpré's eyebrows climbed high on his forehead. "Unfortunately not." He shook his shaggy mane. "Believe it or not, the poor fellow is *trying* to be funny."

"Funny?"

"That's right."

Just then a clamorous clinking and rattling reached my ears. I turned back to the performer to see him shaking his head wildly, tossing his pointed hat from side to side. The sound came from the metal spheres. They were bells! Of course, I thought. Just right for making people laugh. Too bad they sounded so jarring, more like banging swords than ringing bells.

I observed the man for a moment. His hands drooped, his shoulders sagged, and his back stooped. In addition, his entire face—including his brow, his eyes, and his mouth—seemed to frown. The effect was compounded because, despite his thin frame, he had a flabby neck with row upon row of extra chins. So when his mouth turned down once, it turned down five or six times.

Suddenly he drew his heavy cloak around himself as if he were about to deliver a speech. Then, in sad, slow tones, he started to sing—or, more accurately, to wail. His voice seemed to cry, his breathing came like sobs. Like Cairpré, and most of the villagers, I winced. The man may have been trying to be funny, but his singing conveyed all the joy of a funeral dirge.

> *When bells reach your ears,*
> *Abandon all fears!*
> *Your lingering sadness*
> *Will turn into gladness.*
>
> *Be joyful, have cheer:*
> *The jester is here!*
>
> *I frolic and skip*
> *With laughs on my lip!*
> *My bells jingle sweetly,*
> *I thrill you completely.*
>
> *Be joyful, have cheer:*
> *The jester is here!*

As the wailing continued, I turned to Cairpré. "Doesn't he know how he sounds? He is the least funny person I have ever heard."

The poet heaved a sigh. "I think he does know. But he keeps on trying anyway. His name is Bumbelwy. Ever since he was a child, when he first frightened away the birds with his singing, he has dreamed of being a jester. Not just an amusing frolicker, but a true jester, someone who practices the high art of dressing wisdom in the garb of humor. Bumbelwy the Mirthful, he calls himself."

"Bumbelwy the Painful suits him better."

"I know, I know. As I've said before, *Bread yearns to rise beyond its size.*"

The townspeople, meanwhile, seemed every bit as dismal as Bumbelwy himself. Many held their heads in their hands; all wore scowls. One young girl shook loose of a woman's arms and ran into a nearby house, her black hair streaming behind her. While the woman stayed in her seat, she looked as if she envied the girl.

I turned back to Cairpré, scowling myself. "Why does anyone listen to him?"

"One of his, ah, humorous recitals, as he calls them, can ruin your next three meals. But like every other resident of Caer Neithan, he gets to perform in the village circle each year on the date of his birth." Cairpré shook his head. "And the rest of us have to listen. Even those like me who don't live here but are unlucky enough to be here on the wrong day."

He waved at the village circle, his voice no longer a whisper. "To think of all the truly memorable performances this same spot has seen! *Night Hammer. The Vessel of Illusion. Geraint's Vow.*"

Swiveling, he gestured toward one of the smaller, older-looking houses. "Pwyll, whose despairing smile itself inspired volumes of poems, wrote her first poem there." He pointed to a low house with a wooden porch. "Laon the Lame was born there. And let's not forget Banja. Jussiva the Jubilant. Ziffian. They all called this town home. As have so many other fabled bards."

Again I peered at Bumbelwy, whose long arms flailed as he droned on. "The only place he will ever be a jester is in his dreams."

Cairpré nodded grimly. "All of us have our private dreams. But few of us cling to dreams so far removed from our true capabilities! In days long past, Bumbelwy might have been saved by one of the Treasures of Fincayra, the magical horn known as the Caller of Dreams. Think of it, Merlin. The Caller, when blown by someone immensely wise, could bring a person's most cherished dream to life. Even a dream as far-fetched as Bumbelwy's. That is why it was often called, in story and song, the Horn of Good Tidings."

Lines deeper than the scars on my own face appeared on Cairpré's brow. I knew that he was remembering how Rhita Gawr had perverted the magic of the Caller of Dreams to bring only evil tidings to life. In the case of this very village, he had brought about the most terrifying dream of any poet, bard, or musician: He had silenced completely the voices of all who dwelled here, rendering useless the very instruments of their souls. That was why the Town of Bards had been as quiet as a graveyard when I last came here. Cairpré's tormented expression told me that, while the curse itself had departed with the collapse of the Shrouded Castle, its memory lived on.

The bells on Bumbelwy's hat started jangling again, louder than before. If I had not been holding my staff, I would have covered my ears. Nudging Cairpré, I asked, "Why don't you try the Caller of Dreams on him yourself?"

"I couldn't."

"Why not?"

"First of all, my boy, I'm not about to try to take anything—certainly not one of the Treasures—from the Grand Elusa's cave where they now reside. I'll leave that to someone much braver. Or stupider. But that isn't the main reason. The fact is, I am not wise enough to use the Caller."

I blinked in surprise. "Not wise enough? Why, the poet Cairpré is known throughout the land as—"

"As a rhymer, a quoter, an idealistic fool," he finished. "*Have no illusions, I brim with confusions.* But at least I am wise enough to know one important thing: how little I really do know."

"That's ridiculous. I've seen your library. All those books! You can't tell me you don't know anything."

"I didn't say I don't know anything, my boy. I said I don't know *enough*. There's a difference. And to think that I could command the legendary Caller of Dreams—well, that would be a terrible act of hubris."

"Hubris?"

"From the Greek word *hýbris*, meaning arrogance. Excessive pride in oneself. It's a flaw that has felled many a great person." His voice dropped again to a whisper. "Including, I am told, your own grandfather."

I stiffened. "You mean . . . Tuatha?"

"Yes. Tuatha. The most powerful wizard Fincayra has ever known. The only mortal ever allowed to visit the Otherworld to consult with Dagda—and return alive. Even he was susceptible to hubris. And it killed him."

The Flowering Harp felt suddenly heavier, the sling digging into my shoulder. "How did he die?"

Cairpré leaned closer. "I don't know the details. No one does. All I know is he overestimated his own power, and underestimated Rhita Gawr's most fearsome servant, a one-eyed ogre named Balor."

He shook himself. "But let us speak of more pleasant things! My boy, tell me about the Harp. You've made quick work of the Dark Hills if you're already down here in the plains."

I shifted uncomfortably, rubbing my hand over the knotted top of my staff. As I felt the deep grooves, the scent of hemlock spiced the air, reminding me of the woman whose fragrances had filled my childhood. The time had come to tell Cairpré what I wanted to do—and what I had left undone.

Taking a deep breath, I declared, "I haven't finished my work in the hills."

He caught his breath. "You haven't? Did you meet trouble? Warrior goblins on the loose?"

I shook my head. "The only trouble is of my own making."

The bottomless pools of his eyes examined me. "What are you saying?"

"That I've discovered something more important than my task." I faced the poet squarely. "I want to find my mother. To bring her to Fincayra."

Anger flashed across his face. "You would place us all in danger because of that?"

My throat tightened. "Cairpré, please. I will finish the task. I promise! But I need to see her again. And soon. Is that so much to ask?"

"Yes! You are putting all the creatures of this land at risk."

I tried to swallow. "Elen gave up everything for me, Cairpré! She loved her life here. Loved it to the depths of her soul. And she left it all just to protect me. During our time in Gwynedd, I was—well, her only companion. Her only friend. Even though I never did much to deserve it."

I paused, thinking about her sad songs, her healing hands, her wondrously blue eyes. "We had our problems, believe me. But we were much closer than either of us knew. Then one day I left her there, all alone. Just left her. She must be miserable, in that cold stone room. She might even be sick, or in trouble. So while I want to bring her here for me, it's also for her."

Cairpré's expression softened slightly. He laid a hand on my shoulder. "Listen, Merlin. I understand. How many times I myself have longed to see Elen again! But even if we put aside the Dark Hills, to bring someone here from the world beyond the mists—well, to do that is impossibly dangerous."

"Are you certain? The sea has spared me twice."

"It's not the sea, my boy, though that voyage is dangerous enough. Fincayra has its own ways, its own rhythms, that mortals can only guess. Even Dagda himself, it is said, dares not predict who may be allowed to pass through the curtains of mist."

"I don't believe it."

His gaze darkened. "There would be dangers to anyone brought here from outside, and dangers to the rest of Fincayra as well." He closed his eyes in thought. "What you may not understand is that anyone who arrives here—even the tiniest little butterfly—could change the balance of life on Fincayra and cause untold destruction."

"You're sounding like Domnu," I scoffed. "Saying I'm going to be the ruin of all Fincayra."

He swung his head toward the village gates, no longer aglow with golden light. Beyond them, the Dark Hills rolled like waves on a stormy sea. "You could be just that. Especially if you don't finish what you've begun."

"Won't you help me?"

"Even if I knew a way, I wouldn't help you. You're only a boy. And a more foolish one than I had thought."

I pounded my staff on the ground. "I have the power to make the Harp work, don't I? You yourself told the Great Council that I have the heart of a wizard. Well, perhaps I also have the power to bring my mother here."

His hand squeezed my shoulder so hard I winced. "Don't say such things, even in jest. It takes far more than heart to be a true wizard.

You need the spirit, the intuition, the experience. You need the knowledge—enormous knowledge about the patterns of the cosmos and all the arts of magic. And, even more, you need the wisdom, the sort of wisdom that tells you when to use those arts, and when to refrain. For a true wizard wields his power judiciously, the way an expert bowman wields his arrows."

"I'm not speaking about arrows. I'm speaking about my mother, Elen." I drew myself up straight. "If you won't help me, then I will find another way."

Cairpré's brow creased again. "A true wizard needs one thing more."

"What is that?" I asked impatiently.

"Humility. Listen well, my boy! Forget this madness. Take the Harp and return to your work in the hills. You have no idea of the risks you are taking."

"I would take many more to bring her back to me."

He looked skyward. "Help me, O Dagda!" Returning his gaze to me, he asked, "How can I make you understand? There is a proverb, as old as this island itself, saying that only the wisest shell from the Shore of Speaking Shells can guide someone through the mists. It sounds simple enough. And yet no wizard in history—not even Tuatha—has ever dared to try. Does that give you some sense of the danger?"

I grinned. "No. But it does give me an idea."

"Merlin, no! You mustn't. On top of all the other dangers, there is yet another. To you. Attempting such an act of deep wizardry will tell Rhita Gawr exactly where you are—and more, I'm afraid. When he returns, bent on conquering this world and the others, he will pursue you. Mark my words."

I tugged on the sling of the Harp. "I don't fear him."

Cairpré's brambly brows lifted. "Then you had better start. For with hubris like that, you will offer him the sweetest revenge of all. Making you one of his servants, just as he did your father."

My stomach clenched as if I'd been struck. "You're saying I'm no better than Stangmar?"

"I'm saying you are just as vulnerable. If Rhita Gawr doesn't kill you outright, he will try to enslave you."

Just then, a man's shadow fell upon us. I whirled around to face Bumbelwy. Apparently he had finished his recital and approached us, and we had been too absorbed in conversation to notice that he had been listening. He bowed awkwardly, causing his hat to fall to the ground with a noisy rattle. He retrieved the hat. Then, shoulders slumped, he faced Cairpré. "I did miserably, didn't I?"

Cairpré, still glaring at me, waved him away. "Some other time. I'm talking with the boy right now."

Turning his frowning chins toward me, Bumbelwy said glumly, "You tell me, then. Did I do miserably or not?"

Thinking that if I answered him, he would leave, I frowned back at him. "Yes, yes. You were miserable."

But he did not leave. He merely bobbed his head sullenly, clanking the bells. "So I botched the delivery. Too true, too true, too true."

"Merlin," growled Cairpré. "Heed my warnings! I only want to help you."

My cheeks burned. "Help me? Is that why you tried to dissuade me last time from going to the Shrouded Castle? Or why you didn't tell me that Stangmar was really my father?"

The poet grimaced. "I didn't tell you about your father because I feared that such a terrible truth might forever wound you. Make you doubt, or even hate, yourself. Perhaps I was wrong in that, as I was wrong in thinking you couldn't destroy the castle. But I am not wrong in this! Go back to the Dark Hills."

I glanced at the village gates. Shrouded by shadows, they stood as dark as gravestones. "First I am going to the Shore of Speaking Shells."

Before Cairpré could respond, Bumbelwy cleared his throat, making his multiple chins quiver. Then he swirled his cloak about himself with dramatic flair. "I am coming with you."

"What?" I exclaimed. "I don't want you to come."

"Too true, too true, too true. Yet I will come all the same."

Cairpré's dark eyes gleamed. "You will regret your choice even sooner than I expected."

VI

THROUGH
THE MISTS

Like the sour taste that stays in your mouth long after biting into a piece of rotten fruit, Bumbelwy, his bells jangling, stayed by my side. Only with fruit, you can wash your mouth and get rid of the taste. With Bumbelwy, nothing I said or did would make him leave. Although I walked as briskly as I could, not even pausing to strum the Harp, I could not escape his presence.

He followed me out of Caer Neithan's gates, as Cairpré stood watching in silence. He followed me over the rises and dips of the plains, trekking until long after dark, camping with me beneath an old willow, and then continuing through the sweltering sun of the next day. He followed me all the way to the grand, pounding waterway that I knew to be the River Unceasing.

All the while, he mumbled about the heat, the stones in his boots, and the arduous life of a jester. As we approached the river, he asked me several times whether I would like to hear his famous riddle about his bells, promising it would lift my spirits. Whenever I told him that I had no desire to hear his riddle—or, for that matter, his bells—he simply sulked a bit and then asked me all over again.

"Oh, but this is a royal, ranting *romp* of a riddle," he protested.

"A riddler's regular riddle. No, that's backward. Curses, I botched the delivery again! It's a regular riddler's riddle. There, that's right. It's funny. It's wise." He paused, looking even more somber than usual. "It's the only riddle I know."

I shook my head, striding toward the River Unceasing. As we neared its steep, stony banks, thundering rapids boiled beneath us. The spray rose high into the air, lifting rainbow bridges that shimmered in the sunlight. The splashing and roaring grew so loud that, for the first time since the Town of the Bards, I could not hear Bumbelwy's bells. Or his pleas to tell his riddle.

I turned to him. Above the pounding of the river, I shouted, "I have far to go, all the way to the southernmost shore. Crossing the river will be dangerous. You should go back now."

Glumly, he called back, "You don't want me then?"

"No!"

He made a six-layered frown. "Of course you don't want me. Nobody wants me." He peered at me for a moment. "But I want you, you lucky lad."

I stared at him. "Lucky? That's one thing I'm certainly not! My life is nothing but a string of disappointments, one loss after another."

"I can tell," he declared. "That's why you need a jester." Frowning gravely, he added, "To make you laugh." He cleared his throat. "By the way, did I ever tell you my riddle about the bells?"

With a snarl, I swung at his head with my staff. He ducked, stooping lower than usual. The staff skimmed the back of his cloak.

"You're no jester," I shouted. "You're a curse! A miserable curse."

"Too true, too true, too true." Bumbelwy heaved a moaning sigh.

"I'm a failure as a jester. An absolute failure. A jester needs to be only two things, wise and funny. And I am neither." A fretful tear rolled down his cheek. "Can you imagine how that feels? How it makes me ache from my thumbs down to my toes? My fate is to be a jester who makes everyone sad. Including myself."

"Why me?" I protested. "Couldn't you pick somebody else to follow?"

"Certainly," he called above the raging rapids. "But you seem so . . . unhappy. More so than anyone I've ever met. You will be my true test as a jester! If I can learn how to make you laugh, then I can make anyone laugh."

I groaned. "You will never make anyone laugh. That's certain!"

He thrust his chins at me and started to swirl his cloak about himself with a flourish. At the same time, though, he tripped on a stone and pitched sideways, losing his hat and almost skidding over the bank. Grabbing his hat, he jammed it back on his head—upside down. With a snarl, he righted it, but not before he tripped again and plopped down on the muddy ground. Grumbling, he regained his feet, trying to wipe the clumps of mud off his bottom.

"Well then," he declared with a jangle of bells, "at least I can give you the pleasure of my company."

I rolled my eyes, then glanced over my shoulder at the River Unceasing. Perhaps, if I leaped into the rushing water, it might carry me far downstream. Away from this endless torment in the form of a man. Still, as tempted as I was, I knew better. The river at this stretch was flowing far too fast, and jagged rocks protruded like daggers. I would surely damage the Harp, and probably myself as well. Where was Rhia when I needed her? She would know how to speak to the spirit of the river and calm the waves. I cringed, thinking of how we had parted. Yet it was more Rhia's fault than mine. She had been so sure of herself. It had delighted her, no doubt, to see me humbled.

I pulled the Harp higher on my shoulder. At least, once I crossed the river, I wouldn't be surrounded by these parched plains, stretching on and on like the ashen sky above, that reminded me constantly of my unfinished task. South of here, I recalled, the river widened considerably. There I could cross. Then I would continue on to the Shore of the Speaking Shells. With or without Bumbelwy.

To my dismay, it turned out to be with him. The gloomy jester, sleeves flapping and bells clanging, shadowed me past a series of roaring falls, through soggy marshland, and over stretches of smooth stones in the river's floodplain. Finally, reaching the shallows beneath a group of huge, egg-shaped boulders, we stumbled across the River Unceasing. Frigid water slapped against my shins, as the soft bottom sucked at my boots with every step. I felt, somehow, as if the river itself were trying to hold me back.

Emerging from the water, we continued to trek along the western shore. For several hours we plodded along avenues of jagged-edged reeds. To the right, towering trees of Druma Wood stretched skyward, covering the land with a blanket of green as far as the distant Misted Hills. Bright-winged birds flitted among the branches—birds that I knew Rhia could identify. All the while, I did my best to ignore the drooping figure and the jangling bells that followed me.

At last I spied a row of undulating dunes, with a rolling wall of mist behind. My heart leaped. Even with the limits of my second sight, I was struck by the strong colors ahead. Golden sand. Green leafy vines. Pink and purple shells. Yellow flowers.

My boots sank into the loose sand as I climbed the first dune. Reaching the crest, I finally saw the shore itself, rippling with waves.

The tide was low. Beneath the thick curtain of mist, clams and mussels covered the sand. I could hear them squirting and squelching, joined by the chatter and splash of water birds with long, scooped beaks. Tiny mussels by the thousands clung to the rockier places. Huge red sea stars, wide-mouthed whelks, and glistening jellyfish lay everywhere. Crabs skittered, dodging the feet of the birds.

Filling my lungs with the air of the sea, I smelled again the aroma of kelp. And salt. And mystery.

I bent down to grasp a handful of sand. It felt warm and fine as it poured through my fingers. Just as it had before, on the day I first landed on this very spot. Fincayra had welcomed me on that day, giving me refuge from the storms I faced at sea as well as those I carried beneath my brow.

I plucked a few grains of sand and watched them tumble down the slope of my fingertip, bouncing into my palm. They glittered brightly as they rolled, almost as if they were alive. Like my own skin. Like Fincayra itself. Somehow, I realized, I was beginning to feel attached to this island. As unhappy as I had often been here, I felt a surprising pull to its striking terrains, its haunting stories, and—despite the way they had often treated me—its varied inhabitants. And to something else, harder to define.

This island was, as my mother used to say, an *in between place*, a place where immortal and mortal creatures could live together. Not always harmoniously, of course. But with all the richness and power and mystery of both worlds at once. Part Heaven, part Earth. Part this world, part Otherworld.

I stood there, drinking in the sounds and smells of Fincayra's shore. Perhaps, one day, I might feel truly comfortable here. In some ways I already did, at least more than I had ever felt in that miserable village in Gwynedd. If only one particular person were here, Fincayra might even feel like home. Yet right now that person was far away. Beyond the mist, beyond the black rock coastline of Gwynedd.

Swinging the Harp around, I cradled it in my arm. I had not plucked its strings for some time now, since before I had left the arid plains. What, I wondered, could I produce in a place so rich, so teeming with life, as this?

I plucked a single string, the highest one. It tinkled, like an icicle shattering. As the note vibrated in the air, out of the seaward side of the dune popped a single red flower, shaped like an enormous bell. Seeing it sway in the briny breeze, I yearned to touch it, to smell it.

But there was no time. Not now. Dropping the Harp and my staff on the sand, I checked to make sure that Bumbelwy would not disturb them. He was already seated on the beach, frowning as he washed his swollen feet in the waves. His three-cornered hat, its bells silent at least for now, lay beside him. Though he wasn't far away, he seemed fully occupied.

I scanned the beach in both directions. With every slap forward and wash backward of the waves, shells of all sizes and colors rolled across the sand. The sheer breadth and beauty of this beach awed me, just as it had on the day I first landed. On that very day, a shell from this beach had whispered some words to me, words I could barely comprehend. Would I find another one today? And would I understand what it said?

Somewhere out there was the right shell. The trouble was, I had no idea what it might look like. All I knew were Cairpré's words. *There is a proverb, as old as this island itself, saying that only the wisest shell from the Shore of Speaking Shells can guide someone through the mists.*

Beginning with a spotted conch near the base of my staff, I started hunting for shells. Flat ones, round ones, curling ones, chambered ones, all found their way into my hands. Yet none seemed right. I wasn't even certain how to look. I could almost hear Rhia saying something as nonsensical as *Trust in the berries.* Ridiculous, of course. Yet I knew I had to trust in something. I only wished I knew what.

My intellect, perhaps. Yes. That was it. Now, what would the wisest shell look like? It would be striking. Impressive. An emperor of the shore. As large in size as it surely was in wisdom.

Bumbelwy cried out as a large wave splashed over him. As the wave withdrew, grinding against the sand, it revealed the edge of a spiral-shaped shell, bright pink, that was larger than any of the others around. It lay just behind him, although the fellow didn't seem to have noticed it. Could it be the one I was seeking? Just as I started to move closer, Bumbelwy shook himself, grumbling about the cold water, then leaned backward. As his elbow landed on the shell, I heard a loud crunch. He screeched and rolled to the side, clutching his wounded elbow. Shaking my head, I knew that my search had only begun.

Only the wisest shell . . .

I followed the sandy shore, looking for any shells that might seem right. Despite the wide array of shapes, colors, and textures, none were imposing enough. The few that came close I placed against my ear. But I heard nothing except the endless sighing of the sea.

In time I came to a rocky peninsula that jutted seaward, vanishing into the curling mist. As I stood there, wondering whether to search among the wet rocks, an orange crab ran across the toe of my boot.

The crab paused, raising its little eyes as if it were examining me. Then it skittered onto the peninsula and disappeared.

For some reason I felt drawn to this little creature that, like me, wandered this shore alone. Without thinking, I followed it onto the peninsula. Mist enveloped me. I moved carefully across the rocks, trying not to slip. Although the crab seemed to have vanished, I soon spotted another spiral shell. It lay on a flat slab coated with green algae. Even larger than the one Bumbelwy had destroyed, this shell was almost as big as my own head. It glowed with a deep blue luster, despite the unusual shadow that seemed to quiver on its surface. Certain that the shadow was only a trick of the rolling mist, I approached.

With each step I took toward it, the shell seemed more lovely. Gleaming white lines framed its graceful curves. I felt strangely drawn to it, captivated by its radiant hues.

Only the wisest shell . . .

At that moment, a powerful wave surged out of the mist, crashing over the peninsula. Struck by the spray, I felt the sting of salt on my scarred cheeks. The wave receded, pulling the spiral shell off the rock. Before I could grab it, the shell splashed into the water and disappeared in a swirl of mist.

Cursing, I turned back to the flat rock. Although the shell had vanished, the strange shadow still quivered on the algae. I almost reached down to take a closer look, then hesitated. I was not sure why. Just then the orange crab emerged from beneath a nearby rock. It skittered sideways over the peninsula, passing under a ledge before emerging from the other side. As it skirted the rim of a tide pool, it plunged into a tangle of driftwood.

Having lost any interest in following the crab, I turned away. My gaze fell on another tide pool, clear and still. From the bottom, something glistened among the fronds of kelp. Bending lower, I saw only a rather plain shell, brown with a large blue spot, nestled among some purple sea urchins. Still, it aroused my curiosity. Careful to avoid the sea urchins' sharp spines, I reached into the cold water and pulled out the shell.

Unremarkable as it appeared, the shell fit comfortably in the palm of my hand. Almost as if it belonged there. I hefted it, gauging its weight. It felt much heavier than I would have guessed for something so compact.

I brought it to my ear. Nothing. Yet there was something remarkable about this shell. My voice uncertain, I asked, "Are you the wisest shell?"

To my astonishment, I heard a spitting, crackling voice. "You are a fool, boy."

"What?" I shook my head. "Did you call me a fool?"

"A stupid fool," spat the shell.

My cheeks grew hot, but I held my temper. "And who are you?"

"Not the wisest shell, by any means." The shell seemed to smack its lips. "But I am no fool."

I felt tempted to hurl it into the waves. Yet my determination to bring back my mother remained stronger than my anger. "Then tell me where I can find the wisest shell."

The brown shell laughed, dripping water in my ear. "Try someplace where wood and water meet, foolish boy."

Puzzled, I turned the shell over in my hand. "The nearest trees are on the other side of the dunes. There isn't any wood by the water."

"Are you sure?"

"Absolutely sure."

"Spoken like a fool."

Reluctantly, I scanned the peninsula. At length, I noticed the scraps of driftwood where the crab had disappeared. Rotting seaweed draped over the wood like tattered rags. I wagged my head in disbelief. "You don't mean that sorry little pile over there."

"Spoken like a fool," repeated the shell.

Not at all sure I was doing the right thing, I dropped the brown shell into the pool and stepped over to the driftwood. Peeling off the seaweed, I searched for any sign of a shell. Nothing.

I was ready to quit when I noticed a tiny shape in a crack in the wood. It was a sand-colored shell, shaped like a little cone. It could have fit easily on my thumbnail. As I lifted the shell toward me, a black, wormlike creature pushed itself partially out of the opening at the base, then quickly shrunk back inside. Hesitant to bring such a thing too close to my ear, I held it some distance away. Although I could not be sure, I thought I heard a faint, watery whisper.

Cautiously, I brought the object closer. The watery voice came again, like a wave crashing in the tiny shell's innermost chambers. "You, *splashhh*, have chosen well, Merlin."

I caught my breath. "Did you say my name?"

"That I did, *splishhh*, though you know not mine. It is, *splashhh*, Washamballa, sage among the shells."

"Washamballa," I repeated, cradling the moist little cone against my earlobe. Something about its voice made my hopes rise. "Do you also know why I have come?"

"That, *splashhh*, I do."

My heart pounded. "Will you—will you help, then? Will you bring her back to Fincayra?"

The shell said nothing for several seconds. At last its small, gurgling voice spoke again. "I should not help you, Merlin. The risks, *splishhh*, are so great, greater than you know."

"But—"

"I should not," continued the shell. "Yet I feel something in you . . . something I cannot resist. While you have so much more to learn, *sploshhh*, this may well be part of it."

As Washamballa paused, I listened to its watery breathing. I dared not say anything.

"We might succeed, *splashhh*, or we might fail. I do not know, for even success may be a failure in disguise. Do you still, *splashhh*, wish to try?"

"Yes," I declared.

"Then hold me tight, *splashhh*, against your heart, and concentrate on the one you long for."

Clasping the shell in both hands, I pressed it against my chest. I thought about my mother. Her table of herbs, pungent and spicy. Her blue eyes, so full of feeling. Her kindness, her quiet demeanor. Her stories about Apollo, Athena, and the place called Olympus. Her faith—in her God, and in me. Her love, silent and strong.

Mist curled about me. Waves licked my boots. Yet nothing more happened.

"Try harder, *splishhh*. You must try harder."

I felt Elen's sadness. That she could never return to Fincayra. That she could never see her son grow into manhood—and that he, in all those years in Gwynedd, had refused to call her Mother. A simple word, a powerful bond. I winced, remembering how much pain I had caused her.

Slowly, her presence grew stronger. I could feel her embrace, how safe I once felt in her arms. How, for brief moments at least, I could forget all the torments that haunted us. I could smell the shavings of cedar bark by her pillow. I could hear her voice calling me across the oceans of water, the oceans of longing.

Then came the wind. A fierce, howling wind that threw me down on the rocks and soaked me with spray. For several minutes it raged, battering me ceaselessly. Suddenly, I heard a resounding *crack*, as if something beyond the mist had broken. The billowing clouds before me began to shift, gathering themselves into strange shapes. First I saw a snake, coiling to strike. Before it did, though, its body melted into the misty form of a flower. The flower slowly swelled, changing into a huge, unblinking eye.

Then, in the middle of the eye, a dark shape appeared. Only a shadow at first, it grew swiftly more solid. Before long, it looked almost like a person groping in the mist. Stumbling to shore.

It was my mother.

VII

HEADLONG
AND HAPPILY

She collapsed, sprawling on the dark, wet rocks. Her eyes were closed, and her creamy skin looked pale and lifeless. Long, unbraided hair, as golden as a summer moon, clung in ragged clumps to her deep blue robe. Yet she was breathing. She was alive.

Giving the little shell a quick squeeze of thanks, I replaced it among the scraps of driftwood. Then I ran to my mother's side. Hesitantly, I reached toward her. Just as my finger touched her strong, high cheek, she opened her eyes. For a few seconds she gazed up at me, looking confused. Then Elen of the Sapphire Eyes blinked, raised herself up on one elbow, and spoke in the voice I had thought I would never hear again.

"Emrys! It is you."

Though gratitude choked my voice, I replied, "It is me . . . Mother."

At hearing me say that word, a touch of pink flushed her cheeks. Slowly, she extended a hand. Though her skin felt as wet and chilled as my own, her touch sent waves of warmth through me. She sat up, and we embraced.

After a few seconds, she pushed back. Running her fingers gently over my burned cheeks and eyes, she seemed to be looking under my skin, into my very soul. I could tell that she was trying to feel everything I had felt in the months since we parted.

Suddenly, as she touched my neck, she caught her breath. "The Galator! Oh, Emrys. It's gone!"

I lowered my sightless eyes. "I lost it."

How could I tell her that I had lost it on the way to finding my own father? And that, in finally meeting him, I had lost even more?

I raised my head. "But I have you again. We're together, here on Fincayra."

She nodded, her eyes brimming with tears.

"And I have a new name, as well."

"A new name?"

"Merlin."

"Merlin," she repeated. "Like the high-flying hawk."

A pang of sorrow shot through me, as I recalled my friend Trouble, the little hawk who had given his life to save my own. I dearly hoped that he was still soaring, somewhere up there in the Otherworld. Even now, I missed the familiar feeling of him strutting across my shoulder.

And, the truth was, I missed my other friends as well. Friends I had known for a time—and then lost. Cairpré. Honn. T'eilean and Garlatha. Aylah, the wind sister. Even Shim, who had shambled off to the mountains weeks ago. And, yes, Rhia.

I squeezed my mother's hand. "I won't lose you again."

She listened to my vow, her expression both sorrowful and loving. "Nor I you."

I turned toward the dunes. Bumbelwy sat by the water's edge, polishing his bells on his sleeve. He seemed determined to ignore the

sea gulls who kept tugging on his mud-splattered cloak. The Flowering Harp, along with my staff, remained where I had left them on
the sand. Not far beyond, the luscious red flower swayed in the
breeze off the sea.

"Come." I stood, pulling my mother to her feet. "I have something to show you."

We crossed over the rocky peninsula to the fine-grained sand of
the beach. As we moved, arms around each other's waists, I savored
the joy of walking with her again. Of being with her again. And when
I thought about showing her the Harp, and all that I could make it
do, my heart raced.

I was feeling my own power now, just as she had predicted long
ago. She had told me that Tuatha himself came into his powers as he
entered his teenage years. So it made sense that I should, as well. After
all, hadn't I already done something that Tuatha, for all his wizardry,
had never attempted? I smiled to myself. Even the shifting mists surrounding this isle could not resist me.

As we neared the Flowering Harp, she gasped in wonder. Given
her affection for anything alive and growing, I was not surprised to
see that it was not the Harp that had caught her attention. It was the
red flower sprouting from the dune. Indeed, the flower seemed even
more beautiful now than after it had just emerged. The deep cup of
its petals, shaped like a bell, sat gracefully upon its arching stalk.
Bright green leaves, perfectly round, ringed the stem like dozens of
jewels. Dewdrops glistened from the edge of every petal.

"I must smell that flower," she declared.

"Of course." My grin broadened. "After all, I made it."

She halted, turned to me. "You did? Really?"

"With a stroke of my finger," I said proudly. "Come. Let's look closer."

As I drew nearer to the flower, my own urge to smell it grew stronger and stronger. Not just to sip a little of its fragrance, but to immerse my whole face in its petals. To drink deeply of its glorious nectar. To plunge into it, headlong and happily. I hardly noticed the strange, quivering shadow that moved across the petals. Just another trick of the misty light, as I had seen before. And no shadow, however dark, could possibly obscure the radiant beauty of this flower.

My mother's arm fell from my waist, as my own fell from hers. We continued walking toward the flower, wordlessly, as if we were in a trance. Our feet slapped on the wet sand, leaving a trail of dark prints behind us. All I could think about was breathing the flower's wondrous aroma. Only a step away, the briny breeze blew against our faces. Heedless, both of us bent toward the inviting cup.

I hesitated for an instant, wondering if I ought to let her go first. She would enjoy it so much. Then the shadow quivered again—and my urge to smell the flower grew even stronger, so much stronger that I forgot everything else. I lowered my face. Closer. Closer.

Suddenly a green shape leaped over the crest of the dune. It crashed into me, bowling me over backward. I rolled to a stop, covered with sand, then whirled around to confront my assailant.

"Rhia!" Full of rage, I spit some sand from my mouth. "Are you trying to kill me?"

Bouncing back to her feet, she ignored me completely and turned toward my mother. "Stop!" she cried with all the force of her lungs. "Don't do it!"

But Elen paid no attention. With one hand, she pulled her hair back from her face and bent toward the red flower.

Seeing this, Rhia started to dash up the slope of the dune. A terrible scream arrested her—even as it froze the blood in my veins. A dark mass leaped out of the center of the flower, straight into my mother's face. She staggered backward, clutching her cheeks with both hands.

"No!" I shouted to the sky, the sea, the mist. "No!"

But it was too late. My mother stumbled, rolling down the dune. When she stopped, I saw that her entire face was covered by a writhing shadow. Then, to my horror, the shadow slithered into her mouth and disappeared.

VIII

THE LANGUAGE
OF THE WOUND

I rushed to her side. She lay crumpled near the base of the dune. Wet sand smeared her blue robe and one of her cheeks. The sea breeze rose, sending shreds of mist across the beach.

"Mother!"

"She is your mother?" asked Rhia, joining me. "Your real mother?"

"That I am," Elen answered weakly, as she rolled onto her back. Her blue eyes searched my face. "Are you safe, my son?"

I brushed the sand off her cheek. "Safe?" I cried. "Safe? I am destroyed. Totally destroyed. I didn't bring you here to have you poisoned!"

She coughed savagely, as if she were trying to expel the shadow. Yet her face only grew more pained, more frightened.

I turned to Rhia. "I wish you had saved her instead of me."

She pulled at one of the vines woven into her garb. "I'm sorry I didn't arrive sooner. I've been searching all over for you. Finally I came to Caer Neithan, several hours after you had left. When Cairpré told me what you were doing, I followed you as fast as I could." Sadly, she looked down at Elen. "It must feel horrible. Like swallowing a bad dream."

"I—I am all right," she replied, though her wretched expression told differently. She tried to sit up, then fell back onto the sand.

Bells jangled behind me. A familiar voice moaned, "I feel death in the air."

I spun around. "Go away, will you? You're as bad as that poisonous flower!"

His head drooped even lower than usual. "I share your sorrow. I really do. Perhaps I could lighten your burden with one of Bumbelwy the Mirthful's humorous songs?"

"No!"

"How about a riddle, then? My famous one about the bells?"

"No!"

"All right," he snapped. "In that case I won't tell you it was not the flower that poisoned her." He scowled several times over. "And I certainly won't tell you it was Rhita Gawr."

My stomach tightened, even as my mother gasped. I grabbed his wide sleeve and shook him, making his bells rattle. "What makes you say such a thing?"

"*The death shadow.* I have heard it described, many times. Too many times for even a fool like me to forget. It's one of Rhita Gawr's favorite means of gaining revenge."

Elen shuddered and groaned painfully. "He speaks the truth, my son. If I hadn't lost my wits to the spell, I'd have remembered sooner." Her face contorted, even as the breeze swelled again, as if the ocean itself had heaved a great sigh. "Why me, though? Why me?"

I felt suddenly weak. For I knew in my bones that the death shadow had not been meant for my mother. It had been meant for me. Yet because of me—my own stupidity—it had struck her down instead. I should have listened to Cairpré! I should never have brought her here.

"Rhita Gawr saves this method only for those whose death he truly relishes," intoned Bumbelwy. "For it is slow, painfully slow. And horrible beyond anything words can describe. The person afflicted suffers one whole month—through four phases of the moon—before finally dying. But the final moments of dying, I have heard, hold more agony, more torment, more excruciating pain, than the entire month before."

Once again, Elen groaned, drawing her knees into her chest.

"Enough!" I waved my arms at the dour jester. "Stop saying such things! Do you want to kill her sooner? Better not to talk at all—unless you know the cure."

Bumbelwy turned away, shaking his head. "There is no cure."

I started to open my satchel of herbs. "Maybe something in here—"

"There is no cure," he repeated mournfully.

"Oh, but there *must* be," objected Rhia, kneeling beside my mother and stroking her forehead. "There is a cure for every ailment, no matter how horrible. You just have to know the language of the wound."

For a flickering instant, Elen's face brightened. "She is right. There might be a cure." She studied Rhia for a long moment. Then, her voice weak, she asked, "What is your name, young one? And how do you come to know so much about the art of healing?"

Rhia patted her suit of woven vines. "The trees of the Druma taught me. They are my family."

"And your name?"

"Most people call me Rhia. Except for the wood elves, who still use my full name, Rhiannon."

My mother's face creased in pain—but not, it seemed to me, from her ailing body. It might have been a different kind of pain, felt in another kind of place. Yet she said nothing. She merely turned her face toward the billowing mist beyond the beach.

Rhia moved nearer. "Please tell me your name."

"Elen." She glanced my way. "Though I am also called Mother."

I felt a stab of pain in my heart. She still had no idea that this was all my fault. That I had brought her here against Cairpré's strongest advice. That I had tried, in my ignorance—no, my arrogance—to act like a wizard.

Rhia continued stroking Elen's brow. "You feel hot already. I think it will get worse."

"It will get worse," declared Bumbelwy. "Everything always gets worse. Far worse."

Rhia shot me an urgent look. "We must find the cure before it's too late."

Bumbelwy began pacing across the sand, swishing his sleeves. "It's already too late. With this kind of thing, even too early is too late."

"Maybe there's a cure that nobody has found yet," retorted Rhia. "We must try."

"Try all you want. It won't help. No, it's too late. Far too late."

My mind spun in circles, torn between the urgent hopefulness of Rhia and the gloominess of Bumbelwy. Both could not be true. Yet both seemed plausible. I wanted to believe one, but I feared the other was right. A pair of gulls screeched, swooping overhead to land on a bed of sea stars and mussels. I bit my lip. Even if there were a cure, how could we possibly find it in time? Here on this remote beach, with nothing but sand dunes and rolling waves, there was no one to turn to. No one to help.

I straightened suddenly. There *was* someone to turn to! I jumped up and sprinted across the beach to the mist-shrouded peninsula. Ignoring the waves on the slippery rocks, I stumbled several times. Worse yet, in the swirling vapors, I found no sign whatsoever of the pile of driftwood where I had left the wise old shell. Had a powerful wave washed it away? My heart sank. I might never find it again!

Painstakingly, on hands and knees, I combed the wet rocks, turning over slippery jellyfish and examining tide pools. At last, soaked with spray, I spied a shard of driftwood. And there, with it, rested a little shell. Was it the same one? Quickly, I placed the sand-colored cone against my ear.

"Washamballa, is it you?"

No answer came.

"Washamballa," I pleaded. "Answer me if it's you! Is there any cure for the death shadow? Any cure at all?"

Finally, I heard a long, watery sigh, like the sound of a wave breaking very slowly. "You have learned, *sploshhh*, a most painful lesson."

"Yes, yes! But can you help me now? Tell me if there is any cure. My mother is dying."

"Do you still, *splashhh*, have the Galator?"

I grimaced. "No. I . . . gave it away."

"Can you get it back, *splishhh*, very quickly?"

"No. It's with Domnu."

I could feel the shell's despairing breath in my ear. "Then you are beyond any help. *Splashhh*. For there is a cure. But to find it, *splashhh*, you must travel to the Otherworld."

"The Otherworld? The land of the spirits? But the only way to go there is to die!" I shook my head, spraying drops of water from my black hair. "I would do even that if it would save her, I really would. But even if I took the Long Journey I've heard about, the one that leads to the Otherworld, I could never get back here again with the cure."

"True. The Long Journey takes the dead, *splashhh*, to the Otherworld, but it does not send them back again to the land of the living."

A new thought struck me. "Wait! Tuatha—my grandfather—found some way to travel alive to the Otherworld. To consult with the great Dagda, I believe. Could I possibly follow Tuatha's path?"

"That was the path that finally killed him. *Sploshhh*. Do not forget that. For he was slain by Balor, the ogre who answers only to Rhita Gawr. Even now Balor guards the secret entrance, a place called, *splashhh*, the Otherworld Well. And he has sworn to stop any ally of Dagda who tries to pass that way."

"The Otherworld Well? Is it some sort of stairwell, leading up to the land of the spirits?"

"Whatever it is," sloshed the voice of the shell, "to find it is your, *splashhh*, only hope. For the cure you seek is the Elixir of Dagda, and only Dagda himself can give it to you."

A cold wave washed over my legs. The salt stung the scrapes from my falls on the rocks. Yet I barely noticed.

"*The Elixir of Dagda*," I said slowly. "Well, ogre or no ogre, I must get it. How do I find this stairway to the Otherworld?"

Once again the shell sighed with the breath of despair. "To find it you must come to hear a strange, enchanted music. *Splashhh*. The music, Merlin, of wizardry."

"Wizardry?" I nearly dropped the little cone. "I can't possibly do that."

"Then you are, indeed, lost. For the only way to find Tuatha's path is to master, *splashhh*, the Seven Songs of Wizardry."

"What in the world are they?"

The wind leaned against me, fluttering my tunic, as I waited for the shell's reply. At last I heard again the small voice in my ear. "Even I, the wisest of the shells, do not know. All I can say is that, *splishhh*, the Seven Songs were inscribed by Tuatha himself on a great tree in Druma Wood."

"Not . . . Arbassa?"

"Yes."

"I know that tree! It's Rhia's house." I furrowed my brow, recalling the strange writing that I had found there. "But that writing is impossible! I couldn't read a word of it."

"Then you must try again, Merlin. It is your only chance, *splashhh*, to save your mother. Though it is a very small chance indeed."

I thought of my mother, lying in the shadow of the dune, afflicted with the death shadow, her breath growing shorter and shorter. I had done this to her. Now I must try to undo it, whatever the risks. Even so, I shuddered to recall Cairpré's description of the qualities of a true wizard. Qualities that I surely lacked. Whatever the Seven Songs might be, I had almost no chance of mastering them—certainly not in the brief time before the death shadow completed its terrible work.

"It's too much," I said despondently. "I am no wizard! Even if I somehow succeed at the Seven Songs, how can I possibly find this Otherworld Well, elude Balor, and climb up to the realm of Dagda, all within four phases of the moon?"

"I should never, *sploshhh*, have helped you."

I thought about the faint new moon that I had glimpsed last night. Only the barest sliver, it had been nearly impossible for my second sight to find. That meant I had until the end of this moon, and not a day beyond, to find the Elixir of Dagda. On the day the moon died, my mother would die as well.

As the moon grew full, my time would be half gone. As it waned, my time would be almost ended. And when it disappeared at last, so would my hopes.

"I wish you all the luck, *splashhh*, in Fincayra," said the shell. "You will need it, *splashhh*, and more."

IX

ROSEMARY

Since my mother was already too weak to walk, Rhia and I made a rough-hewn stretcher by weaving some vines from the dune between my staff and the branch of a dead hawthorn tree. As we worked, threading the vines from one side to the other, I explained some of what I had learned from the shell, and asked her to lead us through the forest to Arbassa. Yet even as I said the name of the great tree, I felt a strong sense of foreboding at the thought of returning there. I had no idea why.

Rhia, by contrast, didn't seem concerned or surprised to learn that the writing on Arbassa's walls held the secrets I would need to find the Otherworld Well. Perhaps because she had seen Arbassa give so many answers to so many questions before, she merely nodded, continuing to tie off the vines. At last, we finished the stretcher and helped my mother slide into place. Laying my hand on her brow, I could tell that she had grown hotter. Yet despite her worsening condition, she did not knowingly complain.

The same could not be said about Bumbelwy. We had barely started walking, with him taking the rear of the stretcher, when he began doing his own imitation of a speaking shell. When at last he realized that his audience did not find this at all amusing, he switched to describing the intricacies of his bell-laden hat, as if it were some sort of royal crown. When that, too, failed, he began complaining that carrying such a heavy load might strain his delicate back, hampering his abilities as a jester. I didn't respond, although I was tempted to silence both him and his jangling bells by stuffing his hat into his mouth.

Rhia led the way, with the Flowering Harp slung over her leafy shoulder. I took the front of the stretcher, but the weight of my own guilt seemed the heaviest burden of all. Even crossing the dune, passing beside the bell-shaped flower, felt like a strenuous march.

Before entering Druma Wood, we passed through a verdant meadow. Ribbed with streams, the grasses of the meadow moved in waves like the surface of the sea. Every rivulet splashed and rippled, lining the plants along the banks with sparkling ribbons of water. I thought how full of beauty this spot might have seemed to me under different circumstances, beauty not caused by a magical instrument or a great wizard. Beauty that was simply there.

Finally, with a crackling of twigs and needles underfoot, we entered the ancient forest. The bright meadow disappeared, and all went dark. Powerful resins, sometimes pungent, sometimes sweet, spiced the air. Branches whispered and clacked overhead. Shadows seemed to drift silently behind the trees.

Once again, I felt the eeriness of this forest. It was more than a collection of living beings of varied kinds. It was, in truth, a living being itself. Once it had given me my hemlock staff. But now, I felt certain, it was watching me, regarding me with suspicion.

I stubbed my toe on a root. Though I winced with pain, I held tight to the stretcher. My second sight had grown stronger since I was last here, but the dim light still hampered my vision. Sunlight struck just the topmost layers of these dense groves, while only a few rare beams reached all the way to the forest floor. Yet I was not about to slow down to get my bearings. I didn't have time. Nor did my mother.

Following Rhia, we pushed deeper into the forest, bearing the stretcher of vines. The strange sensation that the trees themselves were watching, following our every move, grew stronger with every step. The clacking branches sounded agitated as we passed beneath them. Other creatures seemed aware of us, as well. Every so often I glimpsed a bushy tail or pair of yellow eyes. Squeals and howls often echoed among the darkened boughs. And once, from somewhere very near, I heard a loud, prolonged scraping sound, like sharp claws ripping at a layer of bark. Or skin.

My arms and shoulders ached, but hearing the swelling groans of my mother hurt more. Bumbelwy, at least, seemed moved enough by her suffering to contain his grumbling, although his bells continued to jangle. And while Rhia moved through the woods with the lightness of a breeze, she often glanced back worriedly at the stretcher.

After hours of marching through the dark glades draped with mosses and ferns, my shoulders throbbed as if they were about to burst. My hands, nearly numb, couldn't hold on any longer. Was there no shorter route? Was it possible that Rhia had lost her way? I cleared my dry throat, ready to call out to her.

Then, up ahead, I glimpsed a new light in the branches. As we pushed through a tangle of ferns, which clung to my ankles and thighs, the light grew stronger. The spaces between the trunks widened. A cool breeze, as fragrant as fresh mint, slapped the sweaty skin of my brow.

We entered a grassy clearing. In the center, rising from a web of burly roots, stood a majestic oak tree. Arbassa. Older than old it looked, and taller than any other tree we had seen. Its massive trunk, as wide as five or six trees fused into one, lifted several times my height before its first branches emerged. From there it soared up, up, until at length it merged with the clouds.

Set in the midst of its lower branches, made from the limbs of the oak itself, sat Rhia's aerial cottage. Branches curled and twisted to form its walls, floor, and roof. Shimmering curtains of green leaves draped every window. I remembered first seeing the cottage at night, when it had been lit from within and glowed like an exploding star.

Rhia lifted her arms like rising branches. "Arbassa."

The great tree quivered, raining dew on all of us. With a pang, I recalled my clumsy attempt to make the beech tree in the Dark Hills bend down to me. On that day, Rhia had called me a fool for trying such a thing. Whether or not she had been right, I knew, as I gently lowered my mother's stretcher onto the grass, that I had been far more of a fool on this day for trying something else.

"Rosemary," said Elen, her voice hoarse from moaning. She pointed at a shrub, decked with leafy spires, that was growing near the edge of the clearing. "Get me some of that. Please."

In a flash, Rhia plucked a sprig and offered it to her. "Here you are. It's so fragrant, it reminds me of pine needles in the sun. What did you call it?"

"Rosemary." My mother rolled it between her palms, filling the air with its striking scent. She brought the crushed leaves to her face and inhaled deeply.

Her face relaxed a bit. She lowered her hands. "The Greeks called it *starlight of the land.* Isn't that lovely?"

Rhia nodded, her curls bouncing on her shoulders. "And it's good for rheumatism, isn't it?"

Elen gazed at her in surprise. "How in the world did you know that?"

"Cwen, my friend, used it to help her hands." A shadow crossed Rhia's face. "At least she used to be my friend."

"She made a pact with the goblins," I explained. "And almost killed us in the bargain. She was a tr—Rhia, what did you call her?"

"A treeling. Half tree, half person. The very last one of her kind." Rhia listened for a moment to the whispering oak leaves above us. "She took care of me ever since I was a baby, after she found me abandoned in the forest."

My mother winced in pain, though her eyes remained fixed on Rhia. "Do you . . . do you miss your real family, child?"

Rhia waved her hand lightly. "Oh, no. Not at all. The trees are my family. Especially Arbassa."

Again the branches quivered, showering us with dew. And yet I couldn't help but notice that, despite Rhia's carefree words, her gray-blue eyes seemed sad. Sadder than I had ever seen them.

Bumbelwy, frowning with his eyebrows, mouth, and chins, bent down next to the stretcher and touched my mother's forehead. "You are hot," he said grimly. "Hotter than before. This is just the occasion for my riddle about my bells. It's one of my funniest—especially since I don't know any others. Shall I tell it?"

"No." I pushed him roughly aside. "Your riddles and songs will only make her feel worse!"

He pouted, all of his chins wobbling above the clasp of his cloak.

"Too true, too true, too true." Then he drew himself up a little straighter. "But someday, mark my words, I will make somebody laugh."

"You think so?"

"Yes. It might even be you."

"Right. And the day you do that, I'll eat my boots." I scowled at him. "Get away, now. You're worse than a curse, a plague, and a typhoon combined."

Elen moaned, shifting her weight on the stretcher. She started to say something to Rhia, her blue eyes wide with anxiety. Then, for some reason, she caught herself. Instead, she took another sniff of rosemary. Turning to me, she asked, "Fetch me some lemon balm, will you? It will help calm this headache. Do you know where any grows?"

"I'm not sure. Rhia might know."

Rhia, her eyes still darkened, nodded.

"And some chamomile, child, if you can find it. It often sprouts near pine trees, alongside a little white mushroom with red hairs on the stem."

"The trees will guide me to it." Rhia glanced up at Arbassa's mighty boughs. "But first we'll bring you inside."

She peeled off her snug shoes, made from some kind of bark, and stepped into a small hollow in the roots. Then she spoke a long, swishing phrase in the language of an oak. The roots closed over her feet, so that she stood like a young sapling at Arbassa's side. As she opened her arms to embrace the huge trunk, a leafy branch lowered and laid itself across her back. All at once the branch lifted, the roots parted, and the trunk creased and cracked open, revealing a small, bark-edged doorway. Rhia entered, beckoning us to follow.

As I bent to pick up the front end of the stretcher, I looked at my mother. Perspiration flecked her cheeks and brow. Such torment in her face! Seeing her this way felt like a spear twisting in my chest. Yet . . . I couldn't shake the feeling that not all of the pain she was feeling this day had been caused by me.

Bumbelwy, grumbling to himself, picked up the rear. Together, we stumbled across the maze of roots toward the doorway. When I was only two paces away, the bark-edged door began to close. Just as it had done before, when I first came to Arbassa! Once again, the tree did not want to let me inside.

Rhia shrieked. She waved her hands, swishing a stern reprimand. The tree shuddered. The belligerent door stopped closing, then slowly opened again. Rhia shot me a glance, her expression grim. Then she turned and began to climb the gnarled, spiraling stairway within the trunk. As I followed, ducking my head to pass through the door, I was struck by the smells, rich and moist like autumn leaves after a rain. And by the sheer enormity of the trunk. Arbassa seemed even larger inside than it had outside. Even so, I had to concentrate hard in the dim light not to bump the stretcher against the walls or tilt it so far that my mother might slip off.

Carefully, we climbed the stairs of living wood. Strange writing, as intricate as a spider's web, flowed across the walls. Its interwoven runes filled the entire stairwell from top to bottom. But it was as incomprehensible as before. My hopes sank further.

Finally we came to the thick curtain of leaves that marked the entry into Rhia's cottage. Pushing through, we stepped onto a wide floor of woven boughs. All around us, wooden furniture sprouted straight out of the interlaced branches. I recognized the low table by the hearth, the pair of sturdy chairs, the honey-colored cabinet whose edges were lined with green leaves.

"Oh," breathed Elen, as she shifted slightly to see better. "It's so beautiful."

I nodded to Bumbelwy and we set down the stretcher as gently as possible. Even as he straightened himself stiffly, his frowns lessened ever so slightly. He looked around, captivated by the interior of the cottage. My own thoughts, however, remained in the stairwell below.

As if reading my mind, Rhia touched my arm. "I have some herbs to fetch for your mother." She removed the Flowering Harp from her shoulder, placing it against the wall near the stretcher. "And you, if you still hope to save her, have much work to do."

X

ARBASSA'S
SECRET

.

Deep within Arbassa, I toiled. I tried everything possible to find the key to the puzzle. Time after time, I trudged up the spiral stairs and down again, searching for the right place to start. I backed away, scanning the walls for some sort of pattern. I came very close, laying my forehead against the cool wood, examining each individual rune in turn. To no avail.

Hour after hour, I pored over the mysterious writing on the walls. Writing that might somehow guide me to the cure Elen so desperately needed. Yet while the intricately carved script seemed full of hidden meaning, it left me empty of understanding.

Sunset came and went, and the dim light in the stairwell faded away completely. For some time I struggled to use my second sight, even less reliable than usual in the darkness, until finally Rhia brought me an unusual torch. It was a sphere, as big as my fist, made of thin but sturdy beeswax. Within it crawled a dozen or more beetles that glowed with a steady, amber light. It was enough to illuminate at least a small portion of the script.

Grateful though I was for the torch, I accepted it without a word. The same was true for the two bowls, one filled with water and one with large green nuts, that Bumbelwy brought me sometime later.

Despite the fact that he tripped on the stairs, spilling half the water on my neck, I hardly noticed him. I was too absorbed in my work. And also my guilt. For all my concentration on the strange runes, I couldn't keep myself from hearing the recurrent sighs and moans from the woman lying on the floor above me. The woman I had brought to Fincayra.

Outside, I knew, a pale new moon was rising over Druma Wood, painting Arbassa's boughs with the faintest glow of silver. Now I had one month, less one day, to find the cure. As difficult, perhaps impossible, as that task would be, I could not even begin it until I deciphered the script. And the script showed no sign of sharing its secret.

Wearily, I lay my hand against the wooden wall. Suddenly I felt a brief spark of warmth from the runes. It barely pricked the palm of my hand before it vanished. Yet it left me with the feeling, deep in my bones, that this writing had indeed been carved by the great wizard Tuatha. Could he have known that one day, years later, his own grandson would struggle to read these mysterious words? That the words would offer the only hope of finding the stairway to the Otherworld and the Elixir of Dagda? And could Tuatha have guessed that the Elixir would be needed to save the life of Elen—the woman he had once predicted would give birth to a wizard with powers even greater than his own?

Some wizard I had turned out to be! When I wasn't bearing a magical instrument, what had my powers wrought? Nothing but misery. To me and those in my wake. I had not only snuffed out my own two eyes, I had nearly snuffed out my own mother's life.

I shambled down to the bottom of the stairwell. Despondently, I leaned close to the wall. Reaching out my hand, I touched the very first rune with the tip of my finger. It looked something like a squar-ish sunflower wearing a long, shaggy beard. Slowly, I traced its curves and creases, trying yet again to sense even a glimmer of its meaning.

Nothing.

I dropped my hand. Perhaps it was a matter of confidence. Of be-lief. *I was born to be a wizard, wasn't I? Tuatha himself said so. I am his grandson. His heir.*

Again I touched the first rune.

Again I sensed nothing.

Speak to me, rune! I command you! Still nothing. I slammed my fist against the wall. *Speak to me, I say! That is my command!*

Another painful moan echoed down the stairwell. My stomach knotted. I drew a slow, unsteady breath. *If not for me, then for her! She will die if I can't find some way to learn your secret.* A tear drifted down my cheek. *Please. For her. For Elen. For . . . Mother.*

A strange tingling pulsed through my finger. I caught a whiff of something, not quite a feeling.

Pushing my finger to the rune, I concentrated harder. I thought of Elen, lying alone on a floor of woven boughs. I thought of her love for me. I thought of my love for her. The wood seemed to grow warmer under my fingertip. *Help her, please. She has given me so much.*

In a flash, I understood. The first rune spoke its meaning directly to my mind, in a deep, resonant voice that I had never before heard, yet somehow had always known. *These words shall be read with love, or not read at all.*

Then came the rest. In a flowing, cascading river of words, a river that washed over me and carried me away. *The Seven Songs of Wiz-ardry, One melody and many, May guide ye to the Otherworld, Though hope ye have not any. . . .*

Excitedly now, rune by rune, I read my way up each step of the stairwell. Often I paused, repeating the words to myself before proceeding. When at last I reached the top, the sun's first rays were filtering down the stairwell and trembling over the runes. During the night, the Seven Songs had been carved on the walls of my mind just as they had once been carved on the walls of Arbassa.

XI

ONE MELODY AND
MANY

I climbed the last wooden stair and stepped through the curtain of leaves. My mother still lay on the floor, though no longer on the stretcher. Hearing me enter, she stirred beneath a light, silvery blanket, woven from the threads of moths, and tried with effort to raise her head. Rhia sat cross-legged by her side, her face full of worry. Bumbelwy, leaning against a far wall, looked glumly my way.

"I have read the words," I announced without pride. "Now I must try to follow them."

"Can you tell us a little?" whispered Elen. The pink light of dawn, sifting through the windows, touched the pale skin of her cheeks. "How do they begin?"

Grimly, I knelt by her side. I studied her face, so pained and yet so loving. And I recited:

> *The Seven Songs of Wizardry,*
> *One melody and many,*
> *May guide ye to the Otherworld,*
> *Though hope ye have not any.*

"Though hope ye have not any," repeated Bumbelwy, staring blankly at his hat. "Too true, too true, too true."

As I glared at him, Rhia reached for a small, pine-scented pillow. "What does it mean, *One melody and many?*"

"I'm not sure." I watched her slide the pillow under my mother's head. "But it goes on to say that each of the Seven Songs is part of what it calls *the great and glorious Song of the Stars,* so maybe it has something to do with that."

"It does, my son." Elen observed me for a moment. "What else did the words say?"

"Many things." I sighed. "Most of which I don't understand. About seedlings and circles and the hidden sources of magic. And something about the only difference between good magic and evil being the intention of the one who wields it."

I took her hand. "Then I came to the Seven Songs themselves. They begin with a warning."

> *Divine the truth within each Song*
> *Before ye may proceed.*
> *For truths like trees for ages grow,*
> *Yet each begins a seed.*

I paused, remembering that even the mighty Arbassa, in whose arms we now sat, began as a mere seed. Still, that gave me scant encouragement when I remembered the words that followed:

> *Pursue the Seven Songs in turn;*
> *The parts beget the whole.*
> *But never move until ye find*
> *Each Song's essential soul.*

"*Each Song's essential soul,*" repeated Rhia. "What do you think that could mean?"

I touched the woven boughs of the floor. "I have no idea. No idea at all."

My mother squeezed my hand weakly. "Tell us the Songs themselves."

Still pondering Rhia's question, I recited:

> *The lesson Changing be the first,*
> *A treeling knows it well.*
>
> *The power Binding be the next,*
> *As Lake of Face can tell.*
>
> *The skill Protecting be the third,*
> *Like dwarves who tunnel deep.*
>
> *The art of Naming be the fourth,*
> *A secret Slantos keep.*
>
> *The power Leaping be the fifth,*
> *In Varigal beware.*
>
> *Eliminating be the sixth,*
> *A sleeping dragon's lair.*
>
> *The gift of Seeing be the last,*
> *Forgotten Island's spell.*
>
> *And now ye may attempt to find*
> *The Otherworldly Well.*
>
> *But lo! Do not attempt the Well*
> *Until the Songs are done.*
> *For dangers stalk your every step,*
> *With Balor's eye but one.*

Silence fell over the room. Even Bumbelwy's bells did not stir.
At last, I spoke in a hushed voice. "I don't know how I can pos-

sibly do all the things the Songs require and return here before . . . "

"I die." Elen lifted her hand to my cheek. "Is there any way I could persuade you not to go, my son?" Her arm fell back to the floor. "At least then we'd be together at the last."

"No! I'm the one who did this to you. I must try to find the cure. Even if the chances are one in a million."

Her face, already pale, grew still whiter. "Even if it means your own death, on top of mine?"

Rhia touched my shoulder in sympathy. Suddenly, a whoosh of wings stirred in my memory, and I thought of someone else I had lost, the brave hawk who had died in the fight for the Shrouded Castle. We had named him Trouble, and no name could have been more fitting. Yet his actions rang even louder than his angry screeches in my ear. I wondered whether his spirit still lived in the Otherworld. And whether, if I failed in this quest, I might join him there, along with my mother.

Elen stiffened, clenching her fists, as another spasm of pain coursed through her body. Rhia reached for a bowl of a yellow potion that smelled as rich as beef broth. Carefully, she helped my mother drink a few swallows, spilling a little on the floor. Then, raising the bowl, Rhia made a loud, chattering noise with her tongue.

From on top of the cabinet, a squirrel with huge brown eyes suddenly bounced to the floor and loped to her side. It placed one paw on her thigh, waving its bushy tail. Almost before Rhia had chattered another command, the squirrel took the bowl from her hands. With a high-pitched chatter in reply, it bounded off, carrying the bowl in its teeth.

"That's Ixtma," she explained to my mother. "I found him once in a glade near here, squealing from a broken leg. I set it for him, and since then he often visits, helping however he can. I asked him to refill the bowl for you, after he chops some more chamomile."

Despite her condition, my mother seemed on the verge of laughing. "You are an amazing girl, you are." Then her face tightened, the shadows of leaves quivering on her golden hair. "I only wish I had more time to know you."

"You will," declared Rhia. "After we return with the cure."

"We!" I looked at her in amazement. "Who said you were coming?"

"I did," she replied calmly. She folded her arms across her chest. "And there is nothing you can do to change my mind."

"No! Rhia, you could die!"

"Nevertheless, I'm coming."

The floors and walls of the cottage creaked, as Arbassa swayed from side to side. I could not be sure whether a sudden wind outside had tossed its branches, but I suspected that the wind had sprung from within.

"Why ever do you want to come?" I demanded.

Rhia looked at me curiously. "You get lost so easily."

"Stop that, will you? What about my mother? Someone needs to—"

"Ixtma will do it. We've already arranged everything."

I bit my lip. Turning to Elen, I asked in exasperation, "Are all girls this stubborn?"

"No. Just the ones with strong instincts." Her eyes moved to Rhia. "You remind me of me, child."

Rhia blushed. "And you remind me of . . . " Her voice trailed off. "I'll tell you when we get back."

Bumbelwy cleared his throat. "I shall stay."

I jumped. "What?"

"I said I'll stay. To keep her company, during the excruciating agony of her death. It's going to be miserable, absolutely miserable, that I know for certain. But perhaps I can lighten her load a bit. I'll dust off my most cheery melodies, my most humorous tales. Just the thing for someone gripped by the horror of death."

"You'll do no such thing!" I struck the wooden floor with my fist. "You're . . . coming with us."

Bumbelwy's dark eyes widened. "You *want* me to come?"

"No. But you're coming anyway."

"Merlin, no!" Rhia waved her leaf-draped arms. "Please don't let him come."

I shook my head gravely. "It's not that I want him with us. I want him *away* from her. What he calls humor could kill her in a week instead of a month."

Elen reached a trembling hand toward me and lightly brushed my scarred cheek. "If you must go, I want you to hear what I have to say."

She locked her sapphire eyes on me, so that I could almost feel her gaze penetrating my skin. "Most important, I want you to know that even if I should die before you return, it was worth it all to me just to see you again."

I turned away.

"And something else, my son. I have learned precious little in my time, but this I know. All of us—including me—have within ourselves both the wickedness of a serpent and the gentleness of a dove."

I pushed the hair off my brow. "I have a serpent, that's certain! But I'll never believe you do. Never."

She sighed heavily, her eyes roaming the interwoven branches that framed the room. "Let me say it in another way. You often enjoyed my tales of the ancient Greeks. Do you remember the one about the girl named Psyche?"

Puzzled, I gave a nod.

Once more her blue eyes seemed to search me. "Well, the Greek word *psyche* has two different meanings. Sometimes it means butterfly. And other times it means soul."

"I don't understand."

"The butterfly is the master of transformation, you see. It can change from a mere worm into the most beautiful creature of all. And the soul, my son, can do the same."

I swallowed. "I'm sorry, Mother."

"Don't be sorry, my son. I love you. I love all of you."

Bending low, I kissed her hot brow. She gave me a faltering smile, then swung her head toward Rhia. "And for you, child, I have this." From the pocket of her deep blue robe, she pulled an amulet of twigs bound together with a red thread. "An amulet of oak, ash, and thorn. Take it. You see how the buds are swelling with new life? They are ready to blossom, as are you. Keep it with you, for courage. And to remind you to trust your instincts. Listen to them. For they are really the voice of Nature, mother of us all."

Rhia's eyes glistened as she took the gift and deftly fixed it to her shirt of woven vines. "I will listen. I promise."

"You already do, I think."

"It's true," I declared. "She has even been known to remind other people to trust in the berries."

Rhia blushed, even as she fingered the amulet of oak, ash, and thorn.

"Of course," muttered Bumbelwy, "you have nothing for me."

I scowled at him. "Why should she?"

"Oh, but I do," said Elen weakly. "I have a wish."

"A wish?" The lanky figure came closer and knelt upon the floor of branches. "For me?"

"I wish that one day you will make someone laugh."

Bumbelwy bowed his head. "Thank you, my lady."

"Merlin," whispered my mother. "Perhaps your Seven Songs are like the seven labors of Hercules. Do you remember them? They were thought to be impossible. Yet he did them all, and survived."

Although I nodded, I felt no better. For Hercules' most difficult labor was to carry the weight of the entire world on his shoulders for a time. And the weight I bore now seemed no less than that.

PART TWO

XII

TUATHA

The bark-edged door creaked open, and I emerged from Arbassa. Before leaving the darkened stairwell, however, I took one last breath of the moist fragrance of the inner walls—and one last glance at the runes carved by Tuatha so long ago. I read again the words of warning that had haunted my thinking more than any others:

> *Pursue the Seven Songs in turn;*
> *The parts beget the whole.*
> *But never move until ye find*
> *Each Song's essential soul.*

What could that final phrase mean? *Each Song's essential soul.* It would be difficult enough just to make sense of the Seven Songs, but to master the soul of each seemed utterly impossible. I had no idea even where to begin.

Rhia stepped through the open door onto the grass. Her curly brown hair glowed from a ray of light piercing Arbassa's branches. She bent low and gently stroked one of the roots of the great tree. When she rose, her gaze met mine.

"Are you sure you want to come?" I asked.

She nodded, giving the root a final pat. "It won't be easy, that's certain. But we have to try."

Listening to Bumbelwy's jangling bells coming down the stairs, I shook my head. "And with him along, it will be even harder."

Rhia cocked her head toward the doorway. "I'd rather hear a broken harp all day than listen to those bells. They remind me of an iron kettle rolling down a hillside."

I thought back to the lilting music of the Flowering Harp, music that had accompanied me for so many weeks. Rather than risk damaging it, I had decided to leave the Harp behind, stowing it safely next to Rhia's hearth. Arbassa would guard it well. Yet I knew that I would miss its melodic strains. And something more.

I studied Rhia's face, as forlorn as my own. "I should never have turned away from my task in the Dark Hills. I placed all of Fincayra at risk. Now I've done the same to my own mother." Grinding the base of my staff into the grass, I sighed. "The truth is, I never deserved the Harp. You saw me strutting around with it, like some sort of wizard. Well, I'm no wizard, Rhia. I'm not powerful enough. Not wise enough."

Her eyebrow lifted slightly. "I think you're already a little wiser."

"Not wise enough to master the souls of the Songs! I don't even know where to begin."

The massive boughs above our heads suddenly stirred. Branches shook and clattered against one another, sending a shower of leaves and twigs to the ground. Although the smaller trees surrounding Arbassa remained perfectly still, the great oak itself was swaying, as if caught in a fierce gale.

A bolt of fear surged through me. I grabbed Rhia's arm. "Come! Before a branch falls on us."

"Nonsense." She wriggled free. "Arbassa would never do that. Just listen."

As I shook the leaves from my hair, I realized that the snapping and swishing branches were indeed making another sound. A sound that repeated itself over and over. *Tttuuuaaathhha. Tttuuuaaathhha.* The swaying slowly diminished. The branches grew quiet. The majestic tree towered above us, just as it had before. Yet one thing had changed. For while I still knew nothing about the souls of the Songs, I now had an idea where I might go to find out.

"Tuatha's grave," I declared. "Our quest begins there."

Rhia bit her lip. "If Arbassa believes it might help, then I believe it, too. But I don't like the idea of going there. Not at all."

Just then Bumbelwy, looking more pained than usual, poked his head out of the doorway in the trunk. He staggered onto the grass, clutching his belly. "What a storm that was! My tender stomach is turned inside out."

The lanky fellow straightened himself, jostling the bells on his hat. "But fear not, no, fear not. Weather like that follows me everywhere, so I am quite used to it."

Rhia and I traded worried glances.

"I am still coming," he continued, rubbing his side. "Even though this new injury will make it more difficult to entertain you on the way. Still, a jester must do his best to try!" He pulled his cloak over his head and started hopping around the roots of Arbassa, his bells jangling in muffled bursts.

I frowned. "Better you try to entertain us than my mother."

Bumbelwy removed the cloak from his head. "Oh, don't worry about her," he said casually. "She still has plenty of time. She has almost a month of unremitting pain before she must die." He glanced thoughtfully at Rhia's aerial cottage. "If you like, I could go back up there and give her a few laughs before we leave."

I raised my staff as if to strike him. "You fool! You have no more ability to make people laugh than a rotting corpse!"

He frowned with all of his chins. "Just you wait. I *will* make someone laugh one day. That I will."

Lowering my staff, I said scornfully, "I can taste my boots already."

The massive trunk of Arbassa creaked, as the doorway slid closed. I gazed at the trunk, following it higher, higher, until it disappeared in a mesh of branches above our heads. For a moment, I peered into the branches, woven like the threads of a living tapestry. Leaves glinted in the sun; moss sprouted like fur under every bough.

"Do you think," I asked Rhia, "that someday Arbassa might open its door to me willingly? Perhaps even gladly?"

At my words, the entire tree shuddered, raining more leaves and broken bits of bark on us.

Rhia's eyes narrowed. "Arbassa is being protective of me, that's all."

I searched her gray-blue eyes. "You don't have to come."

"I know." She pursed her lips in thought. "Are you sure, though, about going to Tuatha's grave?"

Bumbelwy gasped, wringing his hands. "The grave of the great wizard himself? Nobody goes there. Nobody who survives, that is. It is a haunted place, a terrible place. Too true, too true, too true."

"We're going there," I snapped.

"But I can't lead you," protested Rhia. "I don't even know where it lies."

"I do. I have been there once before, maybe even twice, though I need to go there again to be sure." I rubbed the top of my staff, filling the air with the scent of hemlock. "If you can guide us to that big swamp just below the Misted Hills, I can take us from there."

She shook her curls doubtfully. "We will lose precious time by doing this."

Bumbelwy shook his jangling head. "We will lose more than that."

"So be it." I thumped my staff on the grass. "Let's go."

Rhia cast a longing glance at Arbassa's boughs, then turned and strode across the grassy meadow, disappearing into a gap in the trees. I followed behind. Bumbelwy took up the rear, grumbling to himself about haunted graves and vengeful wizards.

For some time we followed a twisting trail marked by the prints of foxes, bears, and wolves, as well as others I could not identify. Then the trail vanished and we struggled to cross a wide swath of fallen trees, downed by some ferocious storm. When, shins bruised and bleeding, we finally found our way back to standing groves of pine and cedar, Rhia led us to higher ground. There the spaces between the needled trees were greater, letting more shafts of light reach the forest floor. That helped my second sight, so at least I could avoid tripping over every root and jabbing against every branch.

Even so, it was not easy to keep up with Rhia. Like me, she was driven by the urgency of our task. And, perhaps, by the tempting possibility of losing Bumbelwy somewhere in the forest. But helped by his long, spindly legs, he managed to stay with us, rattling with every step. Meanwhile, Rhia loped along as gracefully as a deer, sometimes breaking into a quick run up a slope. Watching her reminded me of the Greek story about Atalanta, the girl who could run impossibly fast. Yet even as I grinned at the comparison, I frowned to think about the woman who had first told me the story.

I pushed to keep up. Perspiration stung my sightless eyes. As the sun rode high above us, the land grew wetter. Moss sprouted from the sides of every tree, rivulets bubbled out of the ground, and mud clung to our boots. Dark pools of stagnant water appeared more frequently. It was the smell, not the sight, of this terrain that I recognized. Dank, rotting, and ominous, it dug into my memory like claws into flesh.

"Here," I announced, veering to the east.

Rhia turned to follow me, stepping lightly through the mud, unlike Bumbelwy who skidded and stomped just behind. I led them to a shadowed glade of cedars. The sounds of the forest died away, succumbing to an eerie stillness. Not even the whir of a beetle's wings broke the silence.

At the edge of the glade, I halted. With a backward glance, I told the others to remain where they were. Rhia started to speak, but I raised my hand to quiet her. Slowly, cautiously, I advanced alone.

A sudden wind moved through, tossing the branches of the cedars. Instead of making their usual crackling sound, they vibrated strangely, as if they were singing a low, mournful dirge. A song of loss and longing. A song of death. The glade darkened, until I could barely make out the shape of my boots on the needle-strewn soil. All around me, the wailing of the branches swelled. At last, I entered a small clearing, surrounded by the circle of ancient cedars that I knew marked the grave of Tuatha.

Slowly, very slowly, the clearing brightened. Yet the new light did not come from the sun. It came from the ancient cedars themselves, whose swaying branches had begun to glow with an ominous blue light. As the branches waved in the wind like the beards of old men,

I wondered if those trees might hold the spirits of Tuatha's disciples, doomed to watch over his grave, ever mourning.

Twice before, I now felt sure, I had stood on this spot. Once, not long ago. And once as a small child, when I had been brought here on the back of my father's black horse, Ionn, to witness the funeral of Tuatha. I remembered very little from that event, except the feeling of sorrow that permeated the glade.

My gaze fell to the narrow earthen mound in the center of the clearing. Twelve polished stones, perfectly round, bordered its rim. They gleamed like blue ice. As I drew a bit closer, I was struck by the sheer length of the mound. Either Tuatha had been buried with his hat on, or he had been very tall indeed.

"Both are true, you impudent young colt."

The deep voice sounded in my ears. It was the same voice that I had heard while reading the runes in Arbassa. It was the voice, I knew in my bones, of Tuatha himself. Yet beyond my fear, beyond my dread, I felt a strange sense of longing. Training my mind on the burial mound, I gave words to my thoughts.

"I wish I had known you, great wizard."

The blue stones glowed brighter, until they outshone the circle of ancient cedars. Candles seemed to flame within the stones, candles whose flames arose from the very spirit of Tuatha.

"You mean you wish I had saved you from your own folly."

I shifted uneasily, scraping the ground with the base of my staff. "That, too. Yet I also wish I had known you just to be with you. To learn from you."

"That chance was stolen from us," declared the voice bitterly. *"And do you know why?"*

"Because you were felled by the ogre Balor?"

"No!" thundered Tuatha, making the stones light up like torches. *"You have answered how, not why."*

I swallowed. "I—I don't know why."

"Think harder, then! Or is your skull no less thick than your father's?"

My cheeks burned at the insult, yet I tried not to show my outrage. I furrowed my brow, probing my mind for the answer. Suddenly I remembered Cairpré's words of warning at the gates of the Town of the Bards.

"Was it . . . hubris?"

"Yes!" thundered Tuatha's spirit. *"It was my most grievous flaw, just as it is yours."*

I bent my head, knowing too well the truth of his words. "Great wizard, I do not deserve your help. But Elen does. And if I am to have any hope of saving her, I must know something."

The stones flickered ominously. *"How do I know that you will not abandon her, even as you have abandoned the Dark Hills to the designs of Rhita Gawr?"*

I shuddered. "You have my word."

"The Great Council, too, had your word."

"I will not abandon her!" My gaze swept the circle of cedars, who seemed to be shaking their branches disapprovingly. My voice barely a whisper, I added, "She means everything to me."

For a long moment, I heard nothing but the sighing branches. At last the blue stones glowed anew.

"All right then, fledgling. What is it you wish to know?"

Cautiously, I stepped closer to the mound. "I need to know what it means to find the soul of a Song."

The stones flamed bright. *"Ah, the soul of a Song. So little, yet so much! You see, young colt, as brief as the Seven Songs you have read may seem, they reveal the secret wellsprings of the seven basic arts of wizardry. Each Song is but a beginning, a starting point, leading to wisdom and power beyond your imagination. Far beyond, I say! And each Song holds so many verses that it would take several centuries to learn but a few."*

"But what is the soul of a Song?"

"Patience, you beardless infant!" The stones seemed to smolder. *"The soul is the Song's essential truth. Its first principle. To find it is as difficult as catching the scent of a wildflower from across a wide lake. You cannot see it, or touch it, yet still you must know it."*

I shook my head. "That sounds difficult even for a wizard, let alone a boy."

The branches waved more vigorously, as the voice of Tuatha echoed again. *"You may yet become a wizard, young colt—that is, if you survive. But remember this. As little time as you have, you will be tempted to pass over some of the Songs. Resist such folly! Do not try to find the Otherworld Well until you have found the souls of all the Songs. Heed well my words. Finding only five or six is no better than finding none. Without all seven, you shall lose more than your quest. You shall lose your very life."*

I drew an uncertain breath. "How will I know, great wizard? How will I know when I've found the soul of each Song?"

At that instant, a tower of blue flame shot out of the stones. It sizzled and crackled through the air, striking the top of my staff like a bolt of blue lightning. I shook with the force of the blow, yet somehow I did not drop the staff. My fingers felt only slightly singed.

The deep voice filled my ears again. *"You will know."*

I stroked the staff. It felt no different than before, yet somehow I knew that it was.

"Now you must go, young colt. Remember what I have told you." The light began to fade from the stones. *"May you live to look upon my grave once again."*

"Please," I pleaded, "tell me one thing more. Is the prophecy true that only a child of human blood can defeat Rhita Gawr, or his servant Balor?"

The glow did not return. I heard no sound but the mournful sighing of the branches. "Tell me. Please."

At last the stones glimmered. *"The prophecy may be true, and it may be false. Yet even if it is true, the truth often has more than one face. Now . . . be gone! And do not come back until you are wiser than your years."*

XIII

STRANGE
BEDFELLOWS

As I emerged from the glade, the trees fell eerily silent again. I clung tight to my staff, aware that it, like myself, had been touched by the spirit of Tuatha. And that it, like myself, would never be quite the same.

Rhia and Bumbelwy came toward me as I stepped out of the cedars. Although they walked side by side, the contrast between them could not have been starker. One, who moved with the liveliness of a young fox, wore the greenery of the forest. The other, as stiff and glum as a tree stump, wore a heavy brown cloak and, of course, a hat of drooping bells. Yet both, at least for now, were my companions.

Rhia reached for me, wrapping her forefinger around my own. "What did you learn?"

I squeezed her finger. "A little. Only a little."

"That won't be enough," said Bumbelwy. "Nothing is ever enough."

"Where do we go now?" asked Rhia, glancing at the darkened boughs behind me.

Chewing on my lip, I pondered the first of the Seven Songs. "Well,

I must somehow find the soul of the art of Changing. And to do that, I need to find a treeling. *The lesson Changing be the first, A treeling knows it well.*" I caught my breath. "But didn't you say that Cwen was the last of the treelings?"

She nodded, her face grim. I could tell that she felt even now the sting of Cwen's treachery. "She was the last. The very last. And she's most likely gone, too. Probably bled to death after that goblin sliced off her arm."

I spun the staff's gnarled top in my hand. "But then how can I find the soul of the Song? It has something to do with the treelings."

Rhia ran her hands through her curls. "You do have a taste for challenges, Merlin! Your only hope is to go to Faro Lanna, the treelings' ancestral home. I don't think you will find much there, though."

"How far is it?"

"Far. All the way to the southwestern tip of Fincayra. And we'll have to cross the full length of the Druma, which will slow us down more. The only way to avoid that would be to cut across the Misted Hills to the coast, then head south—but that means passing through the land of the living stones. Not a wise idea!"

Bumbelwy's head jangled in agreement. "Sound advice, young woman. The living stones have an uncanny appetite for travelers." He gulped, wiggling his layered chins. "Especially jesters, I understand."

"They must have strong stomachs," I added sardonically. Facing Rhia, I asked, "That's the region where the Grand Elusa lives, isn't it?"

Bumbelwy shuddered. "Another excellent reason to avoid it! Even the living stones are afraid of that gargantuan spider. Her appetite is worse than theirs. Far worse."

I drew a deep breath of air, scented by the boughs surrounding us. "All the same, Rhia, I want you to take us the shorter way, through the Misted Hills."

Both the girl and the jester started. Even the silent cedars jostled their branches, seeming to gasp.

Rhia leaned toward me. "Are you serious?"

"Completely." I pushed the hair off my brow. "If we can save a day, or even an hour, it could be worth my mother's life."

Bumbelwy, his frowns carved deep into his face, grabbed the sleeve of my tunic. "You mustn't do this. Those hills are deadly."

I pulled free. "If you would rather stay here with Tuatha, go right ahead." As his eyes opened to their widest, I struck my staff on the needle-strewn ground. "Let's go."

We left the shadowed glade, trekking through the marshy terrain. Except for the steady rattle of Bumbelwy's bells, we moved in silence. At least, I thought grimly, the Grand Elusa will hear us coming. But would we hear her? And would she hold back her appetite long enough to remember that she had once welcomed Rhia and me as guests in her crystal cave? My legs felt weak at the thought of her slavering jaws.

As our feet squelched through the muddy soil, the trees thinned and I noticed more landmarks. An odd, chair-shaped boulder splotched with yellow lichen. The twisted skeleton of a dead tree. A patch of flaming orange moss. A strange, triangular pit. In the deepening dusk, more water seeped into the soil, as well as our boots. Soon I heard frogs piping in the distance. Water birds joined the chorus, crying in eerie voices. The dank, rotting smell grew stronger. Before long, we arrived at the edge of a wide stretch of tall grasses, dead trees, and dark pools of quicksand. The swamp.

Waving two mud-splattered sleeves, Bumbelwy protested, "We're not going across that now, are we? It's almost nightfall."

"Either we camp here," I replied, "or find some drier ground in the hills. What do you think, Rhia?"

She pulled a handful of purple berries off a low bush and popped them into her mouth. "Mmm. Still sweet."

"Rhia?"

"Drier ground," she answered at last. "Though the berries here are tasty."

As the cry of a swamp crane echoed hauntingly from the shadows, Bumbelwy shook his head. "A lovely choice. Spend the night in a swamp, and get strangled by deadly snakes, or at the Grand Elusa's doorstep, and get eaten as her breakfast."

"The choice is yours." I started off, leaping over a rotting log. I landed with a splash in a puddle. Seconds later I heard two more splashes—along with bells and a lot of grumbling—behind me.

For a while I followed a strip of caked mud that pointed like a finger into the marsh. Yet that soon faded away, making it necessary to slog straight through the grassy pools. Sometimes I sank into water up to my thighs. Long, blackened fingers of submerged branches clutched at my tunic, while mud oozed into my boots. And every so often, strange shapes stirred in the unknown depths.

The light waned steadily. Tonight there would be no moon, however, for thick clouds had rolled in, obscuring the sky. Just as well, I told myself. Seeing the moon would remind me all the more of my vanishing time, as well as hope.

We pushed on in the near-darkness. After another hour of slogging and splashing, all light vanished. A snake hissed somewhere near my boot. I began to fear that we had somehow veered off course. The murk seemed to stretch on endlessly. My legs felt heavier and heavier. Then, little by little, the terrain began to grow more solid under my feet. At first I hardly noticed the change, but in time I could tell that we were climbing gradually onto rocky ground. The rotten pools disappeared, as did their smell. The cries of frogs and birds faded behind us.

We had crossed the swamp.

Exhausted, we stumbled into a level clearing surrounded by boulders. I declared it our camp for the night. In unison, we flopped down on the mossy ground. To warm my cold hands, I slid them into the opposite sleeves of my tunic. My eyes closed, and I fell asleep.

I awoke when a large drop of rain splashed on my nose. Another drop came, and another. A cloud on the horizon flashed suddenly with light, and thunder rumbled over the ridge. The downpour began. Rain pelted us, driven by the rising wind. The night sky grew even darker, as if the clouds had condensed into great slabs of rock. Waves of water poured down from the sky. Even if I could somehow have changed into a fish, I'd have been no wetter. All I needed now was gills.

Shivering from the cold, I moved closer to one of the boulders, hoping to find at least a little shelter. That was when I realized that the boulder was moving closer to *me*.

"Living stones!" cried Rhia. "We've got to get—"

"Aaaaiieee!" screamed Bumbelwy. "It's eating me!"

I tried to roll away from the boulder. Yet the shoulder of my tunic was caught, holding me fast. I tugged on it, trying to break loose. As water streamed down my face, I pounded my fist against the stone.

My fist hit the wet rock—and stuck there. It wouldn't budge! Then, to my horror, the rock started closing around it. Swallowing my whole hand with lips of stone. I shrieked, but a clap of thunder drowned out my voice. In the blackness, in the torrent, I fought with all my strength to pull free.

Soon the stone had consumed my whole hand. Then my wrist. My forearm. My elbow. Hard as I kicked and squirmed, I could not pull away. Though I could still feel my fingers and hand, the pressure on them was increasing steadily. In no time my bones would disintegrate, crushed in the jaws of a living stone.

A sudden flash of lightning brightened the ridge. In that instant, a huge, hulking figure, broader than the boulders themselves, entered the clearing. Its voice, louder even than the thunder, rose above the storm.

"Huuungry," bellowed the great beast. "I aaam huuungry."

"The Grand Elusa!" shouted Rhia.

Bumbelwy screamed again, the scream of a man about to die.

In a single leap, the Grand Elusa landed at my side, her eight legs splattering mud in all directions. Despite the rain and the darkness, my second sight could not miss her massive jaws opening. As I glimpsed the endless rows of jagged teeth, I struggled all the harder to escape. The jaws closed.

Not on me! With a terrific crunch, the Grand Elusa took an enor-

mous bite out of the living stone itself. The boulder shuddered violently, then released my arm. I tumbled backward onto muddy
ground. Before I knew what was happening, someone fell on top of
me, as a blast of white light seared the ridge.

XIV

THE CRYSTAL
CAVE

Light, sparkling like stars, danced all around me. And around Rhia and Bumbelwy, as well, for we lay in a single heap of arms and legs and torn clothing. I pushed someone's dripping foot out of my face and sat up. Aside from being soaking wet and feeling intensely sore in my hand, I was fine. Wherever I might be.

In a flash, I recognized the rows upon rows of glowing crystals, the shimmering waves of light that vibrated over the walls, and the sheer magnificence of this place. Thousands upon thousands of dazzling facets, each as smooth as ice, glittered on all sides, shining with a light of their own. The crystal cave! On my first visit here, I had known that I had never been anywhere as beautiful. Now I knew it again.

Something cracked behind me. I swung my head around to see the Grand Elusa herself, her body so vast that it nearly filled the entire glowing cavern. She had just taken a bite of what looked like the hind quarters of a wild boar. Her huge eyes, faceted like crystals themselves, observed me as she chewed. After swallowing the last morsel, she licked her arms clean with surprising delicacy.

"Welcooome tooo myyy caaave," she bellowed.

Bumbelwy, his bells jingling as he shivered, clutched my sleeve in terror. "Are—are we n-n-next?"

"Of course not," chided Rhia, her damp curls sparkling like the crystals around us. "She brought us here to get us away from the living stones."

"S-s-so she c-could eat us hers-s-self," stuttered the jester.

"Siiilence." The gargantuan spider scratched the white hump on her back. "I haaave saaatisfied myyy huuunger fooor nooow. Luuucky fooor youuu, liiiving stooones taaake sooome tiiime tooo diiigest. Theee boooar waaas meeerely deeessert."

Using the sleeve of my tunic, I wiped the raindrops off my face. "Thank you. But how did you get us here so fast?"

"Leeeaping." The Grand Elusa edged a bit closer, so that I could see myself reflected dozens of times in the facets of her eyes. "Iiit iiis aaan aaart youuu maaay leeearn ooone daaay."

"Leaping is one of the Seven Songs I have to master! Don't tell me I need to learn how to do what you just did. That alone could take a lifetime."

"Maaany liiifetimes." The great white spider continued to examine me. "Espeeecially fooor ooone whooo caaanot compleeete hiiis taaasks. Wheeere haaave youuu leeeft theee Flooowering Haaarp?"

Perspiration beaded on my brow. "It's safe. In Arbassa. But I can't go back to the Dark Hills now! I have another problem to solve first."

"Aaa proooblem youuu caaaused."

I lowered my head. "Yes."

"Aaa proooblem," thundered the creature, "thaaat youuu caaan stiiill sooolve."

Slowly, I raised my head. "Are you saying I might really have some chance to save her?"

One of her enormous legs tapped against the floor of crystals. "Aaa minuscuuule chaaance iiis stiiill aaa chaaance."

Rhia crawled a little nearer to me. "So Elen might survive?"

"Sheee miiight, aaand heeer youuung maaan miiight aaas weeell." As the Grand Elusa cleared her throat, the rumble echoed between the curving, crystalline walls. "Buuut heee wiiill neeed tooo surviiive thiiis queeest, aaand maaany mooore, befooore heee maaay ooone daaay fiiind hiiis ooown crystaaal caaave."

"My own crystal cave?" My heart leaped at the idea. "Is that really possible?"

"Aaanything iiis possiiible."

The immense spider slid her bulk to one side, revealing an array of glittering objects. The Treasures of Fincayra! I recognized the Orb of Fire, its orange sphere aglow like the crystals; the graceful horn I knew to be the Caller of Dreams; and the great sword Deepercut, with one edge that could slice all the way into the soul, and another edge that could heal any wound. Just behind them, I glimpsed the plow that could till its own field, the Treasure that Honn had described to his son. Near it lay the rest of the Wise Tools—except for the one that had been lost.

"Iiit iiis eeeven possiiible thaaat, ooone daaay, youuu maaay beee wiiise enouuugh tooo caaarry ooone ooof theee Treasuuures aaand nooot destrooooy mooore thaaan youuu creaaate."

I swallowed hard.

"Youuu maaay teeell meee theee Seeeven Sooongs." Not a request but a command, her words boomed in my ears.

I hesitated for an instant, then sucked in my breath and began:

> *The Seven Songs of Wizardry,*
> *One melody and many,*

May guide ye to the Otherworld,
Though hope ye have not any.

Bumbelwy, who was huddled at the far end of the cavern, shook his head morosely, clanging his bells. The spider turned an enormous eye on him, and he instantly stopped.

In the glow of the crystals, I continued, reciting the warning to master each of the Songs in turn. Rhia's bright eyes sparkled like crystals themselves when I spoke the words that were now embedded in my very being: *Each Song's essential soul.* Then I moved through the Seven Songs themselves. When, at the conclusion, I mentioned the eye of Balor, the Grand Elusa shifted her weight uneasily on the faceted floor.

No one spoke for some time. At last the Grand Elusa's voice rang out.

"Aaare youuu afraaaid?"

"Yes," I whispered. "I'm afraid I can't do it all in four phases of the moon."

"Iiis thaaat aaall?"

"I'm afraid of how hard it will be to find the souls of the Songs."

"Iiis thaaat aaall?"

I ran my hand nervously across the crystalline floor, feeling the sharp edges. "I'm afraid of the seventh one, Seeing, most of all. But . . . I don't know why."

"Youuu shaaall fiiind ouuut whyyy, iiif youuu geeet thaaat faaar."

Using three of her arms, she scratched her hairy back. "Youuu maaay leeearn aaa liiittle maaagic, aaas weeell. Iiit iiis aaa piiity youuu wooon't leeearn anythiiing reeeally uuuseful, thooough. Liiike hooow tooo spiiin aaa weeeb. Ooor hooow tooo cheeew aaa stooone."

Rhia giggled. Then her face grew taut. "What does it mean, that part about Balor's eye?"

The spider's white hairs bristled. "Theee ooogre haaas ooonly ooone eeeye. Aaand iiit kiiills anyooone whooo loooks intooo iiit, eeeven fooor aaan iiinstant."

Rhia leaned toward me. "That must be how Tuatha died."

"Yeees indeeed," declared the Grand Elusa. "Aaand hooow youuu tooo wiiill diiie, iiif youuu aaare nooot caaareful."

I frowned. "The truth is, I may never get past the first Song. When you found us, we were trekking to Faro Lanna, in the hope of learning something that might help. But with no treelings left, it is hardly a hope at all."

"Iiit iiis theee ooonly hooope youuu haaave."

"Faro Lanna is so far away from here," said Rhia despairingly. "It's a good week's walk, even if we don't run into any more trouble."

"A week!" I groaned. "We don't have that much time to spare."

A sudden explosion of white light filled the crystal cave.

XV

CHANGING

We found ourselves sitting on a grassy field at the edge of a sheer cliff that dropped straight to the sea. As I peered over the edge, I viewed colonies of kittiwakes and silver-winged terns nesting on the cliff wall, screeching and chattering and tending to their young. A cool breeze smacked my face. The smell of salt water seasoned the air. Far below me, the white line of surf melted into bright blue and then into green as dark as jade. Across a wide channel of water, I could barely make out the shape of a small island, dark and mysterious. Behind it billowed the wall of mist that surrounded all of Fincayra.

I turned to Rhia and Bumbelwy, also investigating our new surroundings. To think that we had, only seconds before, been inside the Grand Elusa's crystal cave! Wherever we were now, it was far away from there. Such a wondrous skill, to move people like that. She had even remembered to send along my staff. I made a mental note to pay close attention to the fifth lesson, Leaping, should I ever make it that far.

Rhia bounced to her feet. "Look there," she cried, pointing toward the small island. "Do you see it?"

I stood, leaning against my staff. "That island out there, yes. Looks almost unreal, doesn't it?"

Rhia continued to stare. "That's because it *is* almost unreal. That's the Forgotten Island. I'm sure of it."

A shiver shook my spine. "The seventh Song! That's where I must go to learn about Seeing." I glanced at her briefly before turning back to the island, shrouded by shifting vapors. "Have you seen it before?"

"No."

"Then how can you be so sure it's the Forgotten Island?"

"Arbassa's stories, of course. It's the only piece of land in all of Fincayra that's not connected to the main island. No one—not even Dagda himself, it is said—has set foot there for ages. And except for the mer people who live in this inlet, no one knows how to cross the powerful currents, and even more powerful enchantments, that swirl around it all the time."

I dodged a gull that swooped just in front of my face. Yet I couldn't take my gaze from the island. "Sounds like people aren't supposed to go there." My stomach churned uneasily. "For whatever reason."

She sighed, still watching the island herself. "Some people believe it has something to do with how Fincayrans lost their wings long ago."

"Too true, too true, too true," intoned Bumbelwy as he walked mopily toward us, jangling with every step. "That was the saddest moment in the whole sorry history of our people."

Was it possible that the dour jester knew how the wings were lost? I felt suddenly hopeful. "Do you know how it happened?"

His long face swung toward me. "No one knows that. No one."

I frowned. Aylah, the wind sister, knew. But she hadn't wanted to tell me. I wished I could ask her again. Yet that was impossible, as impossible as catching the wind. More than likely, she had blown all the way to Gwynedd by now.

Rhia turned at last from the island. "Would you like to know where we are standing right now?"

I gave her a nudge. "You still sound like a guide."

"You still need a guide," she answered with a half grin. "We're in Faro Lanna, the strip of land that once was home to the treelings."

Listening to the surging waves below us, I scanned the plateau. Steep, cream-colored cliffs bounded us on three sides. But for a few piles of crumbling stones, possibly all that remained of walls or hearths, nothing but grass covered the plateau. Far to the north, a line of dark green marked the edge of a forest. Beyond that, the horizon lifted in a purplish haze, possibly all that was visible of the Misted Hills.

A dingy brown butterfly fluttered out of the grass and landed on my wrist. Its legs tickled, so I shook my hand. Then it flew off, landing on the knotted top of my staff. Its motionless wings blended into the deeper brown of the wood.

With a sweep of my arm, I indicated the grassy plateau. "I don't see how we're ever going to learn about the treelings' art of Changing. If they ever lived here, they didn't leave much behind."

"That was their way." Rhia picked up a white pebble and tossed it over the cliff. "The treelings were wanderers, always searching for someplace better to live. Someplace to sink roots, like true trees, and call home. Their only settlements were here, by the cliffs, but as you can tell from those rock piles, they weren't much. Nothing more than shelters for the very old and the very young. No libraries or markets or meeting halls. Most treelings spent their days wandering across Fincayra, only coming back here when they were ready to find a mate or to die."

"So what happened to them?"

"They got so caught up in their exploring, I guess, that fewer and fewer of them ever bothered to come home. Eventually, nobody at all returned. The settlements fell apart or blew away, since there was nobody around to take care of them. And the treelings themselves died off, one by one."

I kicked at a tuft of grass. "I can't blame them for wandering. It's in my blood, too. But it sounds as if they never felt at home anywhere."

Rhia studied me thoughtfully, the wind off the water ruffling her leafy garb. "And is feeling at home somewhere in your blood, as you say?"

"I hope so, but I'm not sure. What about you?"

She stiffened. "Arbassa is my home. My family. All the family I've ever had."

"Except for Cwen."

She bit her lip. "Once she belonged to my family. But no more. She gave that up for a sackful of goblin promises."

The butterfly lifted off from my staff. It flew over to Bumbelwy, who was still gazing glumly across the channel at the Forgotten Island. Just before landing, the butterfly apparently changed its mind and returned to the gnarled shaft of hemlock. I watched its dull brown wings, one of which was badly frayed, slowly opening and closing.

Looking again at Rhia, I declared, "We must find her."

"Who?"

"Cwen. She might be able to tell me what those piles of stones cannot."

Rhia made a face as if she had eaten a handful of sour berries. "Then we are lost. There is no way to find her, even if she did survive losing her arm. Besides, if we did find her, we couldn't trust her." Fairly spitting the words, she added, "She's a traitor, through and through."

Below us, an enormous wave crashed against the cliff, sending the kittiwakes and terns screeching from the spray. "Even so, I have to try! Surely somebody saw her after she left. If treelings are all that rare nowadays, the sight of one would be noticed, wouldn't it?"

She shook her head. "You don't understand. Treelings not only weren't satisfied to stay in any one place. They weren't satisfied to stay in any one body, either."

"You don't mean—"

"Yes! They knew how to change form! You know the way most trees change their colors in the autumn, and take on a whole new garb in the spring? The treelings went far beyond that. They were always swapping their treelike shape for a bear, or an eagle, or a frog. That's why they were named in the Song about Changing. They were masters of it."

My hopes, already as fragile as the butterfly perched on my staff, vanished entirely. "So Cwen, if she's still alive, could look like anything."

"Anything at all."

Bumbelwy, sensing my despair, spoke up. "I could sing you a song, if you like. Something light and cheery."

Since I didn't have the strength to protest, he started to sing, swaying his bell-draped hat in time to the rhythm.

> *Life's unending curse:*
> *It could be far worse!*
> *Yet I'm full of glee.*
> *None gladder than me.*

> *Though death fills the air,*
> *I do not despair.*
> *It could be far worse:*
> *Life's unending curse.*
>
> *Be merry! You see,*
> *Far worse it could be.*
> *So much worse than now!*
> *Just . . . don't ask me how.*

"Stop!" shouted Rhia. "If you really feel that way, why don't you just jump off this cliff and put an end to your misery?"

Bumbelwy frowned triply. "Weren't you listening? That's a joyous song! One of my favorites." He sighed. "Oh dear, I must have botched the delivery. As usual. Here, I'll try it again."

"No!" a voice cried out.

But the voice did not belong to Rhia. Nor to me. It belonged to the butterfly.

With a frantic fluttering, the tiny creature left its perch, rose into the air, and started spinning downward. Just before it hit the grass, a loud *crraackk* split the air. The butterfly vanished.

In its place stood a slim, gnarled figure, part tree and part woman. Her hair, as rough as straw, fell over the barklike skin of her face, framing two dark eyes the shape of teardrops. A brown robe encircled her, covering her body down to her broad, knobby feet that resembled roots. Only one arm protruded from the robe, its hand wearing a silver ring on the smallest of six fingers. The sweet scent of apple blossoms clung to her, in stark contrast to the sour expression on her face.

Rhia stood as stiff as a dead branch. "Cwen."

"Yessss," whispered the treeling, her voice rustling like dry grass.

"It issss Cwen. The ssssame Cwen who took care of you assss a baby, and nurssssed you through many a ssssickness."

"And who tried to give me to the goblins!"

Cwen's lone hand ran through her ragged hair. "That wassssn't my dessssire. They promissssed they would not harm you."

"You should have known they would lie. No one can trust a warrior goblin." She stared at the twisted figure. "Now no one can trust *you*."

"Don't you ssssee I know that?"

A kittiwake landed on the grass nearby and started tugging at some strands with its beak. Though the bird pulled vigorously, the grass wouldn't budge. "Watch thissss," said Cwen, taking a small step closer. In her most gentle voice, she asked, "If I tried to help you build your nesssst, good bird, would you let me?"

The kittiwake screeched and flapped its wings angrily at her. Only after carrying on for some time did it finally settle down and return to work, still watching Cwen warily with one eye.

Sadly, the treeling turned back to Rhia. "You ssssee? Thissss issss my punisssshment."

"You deserve it, every bit."

"I am missssserable, totally missssserable! I thought thingssss could get no worsssse. Then ssssuddenly you appeared." She aimed a knobby finger at Bumbelwy. "With thissss . . . voicccce of doom."

The jester raised his head hopefully. "Perhaps you prefer riddles? I know a terrific one about bells."

"No!" shrieked the treeling. "Pleasssse, Rhia. I am sssso full of remorsssse. Won't you forgive me?"

She crossed her leaf-covered arms. "Never."

I felt a strange pang. The word *never* rang in my ears like a heavy door slammed and barred. To my own surprise, a feeling of sympathy rose inside of me. Certainly Cwen had done something terrible. Something she regretted. But hadn't I also done things I deeply regretted?

I stepped close to Rhia, lowering my voice. "It's hard, I know. Yet maybe you should forgive her."

She stared at me coldly. "How can I?"

"The same way my mother forgave me after what I did to her." At that instant, Elen's parting words came back to me. *The butterfly can change from a mere worm to the most beautiful creature of all. And the soul, my son, can do the same.* I bit my lower lip. "Cwen did something awful, to be sure. But she deserves another chance, Rhia."

"Why?"

"Because, well, she could change. *All of us, all living things, have the potential to change.*"

Suddenly my staff flashed with bright blue light. The wooden shaft sizzled, as if it were burning. A split second later, both the light and the sound disappeared. As I twirled the staff in my hand, I found a marking, as blue as the sky at dusk, engraved upon the shaft. It was in the shape of a butterfly. I knew, in that moment, that Tuatha's spirit still touched my staff. And that, somehow, I had discovered the soul of Changing.

Hesitantly, Rhia stretched her hand toward the treeling. Cwen, her slender eyes glistening, took it in her own. For a moment, they regarded each other in silence.

Finally the treeling turned to me. "Issss there any way I can thank you?"

"Seeing you two like this is thanks enough."

"Are you ssssure there issss nothing I can do?"

"Not unless you know the power of Leaping," I replied. "We must go now to the Lake of the Face, far to the north."

"Ten days' walk," moaned Bumbelwy. "No, more like twelve. No, make it fourteen."

Cwen's teardrop eyes probed me. "I don't know the sssskill of Leaping, but the sssskill of Changing may be usssseful to you."

Rhia caught her breath. "Oh Cwen, if only we could swim like fish…"

"It would ssssave you sssseveral days."

I jumped. "Is it really possible?"

A crooked grin spread over Cwen's face as she wiggled her bony fingers at Bumbelwy. "You, voicccce of doom, will go firssssst."

"No," he pleaded, backing away. "You wouldn't. You couldn't."

"Flippna ssslippna, hahnaway ssswish," intoned Cwen. *"Kelpono bubblim tubblim fissssh."*

All of a sudden, Bumbelwy halted, realizing that he had backed up almost to the edge of the cliff. He looked down at the crashing surf, his eyes wide with fright, his sleeves flapping in the wind. He looked back at Cwen, and his eyes grew wider still.

"P-please," he stammered. "I *hate* f-f-fish! So s-slimy, so v-very wet all over! S-so—"

Crraackk.

An ungainly fish, with enormous eyes and quadruple chins under its downturned mouth, flopped helplessly on the grass before finally plunging over the cliff. Yet I found it hard to laugh, for I knew I would be next.

XVI

LIQUID THRILL

Suddenly I couldn't breathe.

Wind rushed past. I fell down, down, down. I fought to take in some air. No use! The howling wind tore at me. Yet I could not fill my lungs with it, as I had always done before. Then, with a splash, I hit cold water. My gills opened wide. Gills! I breathed again at last. As water moved around me, it also moved through me.

No more arms. No more legs. My body was now a single, stream-lined tail, with flexible fins above and below and on both sides. One of the fins curled around a small stick, which I guessed was all that remained of my staff. What had happened to my satchel, boots, and tunic, I had no idea.

It took me a moment to find my balance, for whenever I tried to move my fins, I flipped over on my side. And it took more than a moment for my second sight to adjust to the dim, scattered under-water light. Except for the layer of water closest to the surface, there was practically no light at all. Only gradations of darkness.

After several minutes of struggling, however, my confidence began to improve. I discovered that swimming required completely differ-ent movements than it had with my human form. Stroking was out of the question. So was kicking, at least in the old way. What I needed to do was sway my entire body from side to side, like a living whip cracking. Every single scale on my skin, from my gills to the tip of my tail, joined in the motion. Soon I found I could whip through the waves. And I could move up or down as well as left or right.

A slender fish, mottled with greens and browns, swam over. I knew at once it was Rhia, for although she had been underwater no longer than I, she moved with the grace of the current itself. We waved our fins in greeting. She made some sort of coughing sound, and I realized that she was laughing at the sight of my miniature staff.

At that moment Bumbelwy, trailing a torn ribbon of kelp from his tail, swam slowly toward us. While he wore no bells, there was no mistaking him. From the front, his sagging chins made him look like an eel wearing a ruffled collar. It was the closest he had ever come to being funny, although he had no idea.

Our first task was learning to keep together. Rhia and I took turns in the lead position, with Bumbelwy always following behind. In time, Rhia and I began to swim with increasing coordination. A sixth sense slowly emerged in us, the same sense that binds an entire school of fish together. After the first full day of swimming, the two of us moved almost as a single, connected being.

A quiet, liquid thrill moved through me as we swam through vast forests of swaying kelp or leaped through the rolling waves. I could taste feelings as well as flavors in the currents; I could sense the joy of a family of dolphins, the lonely struggle of a migrating turtle, the hunger of a newborn sea anemone. Yet I never forgot the seriousness of my quest. Even as I reveled in the experience of being a creature of the water, I knew that all of this was merely a means of saving time—and, perhaps, Elen. Still, I promised myself that if I ever survived this quest and one day actually became a wizard, perhaps even the mentor of a young king or queen, I would remember the virtues of transforming my student into a fish.

One of those virtues was discovering the great amount of food that the sea could provide. Why, the sea was really one enormous, floating feast! Day after day, I ate enough insects, eggs, and worms to feel bloated. Rhia, for her part, proved adept at catching tasty little crayfish. While Bumbelwy drew the line at worms, even he tasted many of the sea's strange delicacies.

At the same time, we tried to stay alert to the danger of becoming someone else's delicacy. Once I swam through a tunnel of bright yellow coral only to find a very large, very hungry fish waiting for me at the other end. As quickly as I darted away, I surely would have been caught but for the even larger creature who suddenly appeared, scaring off my pursuer. Although I just barely glimpsed the creature who had helped me, it seemed to possess the tail of a fish and the upper body of a man.

For six days and five nights we swam steadily northward. Often after dark, the pale light of a swelling half moon danced upon the waves. Yet the moon's beauty escaped me. I saw in its face only the face of someone else, someone I feared losing forever. Less than three weeks remained.

At last came the moment when Rhia veered sharply toward the coast. She led us to a small delta where a freshwater stream emptied into the sea. I could taste, mixing with the salty flavors of the wide waters, the purity of melted snow, the playfulness of otters, and the unwavering patience of a stand of ancient spruce trees. We surged up the stream as far as we could. Then, concentrating my thoughts, I repeated the command that I had learned from Cwen.

All of a sudden I stood knee-deep in a tumbling cascade, clutching my staff in one hand and Rhia's arm in the other. Just downstream, Bumbelwy threw himself on the marshy bank, coughing and sputtering. He had, it seemed, forgotten that people tend not to breathe too well with their heads underwater.

While Bumbelwy recovered, Rhia and I shook some of the water from our clothes and ourselves. Meanwhile, she explained that she believed that this stream flowed down from the Lake of the Face itself. Before long, all three of us were trekking along the stony stream bank, climbing with the rising ground. A tangled forest of alder and birch that clung to the bank made the going difficult. Every time Bumbelwy tried to shake free of the branches that grasped at his cloak, his bells rattled soggily.

At one point I paused, panting hard from the climb. Spying a shaggy-topped mushroom growing among the roots of a birch, I pulled it from the ground. "Strange as it sounds," I said as I took a bite, "I'm going to miss those little white worms."

Rhia wiped her brow and grinned at me. She picked her own mushroom. "Maybe you'll find more worms at the Lake of the Face."

"How did it come to have such a name? Do you know?"

She chewed pensively. "Some say it's from the shape, which is a little like a man's face. Others say it's from the power of the water."

"What power?"

"If you look into it, according to legend, you will face an important truth about your life. Even if it's a truth you would rather not know."

XVII

BINDING

We continued on, following the stony stream bank as it climbed through the alders. Though roots tripped our feet and thorns tore our clothing, our pace hardly slackened. Several hours and scraped shins later, the waterway opened into a snug valley surrounded by steep, wooded hills. The spicy scent of pine trees wafted over us. Amidst the trees, outcroppings of white quartz gleamed in the late afternoon sun.

Yet the valley seemed eerily silent. No birds sang, no squirrels chattered, no bees buzzed. I listened closely, hoping to hear the stirring of something alive. Rhia, reading my thoughts, gave a knowing nod. "Animals and birds stay away from this valley. No one knows why."

"They're smarter than people," observed Bumbelwy, still dripping water from his bells.

I watched Rhia walk down to the shore of the lake in the center of the valley. The lake, its water almost black, was so still that hardly a ripple broke its surface. Its contours resembled, from this angle, the profile of a man whose jaw, strong and defiant, jutted outward—much like my own father's. Remembering him, I stiffened. I wished he had been as strong in reality as in appearance. Strong enough to stand up to Rhita Gawr when he had seen the chance. Strong enough to help his own wife, Elen, when she had needed him.

A shriek jolted me out of my thoughts.

There, by the edge of the lake, stood Rhia, gazing into the dark water. She held her hands in front of her protectively, while her back arched in fear. Yet if something in the lake had frightened her, she made no effort to move or get away. She stared straight into the water, completely transfixed.

I ran down to her. Bumbelwy followed me, alternately tripping over his torn cloak and the mesh of vines that grew along the shore. Just as I reached her, she turned around. Her skin, usually full of color, looked deathly pale. She gasped when she saw me, as if she were suddenly afraid. Then she shuddered and grabbed my arm for support.

I braced myself to support her weight. "Are you all right?"

"No," she answered weakly.

"Did you see something in the lake?"

"Y-yes." She shook herself again, releasing my arm. "And you— you'd better not look."

"Fine," declared Bumbelwy, glancing nervously at the dark water. "Let's go."

"Wait." I stepped to the edge of the lake. As I peered into the still water, I viewed my own reflection, so clear that for an instant I thought that my own twin was in the lake, staring back at me. What, I wondered, could have been so frightening about such a perfect reflection? There were my useless eyes, looking like lumps of coal beneath my brows. And my scarred cheeks, ravaged by flames that I could still almost feel. Stroking my cheeks, I wished that I might someday grow a beard to cover those scars. A beard, curly and white, like the one I imagined that Tuatha himself had worn.

I jumped back. The boy in the lake started sprouting whiskers. First black, then gray, then white as the quartz on the hillside, the whiskers grew long and scraggly. They covered most of the boy's face, growing and growing. Soon they fell all the way to his knees. Was it possible? Was the Lake of the Face telling me that I would one day, like my grandfather before me, wear a beard? That I would one day, like him, be a wizard?

I smiled, feeling increasingly confident about peering into the still, dark water. Whatever Rhia had seen had clearly departed. I leaned closer. The boy in the lake, no longer wearing a beard, slowly turned away from me. He ran toward something. No, someone. A huge, muscular warrior, wearing a red band around his forehead, strode out of the depths. Then, as the warrior came nearer, I realized that he had only one eye. One enormous, wrathful eye. Balor!

To my horror, the ogre dodged the boy with ease, grabbed him by the throat, and lifted him high. My own throat constricted as I watched the boy being strangled by powerful hands. Hard as I tried, I could not turn away from the terrifying scene. The boy struggled wildly, trying not to look in the ogre's deadly eye. Yet the eye's power pulled on him. Finally, he succumbed. With a last jerk of his legs, he hung limp in the ogre's hands.

I fell backward on the ground, gasping for air. My head whirled. My neck throbbed. With each breath, I coughed uncontrollably.

Rhia reached for me, as did Bumbelwy. She squeezed my hand, while he patted my brow sympathetically. Slowly, my coughing subsided. But before any of us could speak, someone called to us across the water.

"So," wheezed a gleeful voice, "are you finding the lake's prophecies difficult to, shall we say, swallow?" A full, breathy laughter followed. "Or are you just feeling, shall we say, choked up?"

Regaining my bearings, I scanned the dark surface of the lake. Near what would be the nose of the profile, I spotted an immense, hairy otter, silver in color except for his face, which was white. He floated leisurely on his back, kicking so effortlessly that he hardly caused a ripple.

I pointed. "There. An otter."

Rhia shook her head in disbelief. "I didn't think anyone lived here."

"I only live where I otter," he answered merrily, squirting a jet of water from between his two front teeth. "Care to join me for a swim?"

"No chance," declared Bumbelwy. He waved his long sleeves like fins, causing his bells to dribble water on his face. "I've had enough swimming for a lifetime."

"Then perhaps I should sing one of my water songs for you?" The otter kicked lazily toward us, patting his belly with both paws. "I have, shall we say, a fluid voice." His breathy laughter came again, echoing over the lake.

Supporting myself with my staff, I stood. "No thanks. The only Song we care about isn't about water." Seized by a sudden inspiration, I asked, "You wouldn't happen to know anything about the magic of Binding, would you?"

Rhia frowned. "Merlin," she cautioned. "You don't know him at all! He could be—"

"An expert in matters of Binding," said the otter relaxedly. "My favorite pastime. Next to floating on my back and watching the clouds, that is."

"You see?" I whispered to her. "He could tell us what we need. And I don't see anyone else around this lake who might be able to help."

"I don't trust him."

"Why not?"

She pressed her tongue against her cheek. "I don't know exactly. It's just a feeling. An instinct."

"Oh, confound your instincts! We're running out of time!" I searched the shoreline for any sign of other creatures who could, perhaps, assist us. There were none. "Why would he lie to us? We have no reason to mistrust him."

"But . . . "

I growled with impatience. "What now?"

She hissed at me like a snake. "It's, well . . . confound it all, Merlin! I can't put it into words."

"Then I'm going with what I think, not what you feel. And I think that any creature who lives in this enchanted lake, all alone, must have some special knowledge. Maybe even special power." I turned back to the otter, who had drifted much closer. "I need to find the soul— the first principle—of the art of Binding. Will you help me, good otter?"

Tilting his head toward the shore, he squirted a jet of water at me. "Why should I?"

"Because I asked you, that's why."

He blew some bubbles in the water. "Oooh, that tickles my ears." More bubbles. "You need to give me a better reason than that."

I jammed my staff into the soil. "Because my mother's life is at stake!"

"Hmmm," he said lazily. "Your mother? I had a mother once, myself. She was a terribly slow swimmer. Oh well, I suppose I could help you. Only with the fundamentals, though."

My heart pounded in my chest. "That's what I need."

"Then pull up some of those vines." He floated closer to the shore. "By your feet."

"Vines?"

"Of course," replied the otter, kicking in a slow circle. "To learn about Binding you need to bind something. Go to it, boy! I haven't got all afternoon. Get your smiling friends to help you."

I turned to Rhia, who was still frowning, and Bumbelwy, who had never stopped. "Will you give me a hand?"

Reluctantly, they agreed. The vines, though supple, were thick and heavy, covered with rows of tiny thorns. Hard to grasp, hard to lift. Pulling them up was difficult work. Untangling them from one another was worse.

At last, we succeeded. Several lengths of vine, each three or four times my height, lay at my feet. Bumbelwy, exhausted, sat down with a loud clang, his back to the water. Rhia stayed by my side, watching the otter warily.

I straightened my back, feeling terribly sore in the place between my shoulder blades. Clearly, all the pulling had strained something. "We've done it. Now what?"

The otter continued swimming in a circle. "Now tie one around your legs. Tight as you possibly can."

"Merlin," Rhia warned. She touched Elen's amulet of oak, ash, and thorn, still attached to her leafy shirt.

Ignoring her, I sat down and wrapped one of the vines around my ankles, calves, and thighs. Despite the thorns, I managed to tie it with a triple knot.

"Good," sighed the otter with a yawn. "Now do the same thing to your arms."

"My arms?"

"Do you want to learn about Binding or not?"

I turned to Rhia. "Help me, will you?"

"I don't want to."

"Please. We're losing precious time."

She shrugged. "All right. But it feels all wrong."

The otter, his fur glistening, clucked with satisfaction as he watched Rhia tie my hands together, then bind them to my chest. "Good. You're almost there."

"I hope so," I replied testily. "These thorns are digging into my skin."

"Just one more vine. You are, shall we say, bound to be pleased."

The otter put one paw in the water and splashed Bumbelwy. "You there, lazy fellow! Wrap one around his whole body. Make sure you cover all the places we've missed so far. Even his head. This is, after all, a delicate enchantment we're talking about. Everything must be exactly right."

Bumbelwy glanced at me. "Should I?"

I gritted my teeth. "Do it."

Somberly, Bumbelwy wrapped me up as tight as a cocoon. When he had finished, only my mouth and part of one ear remained exposed. I lay on my side on the soil, unable to move, ready at last to learn the soul of Binding.

My jaw held closed, I asked, "Whad nah?"

The otter wheezed a little laugh. "Now that you are, shall we say, rapt with attention, I will give you the information you asked for."

"Meg id quig." A vine dug into my hip. I tried to roll to the other side, but couldn't even begin to budge. "Peez."

"The first principle of Binding, as with anything, is . . . " He blew a fountain of water into the air. "Never trust a trickster."

"Whad?"

The otter laughed uncontrollably, clutching his ample belly as he rolled over and over in the shallows. "That's why they call me the Trickster of the Lake." Still laughing, he kicked lazily toward the far shore. "Hope I didn't, shall we say, tie you up too long."

I shrieked with anger. Yet I could do no more. However long it had taken to tie me up with the vines, it seemed to take twice as long to untie me. By the time I stood, pacing the shoreline in frustration, the sun had almost disappeared behind the rim of hills.

"I've wasted the whole day," I moaned, tender from the scrapes on my hands, hip, and forehead. "The whole day! I can't believe I trusted him."

Rhia said nothing, though I knew her thoughts well enough.

I swung around to face her. "You should never have come with me! You should have stayed back at Arbassa, where at least you'd be safe."

Her gray-blue eyes examined me. "I don't want to be safe. I want to be with you."

I squashed a vine under my heel. "Why bother?"

"Because . . . I want to." She glanced sadly at the dark water. "Despite what the lake told me."

"What did it tell you?"

She sighed heavily. "I don't want to talk about it."

Remembering my own vision of Balor's eye, I nodded. "All right. But I still don't know why you want to stay."

Something in the sky caught her attention, and Rhia looked up. Following her gaze, I found two distant shapes, weaving their way across the horizon. Although I could barely see them, I knew at once what they were. A pair of hawks, riding the breeze together. They flew almost as one, bobbing and turning in unison, in the way Rhia and I had moved as fishes.

"Aren't they lovely?" she asked, her eyes following the birds. "If they are like the hawks in the Druma, they not only fly together, they build a nest together, a nest they share for their whole lives."

All at once I understood. What tied the hawks to each other, what tied Rhia to me, had nothing to do with vines. Or ropes. Or chains of any kind.

I turned back to her. "I guess, Rhia, the strongest bonds are invisible. Maybe . . . *the strongest bonds are of the heart.*"

With a flash of blue, my staff ignited. As the flame disappeared, I discovered a new marking engraved on the shaft, not far from the butterfly. It was a pair of hawks, bound together in flight.

XVIII

LIGHT FLYER

The blue light had barely faded from my staff before my thoughts turned to the third Song, that of Protecting. I turned from the lake, its smooth surface gleaming darkly, to the forested valley surrounding us. Crossing the steep, thickly wooded ridge would be only the beginning. For the third Song would require yet another long voyage. *The skill Protecting be the third, Like dwarves who tunnel deep.*

To the land of the dwarves! Their realm, Rhia explained, was visited only rarely—and almost never by choice. For the dwarves, while peaceful to their neighbors, did not welcome any intruders. All that was known about their underground realm was that its entrances lay somewhere near the origins of the River Unceasing, on the high plains north of the Misted Hills. This time we had no choice in how to get to our destination. We would have to walk.

Even pushing ourselves each day until long past sunset, it took the better part of a week to work our way over the hills. Our meals consisted mainly of wild apples, crescent nuts, a sweet vine that Rhia discovered, and the occasional egg or two from an unwary grouse's nest. While we avoided any more encounters with living stones, the trekking proved arduous. Vapors swirled constantly, wrapping us in misty shawls, inhibiting our views from even the higher ground.

During one swamp crossing, Rhia lost one of her shoes in a pit of quicksand. We spent much of that afternoon searching for a rowan tree so that she could weave a replacement from its leathery bark. Two days later, we crossed a high pass, slick with ice and snow, but only after walking the entire night of the full moon.

Finally, bedraggled and exhausted, we came to the high plains of the river's headwaters. Countless star-shaped yellow flowers blanketed the plains, filling the air with a tangy scent. In time we reached the rushing River Unceasing itself. There we encountered a pair of cream-colored unicorns, grazing along its banks. Heading north, we followed the river's serpentine path up a series of wide, alpine meadows that ascended like bright green stairs.

As Rhia reached the edge of one of these meadows, she stopped, pointing at the line of snowy mountains in the distance. "Look, Merlin. Behind those peaks lies the city of the giants, Varigal. I've always wanted to see it, even now that it's only a ruin. Arbassa says it's the most ancient settlement on Fincayra."

"Too bad dwarves, not giants, are our goal." I bent down, pulling up a handful of fluffy-tipped grass. "Giants will have to wait for the fifth Song, the one that involves Varigal somehow. If we make it that far."

As we continued trekking after sunset, a gleaming disk emerged from the layers of clouds. Clipped along one edge, the moon was now waning. I pushed harder, practically running along the grassy bank, knowing full well that more than half of my time had vanished, and I had unraveled only two of the mysterious Songs. How could I possibly complete the remaining five, climb up to the Otherworld, obtain the Elixir, and return to Elen, all in less than two weeks? Not even a real wizard could hope to do so much.

By the glow of the moon, we scrambled over yet another steep rise, grasping at roots and shrubs to keep from tumbling over backward. The River Unceasing, now only a splashing stream, flowed down the slope beside us, its little falls and pools sparkling in the silver light. At last we topped the rise. Before us stretched an enormous, moon-lit meadow, split by the shining ribbon of water.

Bumbelwy fell in a jangling heap by the stream. "I can go no further without rest. And also food. A jester needs his strength."

Panting in the night air, I leaned against my staff. "It is your audience who needs strength."

"Too true, too true, too true." He mopped his brow with the edge of his heavy cloak. "On top of everything else, I am baking to death! This cloak has me perspiring even after the sun goes down. And during these hot days we've been enduring, it's sheer torture."

Perplexed, I shook my head. "Then why don't you leave it behind?"

"Because without it I may freeze. Turn to ice! Why, it could snow anytime. This hour, this minute, this second!"

Rhia and I traded amused glances. Then she bent down and sniffed the star-shaped flowers. Grinning, she picked a fistful of stems, rolled them into a compact, yellow mass, then handed the roll to me.

"Taste it," she implored. "The astral flower is a trekker's sustenance. It is said that lost travelers have lived on nothing else for many weeks."

Biting into the roll of flowers, I tasted a sweet yet sharp flavor, almost like burned honey. "Mmmm. You know who would like this? Our old friend Shim."

"Yes," replied Rhia. "Or, as he would say, *certainly, definitely, absolutely.*" She handed a fresh roll to Bumbelwy, sprawled on his back by the stream. "Shim loved honey as much as I do! Even before he grew into a giant, he ate enough honey for one." With a sigh, she added, "I wonder whether we'll ever see him again."

Kneeling, I placed my cupped hands into the shimmering water. As I brought the water to my face, however, the moon's wavering reflection appeared within my hands. I jerked backward, drenching my tunic.

"Did you see something?" Rhia studied me with concern.

"Only a reminder of all the damage I've done."

She considered me for another moment. Then, in a voice so soft I could barely hear it above the splashing stream, she spoke. "You still have the heart of a wizard."

My hand slapped the water, splattering us both. "Then give me the simple heart of a boy! Rhia, whenever I tap into those . . . yearnings, those powers, those arts of wizardry, I do something terrible! Because of me, my mother lies at the edge of death. Because of me, much of the Dark Hills remains a waste, just waiting for Rhita Gawr and his warrior goblins to return. And because of me, my own eyes are blind and useless."

Bumbelwy propped himself up on one elbow, clanging his bells. "Such despair, my boy! Could I offer my assistance? Allow me to tell you the riddle about the—"

"No!" I shouted, waving him away. I turned back to Rhia. "The truth is, Domnu is a thieving old hag. But she had it right. I could be the worst disaster ever to come to Fincayra."

Rhia said nothing, and bent to take a drink from the stream. As she raised her head, she wiped the water from her chin. "No," she declared at last. "I don't think so. It's not anything I can put my finger on. It's more . . . the berries. I mean, the Harp actually did work for you, at least for a while. The speaking shell, too, did your bidding."

"All I did was find the right shell. Then it used its own power to bring my mother here."

"Even if you're right, what about Tuatha? He wouldn't have allowed you to read the Seven Songs unless there was at least some chance you could master them and travel to the Otherworld."

My head drooped. "Tuatha was a great wizard, a real wizard. And he did tell me that someday I might become one, too. Yet even wizards make mistakes! No, the only way I'll travel to the Otherworld is when I die. And by then my mother will have died, as well."

She hooked her finger, still wet from the stream, around my own. "There's still the prophecy, Merlin. That only a child of human blood can defeat Rhita Gawr and those who serve him."

Turning away, I gazed at the wide meadow beyond the stream. Though some of its grasses glimmered in the moonlight, most of the meadow lay shrouded by shadows. Somewhere out there, I knew, lay the realm of the dwarves. And somewhere beyond that lay the secret entrance to the world of the spirits, guarded by the ogre Balor.

I pulled my hand away. "That prophecy, Rhia, is worth no more than the person it refers to. Besides, I only want to save my own mother, not battle the warriors of Rhita Gawr." Reaching for a pebble, I tossed it into the silvery stream. "And I doubt I can even do that."

"Ah, misery," intoned Bumbelwy, his face as shadowed as the meadow. "At last you see the wisdom in what I have been telling you all along."

I bristled. "Nothing you have told me remotely resembles wisdom."

"Don't be offended, please. I'm only pointing out that there is only one thing left for you to do. Give up."

My cheeks burned. Seizing my staff, I stood up. "That, you poor excuse for a jester, is the one thing I shall not do! I may be certain to fail in this quest, but I will not fail out of cowardice. My mother deserves better than that." Casting a glance at the moonlit meadow before us, I spoke to Rhia. "Come if you like. The dwarves' realm cannot be far from here."

She drew a long breath. "Yes, but it would be foolish to try to find it now. We need a few hours' rest. And Merlin, that meadow . . . it's full of danger. I can feel it. On top of that, the dwarves' tunnels are surely hidden, by the land if not by magic. They will be hard enough to find even by day."

"Just give up," urged Bumbelwy, reaching for some more astral flowers.

"Never," I growled. Pivoting on the walking stick, I turned to go.

"Don't, Merlin!" Rhia stretched her arms toward me. "Ignore him. Wait for daylight. You could easily get lost."

If I could have breathed fire, I would have. "You wait for daylight! I can take care of myself."

I strode into the meadow, the tall grasses swishing against my tunic. Moonlight streaked the land like luminous claw marks, yet most of it lay shadowed. Then, several paces ahead, my second sight detected an unusually dark patch. Since no rock or tree stood near enough to cast a shadow, I realized that it might be a tunnel, or at least a pit. Not so foolish as to walk right into such a thing, I angled to the left.

Suddenly the earth beneath my feet gave way. I plunged downward. Before I could even cry out, total blackness swallowed me.

When I awoke, I found myself curled into a tight ball, covered with a heavy blanket that reeked of smoke. Something was carrying me, grunting constantly, though I had no idea what form of beast it was or where it was taking me. Thick ropes bound my arms and legs, while a wad of cloth filled my mouth. But for the muffled grunts beneath me, I heard no sound but the beating of my own heart. Jostled and bounced like a sack of grain, I felt increasingly dazed and bruised. My torture seemed to last for hours.

Finally, the jostling came to an abrupt halt. I was heaved onto a floor of smooth, hard stone. I lay there, facedown, my head spinning. The blanket was ripped away. With great effort, I rolled over.

An assembly of dwarves, each one no taller than my waist, stared at me with eyes redder than flame. Most wore tangled beards, while all bore jeweled daggers on their waists. Standing beneath a row of sizzling torches, with feet firmly planted and burly arms crossed on their chests, they looked as immovable as the rock walls surrounding them. One, whose beard showed streaks of gray, straightened his back stiffly, leading me to guess that he had been one of the grunting dwarves who had carried me here.

"Cut his bonds," commanded a sharp voice.

Immediately, strong hands rolled me over again and sliced through the ropes. Someone pulled the wad of cloth out of my mouth. Working my stiff arms and parched tongue, I managed to sit up.

Spying my staff on the floor beside me, I reached for it. A dwarf lifted his heavy boot and stomped on my wrist. I shouted in pain, my cry echoing within the rock walls.

"Not so fast."

It was the same sharp voice. This time, though, I located its source: a thickset dwarf seated on a throne carved of jade, inlaid with rows of gems, that rested on a ledge above the stone floor. She had unruly red hair, pale skin, and earrings of dangling shells that clinked whenever she moved. Her oversized nose looked nearly as big as Shim's before he became a giant. She wore a black robe embroidered with runes and geometric shapes sewn in glistening gold thread, plus a peaked hat to match. In one hand she held a staff, almost as tall as my own.

As I started to stand, the dwarf raised her free hand. "Do not try to get up! You shall be low, lower than me. And do not reach again for your staff."

She leaned toward me, clinking her white shell earrings. "A staff be dangerous, you know. Even in the hands of an upstart enchanter like you, Merlin."

I caught my breath. "How do you know my name?"

She scratched her prominent nose. "No one knows your true name. Not even you, it be clear."

"You called me Merlin."

"Yes," she said with a snorting laugh that seemed to make the torches flame brighter in the cavern. "And you may call me Urnalda. But neither be a true name."

Furrowing my brow in bewilderment, I tried again. "How did you know to call me Merlin?"

"Ah." The white shells clinked as she nodded. "That be a better question." She raised a stubby finger to touch an earring. "The shells told me. Just as a shell told you a few things, some that you be too headstrong to hear."

I shifted my weight on the hard stone floor.

"Not only that, you be an intruder." Urnalda waved her arms, sending their shadows racing across the walls. "And I do so despise intruders."

At this, several of the dwarves reached for their jeweled daggers. One, whose forehead showed a jagged scar, chortled loudly. The sound hovered in the air of the underground room.

Stroking her staff, Urnalda considered me for a long moment. "Even so, I might yet choose to help you."

"Truly?" I glanced at the dwarves, who groaned in disappointment. Then, recalling my experience with the Trickster of the Lake, I felt suddenly suspicious. "Why might you help me?"

She snorted. "Because one day, if you be successful, you might wear a hat such as mine."

Not comprehending, I examined her peaked hat more closely. Its point slouched to one side. Lower down, dozens of tiny holes pierced its surface, allowing Urnalda's red hairs to poke through. But for the silver embroidery, which might have been more attractive if it showed stars and planets instead of runes, it was quite simply the most ridiculous hat I had ever encountered. Why would I ever want a hat like that?

The dwarf's eyes narrowed, as if she could read my thoughts. In a deeper voice than usual, she declared, "This be the hat of an enchanter."

I winced. "I didn't mean to insult you."

"That be a lie."

"All right, then. I am sorry I insulted you."

"That be true."

"Please. Will you help me?"

Urnalda tapped thoughtfully on her staff before finally uttering a one-word answer. "Yes."

A black-bearded dwarf, standing beside her throne, grumbled angrily. In a flash, she turned on him and raised her hand as if to strike. He froze, petrified. Slowly, she dropped her hand—even as his beard dropped right off his face. He squealed, covering his naked cheeks with his hands. Meanwhile, other dwarves hooted and guffawed, pointing at the fallen beard on the floor.

"Silence!" Urnalda shook herself angrily, jostling the shell earrings, as well as the throne on the ledge. "That will teach you to doubt my decisions."

She turned back to me. "I will help you because you might yet defy all the odds and survive. Mayhaps even live to become an enchanter yourself." Slyly, she squinted at me. "And if I help you now, you might one day help me."

"I will. I promise I will."

The torches sizzled, wavering, making the rock walls themselves appear to vibrate. Urnalda leaned forward, her shadow enlarging on the chiseled surface behind her. "Promises be serious things."

"I know." I gazed at her solemnly. "If you help me find the soul of Protecting, I will not forget."

Urnalda snapped her fingers. "Bring me a light flyer. And a carving stone, with hammer and chisel."

Still wary of some sort of trick, I asked, "What is a light flyer?"

"Be still."

But for the sizzling of torches, silence filled the cavern. For several minutes, no one stirred. Then heavy boots clomped into the underground room, as a pair of dwarves approached the throne. One of them hunched under a huge black stone, as rough as the walls themselves, that must have weighed twice as much as he did. At a nod from Urnalda, he lowered his shoulders and dropped the stone with a thud on the floor.

The second dwarf bore a hammer and chisel in one hand, and some sort of small, glowing object in the other. It seemed to be an upside-down cup made of clear crystal, resting with its rim against his palm. Within the crystal, an unsteady light flickered. At Urnalda's nod, he set the tools by the stone. Then he carefully placed the cup on the floor, taking care to slide his hand away quickly so that something inside it would not escape.

Urnalda gave a snorting laugh, and the torches flamed brighter. "Inside that crystal cage be a light flyer, one of Fincayra's rarest creatures." She grinned crookedly at me, a look I did not like. "Your next Song be Protecting, be it not? To learn what you need to know, you must find the best possible way to protect the light flyer from harm."

Observing the hammer and chisel, I swallowed hard. "You mean carve a cage . . . from that big stone?"

She scratched her nose pensively. "If that be the best way to protect the fragile little creature, then that be what you must do."

"But that could take days. Or weeks!"

"It took dwarves many years to carve the tunnels and halls of our realm."

"I don't have that much time."

"Silence." She pointed her staff at a hole in the ceiling, which glowed with a subdued light of its own. "That tunnel, like the one you fell down, provides us with air as well as light. There be hundreds of them, each one carved as smooth as the floor you be seated on, each one concealed on the surface by enchantment. That be why dwarves stay so well protected. That be why you came here to learn the soul of the Song."

"Are you sure there is no other way?" I protested.

The earrings swayed from side to side. "There be no other way to learn the lesson yourself. Your task be to protect the little creature from harm. Now begin."

With a final clink of her shells, Urnalda left the room, followed by her entourage. I gazed at the sizzling torches on the walls, watching the shadows cast by her throne grow, then shrink, then grow again. That very throne, like the walls themselves, had been hewn from unforgiving stone. The same stone that the dwarves, over centuries, had molded into an entire realm.

And now it was my turn to mold stone.

XIX

PROTECTING

The hammer and chisel gleamed coldly in the wavering light of the torches. Grasping the tools, I regained my feet and approached the massive black stone. It came almost to my waist. I raised the hammer and struck my first blow. My hand, my arm, my whole chest shook. Before the ringing of the hammer died away, I struck a second blow. Then a third.

Time passed as I worked, but without its usual rhythms. For in the subterranean throne room of Urnalda, the only sign of day or night came from the air tunnel in the ceiling above my head. While by night its circular mouth gleamed with the silver light of the moon, by day it glowed bright with the golden light of the sun.

Yet day or night made no difference to me. The torches on the walls sizzled constantly. I hammered incessantly—on the flat top of the chisel, on the black stone directly, and occasionally on my poor swollen thumb. The hammer rang to the rhythm of my own breathing. Chips flew into the air, and sometimes my face. Yet I continued, stopping only long enough to eat some of the thick, smoky porridge provided by the dwarves, or to nap fitfully on the blanket.

Three bearded dwarves guarded me at all times. One stood over my staff on the stone floor, his burly arms folded on his chest. In addition to his dagger, a double-sided axe hung from his belt. The other two, holding tall spears fitted with blades of blood red stone, positioned themselves at either side of the entry tunnel. All wore the same grim expressions, which only deepened whenever Urnalda herself entered the hall.

She sat upon her throne on the ledge, for hours it seemed, watching me work. She seemed lost in thought, despite the constant banging of the hammer in my blistered hands. Or perhaps she was trying to probe my innermost thoughts. I did not know—and did not care. All I knew was that I would not, as Bumbelwy had suggested, give up. When I thought of his proposal, or of my mother's condition, sparks flew from the stone. Yet I felt increasingly aware of the limits of my time. And of my ability as a stone carver.

The glow from the light flyer flickered and wavered, playing on the black stone as I worked. Bit by bit, more pieces of the stone chipped away. In time I had made a shallow groove. If my thumb and aching arms held out, I would widen this into a hollow large enough to invert and cover the light flyer. How much more time that would require I could not tell. Judging from the shifting light in the air tunnel overhead, two days and nights had already passed.

Throughout my labor, I kept hearing in my mind Urnalda's final command: *Your task be to protect the little creature from harm.* Once in a while, as the hammering continued, I wondered whether there was a clue buried in those words. Could there be some other way to keep the light flyer safe? Some way I was missing?

No, I told myself, that couldn't be. Urnalda herself had credited tunnels of stone with keeping the dwarves safe. While even stone will not last forever, it is stronger than anything else. The message was clear. *I must build a cage of stone, just as the dwarves built this underground realm. I have no choice.*

Still, as I hammered and pried, trying to split the stone along its cracks, I wished there were some easier way. Like the way I had wielded the great sword Deepercut, in the battle of the Shrouded Castle! I had used not my hands, but some hidden powers of my mind, to make the sword fly through the air. Somehow in that moment, without knowing how, I had tapped into the magic of Leaping. Just as the Grand Elusa had done, sending us to the abandoned land of the treelings. Could I possibly tap into that same power again? Could I make the hammer and chisel do my work now, thereby sparing my stiff back, sore arms, and blistered thumb?

"Be not a fool, Merlin."

I looked up from the stone to face Urnalda, watching me from her jade throne. "What do you mean?"

"I mean be not a fool! If, indeed, you made Deepercut fly to you, it be less because of you than because of something else. That sword be a Treasure of Fincayra. It be possessed of its own powers." She leaned forward on her jade throne, clinking her earrings. "You did not wield the sword as much as it wielded you."

I dropped the hammer, which clanged on the stone floor. "How can you say that? I did it! I used the sword! With my own power. Just as I—"

Urnalda smirked. "Finish your sentence."

My voice fell to a whisper. "Just as I used the Flowering Harp."

"Exactly." The torches wavered as she examined me, scratching her bulbous nose. "You be a slow learner, but there may yet be hope for you."

"I have a feeling you're talking about more than my skill with stone."

She snorted, straightening her hat. "Of course. I be talking about your skill at Seeing. No wonder that, of all the Seven Songs, you fear that one the most."

I blanched.

Before I could say anything, she declared, "You be a slow learner with stone, too. You would never succeed as a dwarf in the tunnels! Which be why I doubt the prophecy can turn out to be true."

"What prophecy?"

"That you will one day rebuild a great stone circle, as great as *Estonahenj*."

I sputtered like one of the torches. "Me? Rebuild something of that size? That's likely! Just as likely as I will pick up *Estonahenj*, stone by stone, and move it across the ocean to Gwynedd."

Her red eyes gleamed strangely. "Oh, it be prophesied that you will do that, too. Not to Gwynedd, but to a neighboring land called Logres, or Gramarye by some. But that prophecy be even less likely than the other one."

"Enough," I declared. I blew on my blistered palm, then reached again for the hammer. "Now I've got to get back to my real work. Carving a stone cage, as you commanded me to do."

"That be a lie."

My hammer raised, I froze. "A lie? Why?"

Shadows skipped around the room, as her earrings clattered softly. "I commanded you, Merlin, yet that be not my command."

"You gave me this stone."

"That be true."

"You told me to protect the light flyer from harm."

"That be true."

"And that means carving something stronger than that crystal cup over there."

"That be your decision. Not mine."

Slowly, hesitantly, I lowered the hammer. I set it down, along with the chisel, and moved closer to the crystal. The creature within it trembled like a tiny flame.

"May I ask you a question, Urnalda? About the light flyer?"

"Ask."

I watched the wavering light of the crystal. "You said it's one of the rarest creatures in Fincayra. How does it . . . survive? How does it stay safe?"

Urnalda's face, lit by the torches, showed the hint of a crooked grin. "It be safe by roaming in the bright sunlight where it cannot be seen. Or, at night, by dancing in the places where moonbeams meet water."

"In other words . . . by being free."

The shell earrings clinked gently, but she said nothing.

I reached to touch the crystal cup. Spreading my fingers over its glowing surface, I felt the warmth of the creature caught inside. With a sudden flick of my wrist, I turned the cup over.

A shimmering spot of light, no bigger than an apple seed, floated into the air of the cavernous hall. I heard only a faint hum as it rose past my head. The light flyer lifted swiftly to the ceiling, slipped into the mouth of the air tunnel, and was gone.

Urnalda pounded with her fist on the arm of her throne. The two dwarves guarding the entrance instantly lowered their spears, aiming the blades straight at me. Again she pounded. "Tell me why you did that."

I drew a halting breath, "Well, because even a cage of stone will eventually crumble. *The best way to protect something is to set it free.*"

At that instant, blue flame erupted from my staff. The dwarf standing over it yelped and leaped his own height into the air. Even before he fell back to the floor, I could make out the new marking, etched in blue, on my staff. It was a cracked stone.

XX

RIVERS COOL
AND WARM

By the time I found the others at their camp by the headwaters, not far from where I had left them, we had been separated more than three full days. The meadow grasses, painted several shades of green, rippled in the breeze. Seeing me approach, Rhia ran to meet me. Her worried face relaxed as soon as she glimpsed the third marking etched on my staff.

She touched my hand. "I was so worried, Merlin."

My throat tightened. "With good reason, I'm afraid. You told me I might get lost, and I guess I did."

"You found your way back, though."

"Yes," I replied. "But it took me too long. Ten days, no more, remain."

Bumbelwy joined us, almost tripping on his cloak as he hopped over the splashing stream. Although he wore his usual stack of frowns, he seemed genuinely glad to see me. He clasped my hand and shook it vigorously, jangling his bells in my ears. Then, sensing that he was about to try again to tell his famous riddle of the bells, I turned and walked away briskly. Both he and Rhia followed. Before long we had put some distance between ourselves and the realm of the dwarves. Yet far more distance lay ahead.

For the fourth Song, Naming, had something to do with the Slantos, a mysterious people who lived at the extreme northeastern tip of Fincayra. While to get there we would not need to climb any more snowbound passes, we would have to cross the entire breadth of the Rusted Plains. That alone would take several days. Then we would be hard-pressed to find a route past the sheer cliffs of Eagles' Canyon, not to mention the northern reaches of the Dark Hills. And while I knew that danger lurked in all these places, it was the notion of crossing the Dark Hills that left me most unsettled.

To cross the plains, we rose each day at dawn, when the first morning birds and the last evening frogs sang together in chorus. We stopped only occasionally to pick berries or roots—and once, thanks to Rhia's ability to speak the buzzing language of bees, to eat a bit of honeycomb, dripping with sweet syrup. She also seemed to know just where we might find water, leading us to hidden springs and quiet pools. It was as if she could somehow see into the landscape's secret mind as easily as she could see into my own. The moon offered enough light to trek into the night, so trek by moonlight we did, across the sweeping plains. Yet the moon, like our time, was quickly disappearing.

Finally, after three long days, we reached the edge of Eagles' Canyon. We sat on the rocky rim, gazing out over the broad stripes of red, brown, maroon, and pink that lined the cliffs and buttresses. Gleaming white pinnacles protruded from the opposite wall. Far below, a shallow river snaked along the base of the cliffs.

Tired though I was, I couldn't help feeling a rush of strength when I recalled the stirring cry of the canyon eagle that had marked the beginning of the Great Council of Fincayra. If only I could soar like an eagle myself! I could sail over this colorful gorge, as swiftly as the wind. Just as I had done, ages ago it seemed, on Trouble's feathered back.

But an eagle or a hawk I was not. Like Rhia and Bumbelwy, I would have to descend into the canyon by foot and find some route up the other side. With my second sight, I followed the line of cliffs, searching for some way to cross. We were, at least, far enough north that the walls were not completely impassable. Farther to the south, they lifted into a yawning chasm that sliced through the very center of the Dark Hills.

Rhia, the most surefooted of the three of us, led the way. She soon discovered a series of narrow ledges that crisscrossed the cliff walls. By following each ledge until we found a place to drop down to the one just below, we gradually moved lower into the canyon, sometimes sliding on our backs, sometimes climbing over crumbly outcroppings. Finally, soaked with perspiration, we reached the bottom.

The river, though muddy, was much cooler than we were. Bumbelwy, sweltering under his thick cloak, plunged straight in. Rhia and I followed suit, kneeling on the round stones that lined the river bottom, soaking our heads and rinsing our arms, splashing water on each other. Once, though I could not be certain, I thought I heard the distant screech of an eagle from somewhere above us on the cliffs.

At last, feeling refreshed, we began the arduous climb out of the canyon. Before long I needed to use both hands, and thrust my staff into the belt of my tunic. As the slope grew steeper, Bumbelwy's grumbling grew worse. Yet he struggled to keep up, climbing just below Rhia, finding his handholds in the footholds she had just vacated.

As we scaled a particularly steep buttress, my shoulders ached from the strain. I leaned back as far as I dared without losing my grip, hop-

ing to glimpse the top of the canyon wall. But I found only more layered maroon and brown cliffs rising far above us. Glancing below, I
viewed the muddy river, which seemed no more than a thin trickle
on the canyon floor. I shuddered, tightening my grip on the rock.
For as little as I wanted to climb upward, I wanted even less to tumble so far downward.

Rhia, who was slightly to my left on the buttress, suddenly called
out. "Look! A sharr. On the pink rock there."

Careful not to lose my balance, I turned to find a light brown, kit-
tenlike animal, basking in the sunshine. Like a cat, it lay curled in a
little ball, purring quietly. Unlike a cat, it had a pointed snout, lined
with soft whiskers, and two paper-thin wings folded across its back.
The delicate wings fluttered with every purr.

"Isn't it lovely?" asked Rhia, gripping the wall of stone. "Sharrs
are found only in high, rocky places like this. I've seen only one before, from much farther away. They're very shy."

Hearing her voice, the sharr opened its blue eyes. It tensed, watching her intently. Then it seemed to relax. The purring resumed.
Slowly, Rhia shifted her footholds. Then, grasping the crumbling cliff
with one hand, she reached toward the creature.

"Careful," I warned. "You might fall."

"Shhh. You'll frighten it."

The sharr shifted slightly, placing its furry paws on the rock as if it
were preparing to stand. Each of the paws had four little toes. As
Rhia's hand came nearer to its face, the sharr's purring grew louder.

Just then I noticed something strange about the paws. At first I
couldn't identify what it was. For some reason, they seemed a
bit . . . odd.

All of a sudden, I knew. The toes were webbed. Like the feet of a duck. Now, why would a creature of the high, rocky canyons have webbed feet? In a flash, I understood.

"Don't, Rhia! It's a shifting wraith!"

Even as I started to shout, however, the sharr began to transform. Quick as lightning, the wings evaporated, the blue eyes reddened, the fur became scales, and the cat's body changed into a serpent with daggerlike teeth. The air crackled as it threw off a brittle, transparent skin, like a snake that is shedding. All this happened in the blink of an eye. Hearing my shout, Rhia had barely enough time to duck before the serpentine creature, jaws open wide, leaped at her face, claws extended. With a savage scream, the attacker flew just over her head, plunging into the canyon far below.

Although its jaws missed her, the shifting wraith's tail whipped against her cheek. Thrown off balance, she lost her footing. For an instant she clung to the buttress with one hand, swaying precariously. Then the stone beneath her hand crumbled. She fell, right on top of Bumbelwy.

Clinging tight to the rock face, his fingers turning white, the lanky jester howled at the impact. Yet somehow he held on, managing to break Rhia's fall. Still, she was left hanging upside down on his back, struggling to right herself.

"Hold on, Bumbelwy!" I cried, watching them from above.

"I'm doing my best," he groaned. "Though that's never good enough."

Suddenly, the stone supporting his hands broke loose, splitting into shards that clattered down the cliff. The two of them screamed in unison. Arms and legs flailing, they slid down the rock face, striking a narrow ledge that stopped their fall. There they hung, high above the canyon floor.

Like an ungainly spider, I climbed down the cliff, my staff swinging from my belt. Rhia and Bumbelwy were sprawled below me on the ledge, moaning painfully. The jester's bell-draped hat lay beside him, covered with red dust. Rhia tried to sit up, then fell back, her right arm dangling at her side.

Working my way across the narrow ledge, I reached her at last. As I helped her sit up, she gasped when I brushed against her twisted arm. Her eyes, full of pain, searched my face. "You warned me . . . just in time."

"I wish it had been a few seconds sooner." A sudden flurry of wind sprayed us with dust from the cliff wall. After it subsided, I took a pinch of herbs from my satchel and dabbed the scratch on her cheek.

"How did you know it was a wraith?"

"The webbed feet. Remember when we found that alleah bird in the forest? That was when you showed me that shifting wraiths always have something odd about them." I indicated myself. "A lot like people, I suppose."

Rhia tried to lift her arm and winced painfully. "Most people aren't that dangerous."

Moving carefully on the ledge, I came around to her other side to get a better view of the wounded arm. "It looks broken."

"And let's forget about poor old Bumbelwy," the jester whimpered. "I did nothing useful. Nothing at all."

Despite her pain, Rhia almost grinned. "Bumbelwy, you were wonderful. If my arm weren't ready to fall off, I'd give you a hug."

If only for a moment, the dour jester stopped moaning. He blushed ever so slightly. Then, seeing her injured arm, he frowned with his brow, cheeks, and chins. "That looks rather bad. You'll be incapacitated for life. Never able to eat or sleep again."

"I don't think so." Gently, I laid the arm across Rhia's lap, feeling for the break.

She winced. "What can you do? There's nothing—oh, that hurts!—around here to use for a splint. And without two—oh!—arms, it's going to be impossible climbing out of here."

"Impossible," echoed Bumbelwy.

I shook my head, knocking some pebbles from my hair. "Nothing is impossible."

"Bumbelwy's right," protested Rhia. "You can't fix this. Oh! Even that satchel of herbs . . . can't help. Merlin, you should leave me here. Go on . . . without me."

My jaw clenched. "Absolutely not! I've learned more about Binding than that. We are together, you and I, like those two hawks on the wind."

A frail light flickered in her eyes. "But how? I can't climb . . . without my arm."

I stretched my sore shoulders, then drew in a deep breath. "I'm hoping to mend your arm."

"Don't be ridiculous." Bumbelwy crept closer on the ledge. "To do that you'd need a splint. A stretcher. And an army of healers. It's impossible, I say."

Feeling the break, I placed my hands gently on top of it. Although it made no difference to my second sight, I closed my eyes in concentration. With all my power, I imagined light, warm and healing, gathering within my chest. As my heart brimmed with the light, I allowed it to flow down my arms and into my fingers. Like invisible rivers of warmth, the light flowed out of me and into Rhia.

"Ohhh," she sighed. "That feels good. What are you doing?"

"I'm just doing what a wise friend once told me to do. Listening to the language of the wound."

She smiled, leaning back against the rocky ledge.

"Don't be fooled," warned Bumbelwy. "If you feel better now, it's only because you're going to feel ten times worse later on."

"I don't care, you old bother! It feels stronger already." She started to lift her arm.

"Don't," I ordered. "Not yet."

As the warm light continued to pour out of my fingertips, I concentrated on the bones and muscles beneath her skin. Patiently, carefully, I felt each strand of tissue with my mind. Each strand I touched with gentleness, coaxing it to be strong again, to be whole again. One by one, I bathed the sinews, smoothed them, and knitted them back into place. Finally, I removed my hands.

Rhia raised her arm. She wiggled her fingers. Then she flung her arms around my neck, squeezing with all the strength of a bear.

"How did you do that?" she asked as she released me.

"I really don't know." I tapped the knotted top of my staff. "But I think it might be another verse in the Song of Binding."

She released me. "You have truly found the soul of that Song. Your mother, the healer, would be proud."

Her words jolted me. "Come! We have less than a week left. I want to get to the Slantos' village by tomorrow morning."

XXI

THE SHRIEK

By the time we finally pulled ourselves over the rim of the canyon, the sun had just set. Shadows gathered on the sheer buttresses, while the Dark Hills rising before us looked almost black. As I gazed at the hills, the lonely cry of a canyon eagle echoed somewhere nearby, reminding me of the eagle's cry that had begun the Great Council of Fincayra. And of the fact that those hills would have been restored to life by now had I kept my promise with the Flowering Harp.

The three of us trekked in the deepening dusk. The flat rocks under our feet quickly turned into dry, flaky soil, the kind of soil that I had learned to identify with the Dark Hills. But for the occasional rustling of leaves from withered trees, we heard only the crunching of our boots, the rattling of Bumbelwy's bells, and the rhythmic punching of my staff on the ground.

Darkness pressed closer. I knew that whatever brave animals might have returned to these hills since the collapse of the Shrouded Castle must have found secure places to hide after sundown. For that was the time when the warrior goblins and shifting wraiths—and whatever other creatures lived beneath the surface—might be tempted to emerge from their caves in the rock outcroppings and crevasses. I shuddered, remembering that at least one such creature had dared to appear in broad daylight. Rhia, uncannily aware of my feelings as usual, gave my arm a gentle squeeze.

Night fell as we continued to ascend the Dark Hills. Twisted trees stood like skeletons, their branches rattling in the wind. Staying on our northeasterly course was made more difficult because heavy clouds obscured most of the stars and the remaining moon. Even Rhia walked more slowly in the gloom. Although Bumbelwy didn't complain openly, his mutterings grew increasingly fearful. My own weary legs tripped often over stones and dead roots. At this rate, we were more likely to get lost than attacked.

When at last Rhia pointed out a narrow gully running down the slope, all that remained of a once-surging stream, I agreed that it would be wise to rest there until dawn. Minutes later, the three of us lay on the hard soil of the ravine. Rhia found a rounded rock she could use as a pillow, while Bumbelwy curled himself into a ball, declaring, "I could sleep through an erupting volcano." Given the danger, I tried my best to stay awake, but was soon slumbering along with the others.

A high-pitched shriek rang out. I sat up, fully awake, as did Rhia beside me. Both of us held our breath, listening, but heard nothing beyond Bumbelwy's snoring. A feeble glow behind the clouds was all that we could trace of the moon, and its light barely brushed the surrounding hills.

The shriek came again. It hung in the air, a cry of sheer terror. Although Rhia tried to stop me, I grabbed my staff and stumbled out of the gully. She followed me onto the darkened slope. Searching the shadows, I stretched my second sight as far as I could, trying to detect any movement at all. Yet nothing stirred, not even a cricket.

Suddenly I spotted a hulking figure traversing the rocks below us.

Even if I had not glimpsed the pointed helmet, I would have known instantly what it was. A warrior goblin. Over the goblin's muscular shoulder writhed a small, struggling creature whose life was clearly about to end.

Without pausing to think, I dashed down the slope. Hearing my footsteps, the goblin whirled around. He tossed aside the prey on his shoulder and, with amazing speed, drew his broad sword. As he raised it over his head, his fiery eyes narrowed with rage.

Weaponless except for my staff, I planted my feet and hurled myself straight at him. My shoulder crashed into his armored chest, throwing him backward. Together, we rolled and bounced down the rock-strewn slope.

I came to a stop, my head still whirling. But the warrior goblin had recovered faster. He stood over me, snarling, his three-fingered hand still grasping the sword. As the moon above us broke out of the clouds, the blade gleamed darkly. Just as he brought down the sword, I rolled to one side. It slammed into the ground, splintering an old root. The warrior goblin growled wrathfully. He raised the sword again.

I tried to stand, but tripped on a gnarled stick. My staff! In desperation, I lifted it to shield my face, even as the goblin's sword came slicing toward me. I knew the thin shaft would hardly slow the blade at all, yet I could do nothing more.

As the blade struck the wood, a sudden explosion rocked the slope. A tower of blue flame soared high into the sky. The goblin's sword lifted with it, spinning like a branch borne aloft by a gale. The warrior goblin himself roared in anguish. He stumbled backward, collapsing on the hillside. He wheezed once, tried to raise himself, then fell back, as still as stone.

Rhia ran to me. "Merlin! Are you hurt?"

"No." I rubbed the shaft, feeling the slight indentation where the sword had struck it. "Thanks to this staff. And whatever virtue Tuatha gave to it."

Rhia kneeled, her curls frosted with moonlight. "I think it was as much you as the staff."

I shook my head, observing the motionless form of the warrior goblin. "Come now, Rhia. You know better."

"I do," she declared crisply. "And I think you are denying it because you want so much for it to be true."

Stunned, I gazed at her. "You read me, in the same way I came to read those runes on Arbassa's walls."

Her bell-like laughter rang out. "Some things I still can't understand, though. Like why, instead of hiding when you saw the goblin, you charged straight at him."

Before I could reply, a small voice spoke behind us. "You must be magical."

Rhia and I spun around to see a short, round-faced boy, crouching on the ground. He couldn't have been older than five. I knew at once that he was the unfortunate creature whose shriek had awakened us. His eyes, themselves glowing like little moons, seemed full of awe.

I glanced at Rhia. "That's why." Turning back to the boy, I beckoned. "Come here. I won't hurt you."

Slowly, he rose to his feet. Hesitantly, he approached, then stopped himself. "Are you good magical or bad magical?"

Rhia stifled a laugh, wrapping her leafy arms around the boy. "He is very good magical. Except when he is being very bad."

As I growled playfully at her, the boy frowned in confusion. He wriggled away from Rhia and started backing down the shadowy slope.

"Don't listen to her. I am an enemy of warrior goblins, just like you." Leaning on my staff, I stood. "My name is Merlin. This is Rhia, who comes from Druma Wood. Now tell us your name."

The boy studied me, patting his round cheek thoughtfully. "You must be good magical, to slay the goblin with only your staff." He sucked in his breath. "I am Galwy, and I've lived all my life in the same village."

I cocked my head. "The only village near here is—"

"Slantos," finished the little fellow.

My heart raced.

Galwy looked away sheepishly. "I didn't mean to stay outside the gates after dark. Really, I didn't! It's just that the squirrels were playing, and I followed them, and when I realized how late it was . . . " He glared at the twisted form of the fallen warrior goblin. "He wanted to hurt me."

I stepped to the small boy's side. "He won't hurt you now."

Eyes shining, he tilted his head to look up at me. "I think you really are good magical."

XXII

AMBROSIA
BREAD

When we returned to the ravine, we found Bumbelwy still snoring. Although the explosion of flame had not been a volcano, his prediction of sleeping soundly had certainly proved true. Rhia and I carefully tucked Galwy, who was so tired he could barely stand, under a portion of the jester's cloak. Then, feeling our own exhaustion, we joined them on the ground. Clutching my staff, I soon fell asleep.

Before long, the first fingers of morning light tickled my face. I woke to find Bumbelwy already doing his best to impress young Galwy with his skills as a jester. From the solemn expression on the boy's round face, I could tell he hadn't progressed very far.

"That is why," the dour fellow was explaining, "they call me Bumbelwy the Mirthful."

Galwy stared at him, looking as if he were about to cry.

"Let me show you another of my jesterly talents." Bumbelwy gave his head a vigorous shake, clanging his bells, and drew his cloak tightly about him. "I will now tell you the famous riddle of the bells."

Rhia, who was also watching, started to protest. But I held up my hand. "Let's hear this confounded riddle. We've been hearing *about* it for weeks."

She smirked. "I suppose so. Are you ready to eat your boots if any of us laugh?"

"Ready." I licked my lips in mock satisfaction. "Then, with any luck, we'll find something more tasty at the Slantos' village."

Bumbelwy cleared his throat, making his drooping chins quiver. "I am now ready," he announced. He paused expectantly, almost as if he could not quite believe that he was finally being allowed to tell his riddle.

"We're waiting," I declared. "But not all day."

The jester's wide mouth opened. Then shut. Opened again. Shut again.

I leaned forward. "Well?"

Bumbelwy's eyebrows arched in consternation. He cleared his throat once more. He stomped his foot on the dry ground, rattling his bells again. But he did not speak.

"Are you going to tell this riddle of yours or not?"

The jester bit his lip, then shook his head glumly. "It's been . . . so long," he grumbled. "So many people, over so many years, have stopped me from telling it. Now that I may, I can't . . . remember it." He heaved a sigh. "Too true, too true, too true."

As Rhia and I rolled our eyes, Galwy smiled broadly. He turned to me. "Could you take me back to the village now? With you, I feel safe."

I tapped Bumbelwy's hunched shoulder. "Perhaps, one day, you'll remember it."

"If that ever happens," he replied, "I'll probably botch the delivery."

Moments later, we were trekking toward the rising sun. As usual,

Rhia and I led the way, although now I bore Galwy on my shoulders. Bumbelwy, more somber than ever, kept to the rear.

To my relief, we soon began a long, rolling descent, leaving behind the parched slopes and shadowed rock outcroppings of the Dark Hills. I could not rid myself of the uneasy feeling that the goblin we had encountered was only one of the first of Rhita Gawr's warriors to emerge from hiding. Nor could I forget how little I had done to make this land habitable for other creatures.

Before long, we entered a wide, grassy plain. Piping birds and humming insects appeared, as clusters of trees with hand-shaped leaves grew more common. A family of foxes, bushy tails all erect, crossed our trail. Sitting in the boughs of a willow tree sat a wide-eyed squirrel who reminded me of Rhia's friend Ixtma—and of the dying woman in his care.

The first sign of the village was the smell.

Grounded in the rich, hearty aroma of roasting grains, the smell strengthened as we crossed the grassy plain. With every step, it intensified, reminding me of how long it had been since I had eaten a crust of freshly baked bread. I could almost taste the grains. Wheat. Corn. Barley.

Other aromas, too, wove through this fragrant fabric. Something tangy, like the bright orange fruits that Rhia and I devoured long ago beneath the boughs of the shomorra tree. Something sharp and fresh, like the crushed mint that Elen often added to her tea. Something sweet, like the honey that bees made from clover blossoms. And more. Much more. The smell contained spicy flavors, robust flavors, and soothing flavors as well. It also contained, more often than not, a hint of something that was not really a flavor at all. More like a feeling. An attitude. Even . . . an idea.

When at last we entered the valley of the Slantos, and their low, brown buildings came into view, the smell grew overpowering. My mouth watering, I remembered tasting the Slantos' bread once before, in the underground den of Cairpré. What had he called it? *Ambrosia bread.* Food for the gods, the Greeks would have surely agreed. I remembered biting into the stiff crust, as hard as wood at first. Then, after some vigorous chewing, the bread had exploded with zesty flavor. A wave of nourishment had coursed through me, making me feel taller and sturdier. For a moment, I had even forgotten about the perpetual soreness between my shoulder blades.

Then I remembered something else. Cairpré, through a mouthful of ambrosia bread, had given me a stern warning. *No one from other parts of Fincayra has ever tasted the Slantos' most special breads, and they guard those precious recipes with their lives.* I gripped my staff as a new wave of fear surged through me. If the Slantos were not even willing to part with their recipes, how in the world was I going to get them to part with something much more valuable—the soul of the Song of Naming?

At the sight of the village gates in the distance, Galwy released a whoop of joy, jumped down from my shoulders, and scampered ahead of us, his arms flapping like the wings of a young bird. Beyond the gates, smoke poured from the hearths of many low buildings. The structures, while varied sizes, were all made from wide, brown bricks lined with yellow mortar. I almost smiled, noting that they looked like giant loaves of buttered bread themselves.

Bumbelwy, who had remained silent all morning, smacked his lips. "Do you think they're in the habit of giving visitors a crust of bread? Or do they turn people away hungry?"

"My guess," answered Rhia, "is that they're not in the habit of having visitors at all. The only people on this side of Eagles' Canyon are in—" Abruptly, she caught herself, glancing at me.

"In prison, in the caverns south of here, you were about to say." I pushed some stray black hairs off my face. "Like Stangmar, the man who was once my father."

Rhia eyed me sympathetically. "He's still your father."

I strode more briskly toward the gates. "Not anymore. I don't have a father."

She swallowed. "I know how you feel. I never even knew my father. Or my mother."

"At least you have Arbassa. And the rest of Druma Wood. As you've said before, that's your real family."

She worked her tongue, but said nothing.

As we arrived at the wooden gates, which were affixed to two tremendous spruce trees, a guard stepped out of the shadows by one of the trunks. Shaking the thinning locks of sand-colored hair that fell over his ears, he scowled at each of us in turn. Though his sword remained in its scabbard, one of his hands grasped the hilt. Even more than the roasting grains that filled the air, I began to smell the likelihood of trouble.

Warily, he examined my staff. "Be that the magical staff that felled the goblin?"

I blinked in surprise. "You know about that already?"

"Half the village knows by now," snorted the guard. "Young master Galwy has been telling everyone he can find."

"You'll let us pass, then?"

The guard shook his locks again. "I didn't say that." He pointed at the staff, eyeing it cautiously. "How do I know you won't use that to harm any villagers?"

"Well, for the same reason I'm not using it to harm you right now."

His face tightened, and he gave his sword an anxious tug. "You'll have to do better than that. You could be an infiltrator, after our secrets. Or an errand boy for the goblins, for all I know."

Rhia, bristling, stepped forward. "Then why would he have slain the goblin last night?"

"As a ruse, leafy girl." He ran a hand through his thinning hair. "Tell me, then. Why would a boy, a girl, and a . . . " He paused, observing Bumbelwy. "And a beggar, of whatever kind, travel all the way to Slantos? Not by chance, I'll wager."

"No," I answered carefully. "Your village is famous, far and near, for its breads. My friends and I would like to learn some of the bread maker's art."

His eyes bored into me. "I suspect that's not all you'd like to learn."

Remembering Cairpré's warning, I swallowed. "I seek nothing that won't be given freely."

The guard lifted his face to the spruce boughs above him, as if somehow seeking their counsel. He drew a long, slow breath. "Well, all right. I shall let you in—not for what you've said, which leaves me quite suspicious, I'll tell you. But for what you did to help master Galwy."

With a final shake of his dangling hair, he moved aside, stepping into the shadows under one of the trees. Although I could feel his eyes watching me warily, I didn't look back again. Nor did the others.

Immediately upon stepping through the gates, I spotted a high, spiraling structure in the middle of the common. Children squealed and jumped, playing around its base, while a steady stream of adults shuttled to and from it. Laden with buckets, baskets, and jugs, they resembled a colony of ants, hauling all the burdens of their society on their backs. Then I noticed a strange rippling on the gold-colored surface of the structure. As if it were moving somehow. As if it were alive.

Except for the few who pointed to my staff, whispering furtively, most of the villagers seemed too preoccupied with their tasks to pay any attention to us. Stepping over a cluster of children playing some sort of game with sticks, I moved cautiously closer to the structure. It seemed to be the source of at least some of the delicious smell that emanated from this village. And its surface was, indeed, moving. A thick, golden liquid flowed slowly from a spout at its highest point, down several spiraling troughs, all the way to a wide pool at its base. Out of this pool, people labored to draw the golden liquid by the bucketful, which they carried briskly into the buildings. At the same time, other people poured flour, milk, and other ingredients into the many vents that ringed the base.

"A fountain." I stared, utterly amazed. "A fountain of bread."

"Dough, you mean." Rhia bent over the churning pool. "They must use the golden stuff—doesn't it remind you of honey, but thicker?—as dough to start some of their breads."

"All of our breads, in fact."

We whirled around to see a plump, fair-haired man with ruddy cheeks, who was filling two large pitchers from the fountain. His ears, like other Fincayrans, were slightly pointed at the top. Yet his voice, like his face, seemed quite unusual, both scornful and mirthful at once. He was, I felt sure, one or the other. Which one I could not tell.

When the pitchers had nearly overflowed, he pulled them out of the pool. Resting them on his sizeable belly, he observed us for a moment. "Visitors, eh? We don't like visitors."

Unsure whether he was being unfriendly, or merely playful, I spoke up. "I would like to learn a little about bread baking. Could you help me?"

"I could," he answered gruffly. Or teasingly. "But I'm too busy now." He started to walk away. "Try some other day."

"I don't have another day!" I ran over to his side, keeping with him as he strode toward one of the buildings. "Won't you please show me a little of your art?"

"No," he declared. "I told you I'm—"

He tripped, tumbling over two scruffy boys, about the same age as Galwy, who were fighting over a loaf of blue-speckled bread. While only one of the pitchers fell to the ground, it smashed into dozens of pieces, all oozing with golden liquid from the fountain.

"Now see what you've done!" With a growl that was clearly serious, not playful, he stooped down to gather the broken pieces. Seeing me start to assist, he waved me away angrily. "Go away, boy! I don't need your help."

Glumly, I turned back to the bread fountain. I trudged toward it, barely noticing the rich aromas it continued to spill into the air. Rhia, having seen what happened, shook her head in dismay. She knew, as did I, that all of our efforts up to this point would be worthless unless we could find what we needed here in Slantos.

As I passed the two squabbling boys, who looked like twin brothers, I could tell that their argument was about to explode into a full-scale fight. Fists clenched, voices snarled. One boy tried to step on the blue-speckled loaf, which lay at the other one's feet. The second boy's nostrils flared. He roared angrily and charged at his enemy.

Slipping my staff through my belt, I stepped between them. Holding one boy by the collar of his tunic, and the other by the shoulder, I tried my best to keep them apart. Both shouted and struggled against me, kicking wildly at my legs. Finally, when my arms were about to give out, I released them and quickly snatched up the loaf of bread.

I raised the loaf, now more dirty brown than blue. "Is this what you're fighting about?"

"It's mine!" cried one.

"No, mine!" shouted the other.

Both of them lunged at the bread, but I held it just out of reach of their grasping hands. Ignoring their angry squeals, I waved it above them. Still warm, it smelled of sweet molasses. "Now," I demanded, "would you like to know how you can both have some?"

One boy cocked his head skeptically. "How?"

I glanced furtively over my shoulder. "I can tell you, but only on the condition that you keep it a secret."

The boys considered the idea, then nodded their heads in unison.

I kneeled down, then whispered something to them. Eyes wide, they listened intently. Finally, when I had finished, I handed them the loaf. They sat down on the spot, and within seconds, both of their mouths were bulging with bread.

"Not bad."

I looked up to find the plump man gazing at me. "Tell me, boy. How did you ever get them to share the loaf?"

Standing up, I pulled my staff from my belt. "Simple, really. I merely suggested that they each take turns having a bite." I grinned slightly. "And I also told them that if they couldn't manage that, I would eat the bread myself."

The man released a deep, guttural sound that could have been either a laugh or a groan. Scrunching up his face, he appeared to regard me with new respect. Or new concern. It was hard to tell. At last he spoke, removing any doubt. "If you'd like to learn a little about bread baking, boy, follow me."

XXIII

NAMING

The man strode to one of the loaf-shaped buildings at the far edge of the common. Before entering, he tossed the fragments of his broken pitcher into a pail outside the door. Then he wiped his plump hand on his tan tunic, already stained by many other wipings. Laying the hand on the wall by the door, he gave the brown bricks a grateful tap.

"Ever seen bricks like this?"

"No. Are they made from a special kind of mud?"

His expression turned grumpy. Or amused. "Actually, they're made from a special kind of flour. The ingredients give it unusual hardness, you see." He tapped the bricks again. "Knowing your ingredients, boy, is the first principle of baking bread."

Something about how he said *knowing your ingredients* made me think he meant something more than merely recognizing different grains and herbs. Tempted though I was to ask him to explain, I held my tongue for fear of pushing too hard.

"This one," he continued, "we call brickloaf. Baked six times for extra strength." He pressed his stubby fingers against the wall. "These bricks will outlive me by a hundred years."

Rhia, who had followed us, gazed at the bricks in wonder. "I've eaten some hard bread before, but not that hard."

The rotund man turned to her. Suddenly he started to laugh, so hard that his belly shook and golden liquid sloshed out of his remaining pitcher. "A good one, forest girl."

She smiled. "You may call me Rhia."

"And me Merlin."

The man nodded. "And me Pluton."

"Pluton," I repeated. "Isn't that a Greek name? From the story of Demeter and the first harvest of corn?"

"Why yes, boy. How do you come to know about the Greeks?"

My throat went dry. "My mother taught me."

"Indeed, as did mine. No child is born in Slantos who doesn't learn the tales of harvesting and baking from many different lands. And it's not unusual to give a child a name from one of those tales." He gave me an ambiguous look. "Of course, that's not my true name."

Rhia and I traded glances. Remembering Urnalda's comment about true names, I felt tempted to ask more. Besides, it troubled me that I could see no connection between the domestic art of bread baking and the magical art of Naming. But I held back. Things had taken a positive turn, and I did not want to alter that. Better to wait for another moment to learn about Naming.

Pluton lifted the door latch. "Come on in, both of you."

As we started to follow him inside, I suddenly remembered Bumbelwy. Scanning the bustling common, I quickly found him, still standing by the bread fountain. He was leaning against its base, peering hungrily at the pool of golden liquid. Children, probably curious about his belled hat, were gathering around him. He seemed unlikely to get into any trouble, and I didn't want to stretch Pluton's hospitality any further than necessary, so I decided just to leave him there.

As we entered the building, a new wave of aromas washed over us. I smelled roasting barley, some nectar as sweet as roses in bloom, and several spices I could not identify. The main room looked like the kitchen of a bustling inn, with pots boiling on the hearth, dried herbs and roots and bark shavings dangling from the ceiling, and bags of grain and flour sitting on the shelves. The room held six or seven people busily stirring, pouring, slicing, mixing, testing, and baking. From their expressions, it was clear that they both enjoyed their work and took it quite seriously.

Sunlight streamed into the room through rows of narrow windows. Yet the main source of light was the hearth itself, a complex of stone ovens and fire pits that covered almost an entire wall. Rather than burning wood, the hearth's fires used some sort of flat, gray cakes as fuel. No doubt they came from another mysterious recipe of the Slantos.

Above the hearth, high enough to be well out of reach, hung a massive sword, its hilt blackened by many years of fires beneath it. The metal scabbard had rusted with age; the leather belt had been eaten away. Something about the old sword made me curious to examine it more closely. Yet with the swirl of activity in the room, I soon forgot about it.

A tall girl, with apple cheeks and black hair that fell to her shoulders, approached Pluton. She looked quite different from anyone else I had seen in the village, partly because of her dark hair, partly because of her slender form. Her eyes, as black as my own, glowed with intelligence. The girl reached for the pitcher of golden liquid, then froze when she noticed Rhia and me standing to the side.

Pluton flicked his hand toward us. "This is Merlin, and Rhia. They're here to learn a bit about baking." Indicating the girl, he added brusquely, or just distractedly, "This is my apprentice, Vivian. Came to me when her parents, whom I'd known from my travels in the south, died in a terrible flood. How long ago was that now?"

"Six years, Breadmaster Pluton." She took the pitcher, her hands embracing it with the care of a mother holding a newborn. Still watching us warily, she asked, "Are you not concerned about them?"

"Concerned? My, yes." He studied her inscrutably. "But no more concerned than I was about you."

She stiffened, but stayed silent.

"Besides," Pluton continued, "I heard a story in the common about a boy who beat off a huge warrior goblin with nothing more than his staff. Saved one of our own children, he did." He cocked his head toward me. "Might that have been you?"

A bit embarrassed, I nodded.

He waved his stout hand at my staff. "And might that have been your weapon?"

Again I nodded.

"Not much of one against a goblin," he said casually. "Unless of course it's touched by magic."

At that, Vivian caught her breath. Her coal-dark eyes fixed on my staff. Instinctively, I turned the shaft around so that the markings from the Songs faced the other way.

Pluton reached out and took a steaming loaf of yellow-crusted bread from the tray of a man walking past. Breaking it into two halves, he filled his lungs with the freshly roasted smell. Then he handed the halves to Rhia and me. "Eat now," he suggested, or commanded. "You'll need your strength."

Without any hesitation, both of us bit into the crusts. As the warm, chewy bread touched our tongues, tasting of corn and butter and dill and many things more, our gazes met. Rhia's eyes sparkled, like the ocean sky at sunrise.

Pluton turned to Vivian. "We'll keep them to the simplest tasks. Stirring, mixing, slicing. No recipes."

He picked up a pair of wooden buckets, dusted with flour, and handed them to Rhia. "You can fill these, one with barley and one with wheat, from those sacks over there. Then carry them to the grinding wheel, in that room beyond the high shelves. You can learn a bit about milling and sifting in there."

He brushed some flour off his tunic. "And you, boy, can do some chopping. Over there at the table preparing heart bread."

Vivian seemed startled. "Really, Breadmaster?"

"That's right," declared Pluton. "He can chop some seeds." Ignoring her look of surprise, he turned to me. "If you do a good job, boy, I'll show you more. Might even let you taste a little heart bread itself, which will fill your belly even as it fills your heart with courage."

Swallowing the remains of my crust, I said, "Thank you, but I need no bread beyond what you just gave me. It's delicious."

His round face glowed. "As I said, it all comes from knowing your ingredients." A secretive smile touched his lips, then vanished. "You'll need a chopping knife for the seeds, and we're quite short on them right now. Ah, good, there's one left at the table. Vivian, why don't you take him over there and show him how it's done? I'll come by to check on his progress shortly."

Hearing this, the girl brightened. Smoothly, she stepped between Rhia and me. In a voice far gentler than before, she whispered to me, "Most people call me Vivian, but my friends call me Nimue." A warm smile graced her apple cheeks. "I'd be glad to help you. Any way I can."

"Ah, thank you, Viv—I mean, Nimue," I mumbled. Was I merely flattered by her attention, or was there something else about this girl that made my heart beat faster?

Rhia, the light gone from her eyes, nudged her aside. "You can start by getting him a knife." She shot me a harsh look of warning.

Her intrusion annoyed me. What did I need to be warned about, anyway? She was treating me like a child again.

"Come," said Nimue, brushing past Rhia. Gently taking my hand, she slowly slid her fingers up the length of my forearm. A new warmth filled me as she led me over to a table covered with vegetables, seeds, roots, and herbs. An elderly woman sat at one end of the table, deftly sorting the ingredients into piles. At the other end stood a young man, thinly bearded, peeling the skin off an enormous nut that looked like a giant acorn.

"Let's start here." Nimue guided me to the middle of the table. She slid over a bowl containing a stack of square, purple vegetables, steaming from having just been cooked. Pulling a battered knife from a block of wood on the table, she deftly sliced open the vegetable and removed a flat seed that glowed with a deep red luster. Then, laying her warm hand over my own, she showed me the sharp, twisting motion that would allow me to chop the seed into tiny pieces.

"There now," she said kindly, allowing her hand to linger on mine. "You are most fortunate, you know. Heart bread is one of Breadmaster Pluton's great specialities. He hardly ever lets an outsider help prepare it, certainly not chop the essential seeds." She flashed her most lovely smile. "He must see something special in you."

With a slight squeeze, she lifted her hand. "I'll come back to check on you in a while." As she started to step away, she pointed to my staff, propped against the side of the table. "That staff of yours is going to fall. Should I put it somewhere safe for you?"

A vague shiver ran through me, though I wasn't sure why. After all, she was only trying to be helpful. "No thank you," I replied. "It's fine where it is."

"Oh, but I wouldn't want it to get damaged. It's so very . . . handsome."

She reached out to touch it. Just then the elderly woman happened to bump her knee against the table. The staff slid sideways along the edge, falling against my hip. I grasped it by the shaft and slid it into the belt of my tunic.

"There," I said to Nimue. "It's safe now."

For the briefest instant, her eyes seemed to flash with anger, though the look of kindness returned so swiftly that I couldn't be sure. In any case, she quickly turned and walked away. After a few paces, she looked back, smiling warmly.

I could not help but smile in return. Then I turned back to the table and took one of the purple vegetables. Still steaming, it sliced open easily. Carefully, I removed the lustrous seed. As I started to chop it, however, the worn blade suddenly split into shards. Rotten luck! I cast aside the useless knife.

I needed to perform my task well, not to bungle it! Pluton, I felt sure, was testing me. Why else would he have given me such unusual responsibility? He had even promised to show me more, if only I did my job well. And if I failed, I couldn't possibly gain his trust. Frantically, I cast about with my second sight, searching for another blade that I could use.

Nothing. Every single knife in the room was being used by someone for carving or slicing. I rose, still carrying my staff in my belt, and looked again. On the shelves. By the hearth. Under the tables.

Nothing.

No blade of any kind.

Then my gaze fell on the tarnished sword hanging above the hearth. It would be clumsy to wield, and grimy to hold. But it was at least a blade.

No, I told myself, the idea was ridiculous. I had never seen anyone use a sword for chopping. I chewed my lip, searching the room again. No knives anywhere. And time was wasting. Pluton would be checking on my progress soon. I turned again to the grimy blade.

Spying a small ladder leaning against the tallest set of shelves, I placed it next to the hearth. Climbing up to its top rung, I reached as high as I could. Yet . . . I couldn't quite reach the hilt of the sword. I looked around for someone taller who might be able to help, but all the people in the room were deeply immersed in their own tasks.

Standing on tiptoes, I tried again. Almost there! I stretched even higher. Almost, almost . . . but no. I simply could not reach it.

I glared at the sword, cursing to myself. Why had it been placed so high, anyway? To be of any help, it needed to be reachable. And I could certainly use its help now. Not just for chopping the seeds for heart bread. Much more was at stake. If I couldn't win over Pluton, I couldn't possibly save Elen.

I concentrated on the old sword, searching for some way to reach it. If only I could make it fly to me, as I had done long ago with Deepercut. But, as Urnalda had taught me, that had been possible only because of Deepercut's own magic.

At that instant, I noticed some very faint scratches on the hilt. They could be nothing but random marks . . . or, perhaps, they could be something more. Runes. Letters. Could this sword, like Deepercut, possess some sort of magic? Yet even as the thought struck me, I knew that the chances were extremely small. Why would a magical sword be hanging, rusted and unused, in a remote village devoted to baking bread?

Still, the runes seemed to beckon to me. Perhaps they described the sword's history. Or, if indeed it were magical, perhaps they gave instructions on how to use it. How to make it fly to me!

Straining to focus my second sight, I tried to make some sense of the scratches. Beneath the layers of dust and soot, I detected a rhythm, a pattern, to the marks. There were straight lines. And curves. And corners. Throwing all my power into the task, I followed the hidden indentations.

The first letter came clear. I could read it! Then . . . the second. And the third. The fourth, the fifth . . . all the way to the end of the word. For that was all the hilt contained. A single, unusual word.

I spoke the word, not out loud, but within the walls of my mind. Pronounced it slowly, carefully, savoring the richness of the name. And, in return, the sword spoke to me. It declared its grand past, and its even grander future. *I am the sword of light, past and present. I am the sword of kings, once and future.*

Suddenly, the sword detached itself from the wall. At the same time, all the grime vanished from the hilt, revealing the brilliant silver forged beneath. Scabbard and belt were reborn, transformed into polished metal and sturdy leather, studded with purple gemstones.

As gracefully as a leaf borne aloft by the wind, the sword floated over the hearth and into my hands.

Only then did I realize that the entire room had fallen silent. No one moved. No one spoke. All eyes were trained on me.

My heart sank, for I felt certain I would now be labeled an infiltrator. Rhia and I would be banished. Or worse.

Pluton, looking either annoyed or astonished, stepped forward. Hands on his wide hips, he regarded me for a while. "Didn't think much of you at first. That's certain."

"I—I'm sorry about your sword."

He ignored me, continuing his thought. "Still, like a good lump of dough, you have risen, boy. Beyond anything I ever expected. You just needed time enough to rise."

"You mean . . . I can use it?"

"You can keep it!" thundered Pluton. "The sword is yours."

I blinked, trying to take all this in. I caught sight of Rhia, watching me with pride. And Nimue, hands on her hips, watching me with . . . something else. Something more like envy.

"But all I did was read its name. It's called—"

"Hush, boy!" Pluton held up his hand. "A true name should never be spoken aloud, unless it's absolutely necessary. You gained power over the sword by recognizing its true name. Now you must guard that name faithfully."

I scanned the room, aglow with light from the hearth, rich with the smells of freshly ground flour and baking bread and a thousand spices. "I think I understand," I said at last. "Here in this village you learn the true names of each and every ingredient before using them. That allows you to master their powers, and release them in your breads. That is why your breads are so full of magic."

Pluton nodded slowly. "Ages ago, that sword came to this place carried by a flock of enchanted swans. It was foretold that it would, one day, fly like a swan itself into the hands of the one person who could read its true name. Because we, of all the peoples of Fincayra, most value the power of true names, the sword was entrusted to us. Until this day. Now it is entrusted to you."

He swiftly affixed the belt around my waist and adjusted the scabbard. "Use this sword wisely and well. And keep it safe. For it was also foretold that one day it would belong to a great, though tragic, king—a king whose power would be so profound that he would pull the sword from a scabbard of stone."

I looked into Pluton's face. "Then he, too, will know its true name. *For a true name holds true power.*"

At that instant, my staff sizzled with a burst of blue light. A new marking appeared, in the shape of a sword. A sword whose name I knew well.

XXIV

NO WINGS,
NO HOPE

Only after Rhia and I had sampled nine different varieties of bread (including ambrosia bread, even better than I had remembered), did we finally extract ourselves from Pluton's kitchen. At last, the master baker stuffed some freshly baked heart bread in my satchel and sent us on our way. No sooner had we stepped out of his door, rejoining the bustle of the common, than we found Bumbelwy, slumped against the base of the great bread fountain.

The lanky jester was holding his swollen belly, moaning painfully. His face, down to the bottommost chin, looked blueish-green. Lumps of golden dough streaked his hooded cloak and clung to his hair, his ears, and even his eyebrows. His three-cornered hat, also clogged with dough, sat soundless on his head.

"Ohhh," he moaned. "Death by overeating! Such a painful end."

Despite myself, I almost laughed. Remembering my pledge about my boots, however, I caught myself.

As he explained to us in halting phrases between moans, Bumbelwy had stood by the bread fountain, watching and smelling the rich, thick liquid flowing out of its spout, until finally he could stand it no longer. He had leaned closer, drinking in the aroma. Then, with both hands, he had scooped some wondrous dough straight out of the pool and into his mouth. Liking the taste, he had taken some more. And some more. What he hadn't realized until too late was that the dough had only begun to rise. So then rise it did—in his stomach. The result was a bellyache too horrible for even him to describe.

Leaning my staff against the fountain, I sat down beside him. Rhia joined us, wrapping her arms around her knees so that she resembled a bundle of green and brown vines. Slantos villagers scurried past, pursuing their tasks with all the speed and purpose of an army.

I sighed, knowing that while we had purpose aplenty, we had no speed. And we still had very far to go.

Rhia reached a leafy arm toward me. "You're worried about the time, aren't you? The moon is waning fast." She hesitated. "No more than five days left, Merlin."

"I know, I know. And for Leaping we must go all the way back to Varigal. We'll have to cross Eagles' Canyon again, and we'll probably find trouble in the Dark Hills again." I ran my finger along the scabbard I now wore on my waist. "More trouble, I'm afraid, than even a magical staff and sword can handle."

Rhia nodded toward Bumbelwy. "And what about him? He can't even sit up, let alone walk anywhere."

I considered the moaning figure, studded with lumps of dough. "This may surprise you, but I just don't feel right about leaving him. He really did his best for you back there on the cliff."

She smiled sadly. "It doesn't surprise me."

"So what should we do?" I stretched my aching shoulders. "If only we could fly."

Rhia swallowed a crust of ambrosia bread. "Like the Fincayrans of old, before they lost their wings."

"I need more than wings," said Bumbelwy, stirring to roll over on his side. "I need a whole new body."

I observed the staff, propped against the base of the fountain. There, etched darkly, were the images of a butterfly, a pair of soaring hawks, a cracked stone, and now a sword. We had come so far, accomplished so much. Yet it all amounted to nothing if I could not discover the souls of the remaining Songs before time ran out.

I recited them to myself, trying to find a hint of hope:

> *The power Leaping be the fifth,*
> *In Varigal beware.*
>
> *Eliminating be the sixth,*
> *A sleeping dragon's lair.*
>
> *The gift of Seeing be the last,*
> *Forgotten Island's spell.*
>
> *And now ye may attempt to find*
> *The Otherworldly Well.*

My heart sank as I considered the vast distances that the Songs required. Even if I did have wings, how could I possibly cover so much ground? Not to mention the challenges that still would remain: finding the Otherworld Well, evading the ogre Balor, and climbing up to the realm of Dagda to get the precious Elixir. All this . . . in five short days.

If only I could compress things somehow! Skip one of the Songs. Go straight to the land of the spirits. Yet even as I considered the notion, I remembered Tuatha's warning to avoid such folly.

I slammed my fist against the ground. "How can we do it all, Rhia?"

She started to reply when a group of four men tottered over to the fountain, staggering under the weight of a huge black cauldron. Oblivious to anyone who might happen to be in their path, they pushed and bumped their way across the common. As they moved between Rhia and myself, they nearly stepped right on poor Bumbelwy. Even as he groaned and rolled aside, they propped the cauldron on the edge of the fountain's pool and began to pour. A creamy brown mixture that smelled of cloves emptied into the pool, gurgling and splattering.

As they departed with the empty cauldron, a small, round-cheeked boy ran up to me. Excitedly, he tugged on my tunic.

"Galwy!" I exclaimed. Then, seeing the worry on his face, I froze. "What's wrong?"

"She took it," he panted. "I saw her took it."

"Took what?"

"The goblin slayer! She took it."

Puzzled, I squeezed his stout little shoulders. "Goblin slayer? What—"

Suddenly I looked at the fountain. My staff was gone!

"Who took it?"

"The girl, the tall one." Galwy pointed at the village gates. "Ran that way."

Nimue! I flew to my feet, shoved my way through the villagers near the fountain, leaped over a sleeping dog, and sprinted through the wooden gates. Standing beneath one of the towering spruces, I scanned what was visible of the grassy plains, although a thick blanket of fog obscured everything beyond the foreground.

No sign at all of Nimue. Or of my staff.

"Leaving already?"

I whirled around to see the guard. He was watching me from the shadows, still grasping the hilt of his sword. "My staff!" I cried. "Did you see a girl just now with my staff?"

Slowly, he nodded. "That one called Vivian, or Nimue."

"Yes! Where did she go?"

The guard tugged on the shreds of hair dangling over his ears, then waved at the rolling fog. "Somewhere out there, beyond the sea mist. Maybe toward the coast, maybe toward the hills. I have no idea. I save my attention for people coming in, not going out."

I kicked at the ground. "Didn't you see she had my staff?"

"That I did. Your staff is hard to miss. But it's not the first time I've seen her convince a fellow to part with something precious, so I didn't think much of it."

My eyes narrowed. "She didn't convince me! She stole it!"

He grinned knowingly. "I've heard that a few times, too."

In disgust, I turned back to the clouded plains. Stretching my second sight to the limit, I tried to find any sign of the thief. Yet all I found was fog and more fog, endlessly shifting. My staff. My precious staff! Filled with the vitality of Druma Wood, touched by the hand of Tuatha, marked by the power of the Songs. Gone! Without the staff's ability to tell me whether I had found the soul of each Song, I had no hope.

Head bowed, I trudged back through the gates and into the common. A man, arms laden with bread, bumped into me and dropped several loaves. But I hardly noticed. I could think of nothing but my staff. As I reached the base of the fountain, I collapsed beside Rhia.

Wrapping her forefinger around my own, she searched my face. "So it's lost."

"Everything is lost."

"Too true, too true, too true," moaned Bumbelwy, rubbing his swollen belly.

Rhia reached for my satchel and opened it. Pulling out Pluton's heart bread, she tore off a chunk and placed it in my hand. A sturdy, robust smell, as rich as roasting venison, filled the air.

"Here. Pluton said it will fill your heart with courage."

"It will take more than courage to save my mother," I muttered, taking a small bite of the bread.

As I chewed, the bits of seeds burst in my mouth, releasing their powerful flavor. And something more. I straightened my back and drew a hearty breath, savoring the new strength that I could feel surging through my limbs. Yet, even as I took another bite, I could not forget the truth. My staff was lost, as was my quest. What could I possibly do—without the staff, without the time, without the wings to fly to the other end of Fincayra?

Tears brimmed in my sightless eyes. "I can't do it, Rhia. I can't possibly do it!"

She slid closer on the ground, brushing aside some hardened lumps of dough. Gently, she touched the amulet of oak, ash, and thorn that Elen had given her. "As long as we still have hope, we still have a chance."

"That's just the point!" I jabbed at the air with my fist, almost hitting the base of the bread fountain. "We have no hope."

At that instant, something warm brushed against my cheek. A light touch, lighter than a caress. Lighter than air. "You still have hope, Emrys Merlin." The familiar voice breathed in my ear. "You still have hope."

"Aylah!" I leaped to my feet, lifting my arms skyward. "It's you."

"There, you see?" said Bumbelwy sadly. "The strain was too much for the poor boy. He's lost his mind. Now he's talking to the air."

"Not the air, the wind!"

Rhia's eyes brightened. "You mean . . . a wind sister?"

"Yes, Rhiannon." A soft, whispering laughter rose out of the air. "I am here to take you, all of you, to Varigal."

"Oh, Aylah!" I cried. "Is it possible, before you take us there, to go somewhere else first?"

"To find your staff, Emrys Merlin?"

"How did you know?"

As a spring bubbles out of the ground, pouring over the soil, the wind sister's words tumbled out of the air. "Nothing can long hide from the wind. Not a stealthy girl, nor the secret cave where she hides her treasures, nor even her desire one day to wield great power through magic."

My blood surged angrily. "Can we still catch her before she reaches her cave?"

A sudden gust of wind swept the village common. Hats, cloaks, and aprons lifted into the air, swirling like autumn leaves. All at once my boots, too, rose off the ground. In an instant, Rhia, Bumbelwy, and I were airborne.

XXV

ALL THE VOICES

As we lifted off from the village common, several people standing near the fountain shrieked in fright—though none shrieked as
loud as poor Bumbelwy. For my part, I swung my legs freely in the
open air, alive with the thrill of flight. It was a thrill that I had known
only once before, nestled into the feathers of Trouble's back. Yet this
time the feeling was even more powerful, if also more frightening.
For this time I was borne aloft not by another body, but by the very
wind itself.

Aylah carried us swiftly higher, supporting us on a blanket of air.
As the loaf-shaped buildings of Slantos melted into the fog, the
golden pool of the bread fountain faded into tan, then brown, then
white. Clouds swallowed us whole, leaving nothing visible beyond
ourselves. I could hear the whistling of air all around, yet it wasn't
too loud, for we were flying with the wind and not against it.

"Aylah!" I cried. "Can you still find her in the fog?"

"Patience," she replied, her airy voice springing from both above
and below. The clouds thickened as we dropped lower and banked
to the right.

Rhia turned to me, her face showing her own growing exhilara-
tion. We were riding, it seemed, on a cloud itself, close enough to

touch each other and far enough apart to feel completely free. And, in the case of Bumbelwy, completely miserable. His face, still splattered with dough, turned greener with every jostle and sway.

Suddenly, just below us, a figure emerged from a gap in the fog. Nimue!

She strode purposefully across the grassy plain, her long black hair falling over her shoulders. In her hand, she clutched my staff. I could almost hear her clucking to herself in satisfaction. No doubt she was considering what place of honor to give my staff in her cave of treasures. Or how she might find some way to turn its hidden powers to her advantage. A thin smile spread across my own face as we drew nearer, casting a trio of ghostly shadows on the ground.

Sensing something, she whirled around. She shrieked, seeing me and my companions dropping right out of the sky on top of her. Before she could turn and run, I reached down and grasped the gnarled top of the staff with both hands.

"Thief!" she wailed, clinging tightly to her prize.

We tugged against each other, trying to twist the staff free. As Aylah bore me aloft again, Nimue herself rose off the plain, her legs kicking wildly. My back and shoulders ached from the strain, but I held on. Currents of air slapped against her, shoving her body this way and that. Yet she refused to let go. We dropped a bit lower, just as a tangle of brambles came into view. Straight through it flew Nimue, the thorns tearing at her legs and ripping her robe. Still she did not release her grip.

I felt the staff slip lower in my perspiring hands. Her weight made my shoulders scream with pain. My arms were starting to feel numb. All the while, Nimue twisted and writhed, trying her best to break free.

Banking hard to the left, we veered toward a pile of jagged rocks. An instant before she collided, Nimue caught sight of the approaching obstacle. With a terrified shriek, she let go at last.

With a thud, she dropped to the ground, landing on her back next to the pile of rocks. Weakly, I pulled the staff to me, gazing again at its familiar markings. The sign of the paired hawks glistened with my own perspiration. I felt whole again, my staff and my hope both restored.

As the mist thickened, I glanced down at Nimue. As she sat up, her eyes flashed angrily. She kicked her heels on the turf like an infant, waving her clenched fists at the air, cursing and crying for revenge. Smaller she grew, and smaller. An instant later, she disappeared in a shroud of fog, her shouts replaced by the whistling wind.

I twirled the staff in my throbbing hands. "Thank you, Aylah."

"You are welcome, Emrys Merlin. Ahhh yes."

The wind bore us higher, until the fog began to pull apart, shredding into white waves that rose and fell like the rolling sea. Ships of mist, sails billowing, lifted their prows, only to dash upon vaporous shores. The cloud waves rolled over us, soaking us with spray, churning ceaselessly.

I turned to Rhia, her eyes as joyful as Nimue's had been wrathful. "You were so right about her. I don't know how, but she had me, well, confused at first. I wish I had your . . . what did my mother call them?"

"Berries," she said with a laugh. "Also called instincts." She flapped her arms in the mist, stretching them like wings. "Oh, isn't this wonderful? I feel so free! Like I'm the wind myself."

"You are the wind, Rhiannon." Aylah's wispy arms encircled us.

"You have all living things within yourself. That is what instincts are, the voices of those living things inside you."

I watched the shredding clouds, as Aylah's voice whispered in my own ear. "You, too, have instincts, Emrys Merlin. You simply do not hear them very well. You have all the voices, old and young, male and female."

"Female? Me?" I scoffed, tapping my sword, as the air whooshed past. "I'm a boy!"

"Ahhh yes, Emrys Merlin, you are a boy. And a wonderful thing that is to be! One day, perhaps, you will learn that you can also be more. That you can listen as well as speak, sow as well as reap, create as well as construct. And then you may discover that the merest trembling of a butterfly's wings can be just as powerful as a quake that moves mountains."

Hardly had those words been spoken than a sudden current of air jolted us. Rhia and I rolled into each other, while Bumbelwy cried out, flailing his arms and legs. His bell-draped hat flew into the air, and nearly sailed away before Rhia caught it. As she snatched the hat, several chunks of dough flew off, causing it to rattle noisily again.

All at once we burst out of the clouds. As swiftly as hawks, we rose above their fluffy contours. Far below, Fincayra revealed itself now like a tapestry unfurling, full of dazzling colors and intricate patterns. There lay the Dark Hills, swathed in shadows, the flowing ridges broken only by the occasional cluster of trees or jumble of rocks. There ran the red and maroon gorge of Eagles' Canyon, winding away to the south. And there, dappled with sun, stretched the rolling sweep of the Rusted Plains.

I leaned forward, stretching myself prone on the carpet of wind.

Soaring headlong over the lands below, I felt for a moment as if I had become a fish again, gliding through an ocean of air rather than water. Buoyed by invisible currents, sailing weightlessly, I flew through the very substance of my breathing.

To the north, I followed the contorted coastline of a dark peninsula, until it melted into mist. Twisting rivers sparkled below, as hills started swelling beneath us. Dimly, beyond the hills, I glimpsed the grim profile of the Lake of the Face. An icy finger ran down my spine as I recalled the image I had seen in those dark waters, the image of Balor's deadly eye.

Then, above the whooshing wind, I heard a faint rumbling. It came from somewhere in the snowy mountains ahead, whose crested summits gleamed in the late afternoon light. The rumbling grew louder and louder, rolling like avalanches down the slopes. It seemed that thunder itself must be part of this land.

And indeed it was. For we had arrived in the land of the giants. The rumbling swelled as Aylah set us down on a knoll bristling with short, stubby grass. Rising out of a steeply sloping, rocky ridge, the knoll was one of the few patches of green around. The ground beneath us, like the cliffs on all sides, shook from the noise. Or from whatever caused the noise.

As soon as Bumbelwy's feet touched down, he tottered unsteadily over to an enormous pile of leaves, branches, and ferns that had been left on the knoll for some reason. It covered nearly half of the knoll, rising like a miniature mountain of brush. He fell into the pile, crawled higher, then sprawled on his back. Above the rumbling, he called, "If I'm going to die in an earthquake, I might at least be somewhere soft!"

He smoothed some broken branches beneath his head. "Besides,

I have some difficult digesting to do. Not to mention recovering from that ride." He closed his eyes, wriggling deeper into the ferns. "Imagine! Almost killed twice in the same day." He yawned, shaking his bells. "If I weren't such an optimist, I'd say something even worse will happen to me before the day is over."

Seconds later, he was snoring.

"I wish you well, Emrys Merlin." Louder than usual because of the rumbling, the voice spoke in my ear. "I wish I could stay with you longer, but I must fly."

"I wish you didn't have to go."

"I know, Emrys Merlin, I know." Aylah's warm breath caressed my cheek. "Perhaps, on another day, we will meet again."

"And fly again?" Rhia lifted her arms as if they were wings, "Like the wind?"

"Perhaps, Rhiannon. Perhaps."

With a sudden swirl of air, the wind sister departed.

XXVI

LEAPING

A great thud sounded, from somewhere in the steep-walled valley below the knoll. The ground shook again, knocking both Rhia and me over backward. A plump thrush, its purple wings dotted with white, shrieked and flew away from its perch in the bristly grass. Sitting up, I looked over at Bumbelwy, still snoring peacefully in the pile of leaves and brush. What it might take to awaken him, I could not imagine.

Crawling on hands and knees, Rhia and I crept slowly to the edge of the knoll. Peering over, we gazed into the valley below. At that instant, an entire section of cliff above the valley cracked open, dangled precariously, then tumbled down in a cloud of rubble and dust. Another rumble filled the air, and the ground beneath us shook violently again.

Then, as the dust cleared, I recognized the figures laboring below. Even from this distance, the giants looked enormous. And frighteningly powerful. While some of them split boulders apart with hammers the size of pine trees, others hauled the chunks of rock to the center of the valley. Lifting even one such stone would have required fifty men and women, yet the giants moved them around like bales of summer hay.

Not far away, more giants worked, cutting and shaping the gray and white stones. Still others fit them carefully into the towers and bridges of a growing city. So this was Varigal! Destroyed by Stangmar's army of warrior goblins, Fincayra's most ancient city was being completely rebuilt, rock by rock. Already its rough-hewn walls and spires mirrored the cliff walls and snowy spires that surrounded the valley.

As they labored, the giants chanted in low, rumbling tones. Their words echoed from cliff to cliff, pounding and cracking like stones themselves.

> *Hy gododin catann hue*
> *Hud a lledrith mal wyddan*
> *Gaunce ae bellawn wen cabri*
> *Varigal don Fincayra*
> *Dravia, dravia Fincayra.*
>
> *Hud ya vardann tendal fe*
> *Roe samenya, llaren kai*
> *Hosh waundi na mal storro*
> *Varigal don Fincayra*
> *Dravia, dravia Fincayra.*

I remembered, ages ago it seemed, hearing those same voices chanting the Lledra during the Dance of the Giants that had finally brought the Shrouded Castle crashing down. And I remembered hearing Elen sing that same chant to me when I was barely more than a babe in her arms.

> *Talking trees and walking stones,*
> *Giants are the island's bones.*

While this land our dance still knows,
Varigal crowns Fincayra.
Live long, live long Fincayra.

Giants breathe and tempests blow,
Touch the waves and rivers slow.
In the island's realm of snow,
Varigal crowns Fincayra.
Live long, live long Fincayra.

Bumbelwy snorted, rolling over on his bed of branches. A sprig of fern had caught in his hair and seemed to be growing straight out of his ear. With every breath, his bells rattled like a potful of pebbles. Yet the jester slept on, undisturbed.

I turned back to watch a wild-haired female giant, at the near end of the valley, push the base of a stone tower into place with her bare shoulder. From this distance, she looked much like the giant on whose immense frame the eagle had landed at the start of the Great Council. I suspected that, somewhere down there, my old friend Shim was also working. Or, more likely, doing his best to avoid working. Yet as much as I wanted to see him again, there would be no time to try to find him.

"So," spoke a melodic voice behind us, "why do you come to the land of the giants?"

Rhia and I spun around. Seated on a rounded, mossy rock—a rock that had been empty only seconds before—was a tall, pale woman. Her golden hair, stretching almost to her knees, fell about her like rays of light. She wore a simple, light blue robe, yet her very posture made it seem like an elegant dress. Her eyes shone unusually bright, as if intense flames burned inside her.

Winsome though she was, I steeled myself. *I may not have Rhia's instincts, but I won't let what happened with Nimue happen again.* Reaching for my staff in the grass, I pulled it closer to my side.

The bright-eyed woman laughed gently. "I see you don't trust me."

Rhia, while still sitting on the grass, straightened her back and seemed for a moment to study the woman's face. Then she drew in her breath. "I trust you. We came here to learn about Leaping."

I nearly jumped out of my boots. "Rhia! You don't know her!"

"I know I don't. And yet . . . I do. She makes me want to—well, trust in the berries. There's something about her that, I don't know . . . that reminds me of the stars shining at the darkest time of night."

The woman rose slowly, her hair swirling about her waist. "That is because, dear girl, I am the spirit of a star. You know me, in fact, as one of your constellations."

Despite the quaking ground, Rhia rose to her feet. "Gwri," she said softly, so softly that I could barely hear her above the continuing rumble. "You are Gwri of the Golden Hair."

"Yes. I live in your westernmost sky. And I have watched you, Rhia, as well as you, Merlin, even as you have watched me."

Dumbfounded, I too clambered to my feet. It seemed so long ago, that night under the shomorra tree, when Rhia had first shown me Gwri of the Golden Hair. And how to see constellations in a completely new way. To find their shapes not just in the stars themselves, but in the spaces *between* the stars.

Rhia took a small step closer on the grassy knoll. "Why did you come all the way here?"

Gwri laughed again, more heartily than before. This time a circle of golden light glowed in the air around her. "I came here to help the giants of your land rebuild their ancient capital. For, you see, I also came here ages ago when Varigal was first built. I stood by Dagda's side, providing the light he needed to work through the night when he carved the very first giant from the stony side of a mountain."

"You came such a long way."

"Yes, Merlin. I came here by Leaping."

My legs nearly buckled beneath me, though not because of the quaking ground. "Leaping? Will you—can you tell me what I need to know?"

"You already know the soul of this Song," the star declared. "You only need to find it within yourself."

"We have so little time! The moon is barely a quarter full. And my mother . . . " My throat tightened, reducing my voice to a whisper. "She's going to die. All because of me."

Gwri studied me intently. She seemed to be listening to my innermost thoughts, oblivious to the continuing rumble from the valley below. "Just what did you do?"

"I found the speaking shell, whose power brought her here."

Gwri tilted her head, sending a cascade of hair tumbling over her arm. "No, Merlin. Think again."

Puzzled, I rubbed my chin. "But the shell—"

"Think again."

I caught Rhia's eye. "You mean . . . it was me. Not the shell."

The woman nodded. "The shell needed your power to do it. Your power of Leaping, unformed as it is. One day, perhaps, you may master that power. Then you may send people, or things, or dreams. You could travel through the worlds, or even through time, as you choose."

"Time?" A vague memory stirred within me. "When I was very young, I used to dream about living backward in time. Honestly! Just so I could relive my favorite moments over and over again."

A spare smile touched her face. "Perhaps you will come to master that, as well. Then you could grow younger every day, while everyone around you grows older."

As much as the idea intrigued me, I shook my head. "That's only a dream. I'm afraid I'll never master anything. Look what disaster I caused when I brought my mother to Fincayra."

"Tell me," said Gwri, "what have you learned from that?"

Another quake shook the ground. Rocks from the cliff nearest us broke loose, sending up a cloud of dust as they clattered down to the valley below. I grasped my staff for better balance. "Well, I've learned that Leaping, like all magic I suppose, has limits."

"True. Even the great spirit Dagda has limits! For all he knows about the powers of the universe, he cannot bring someone back to life who has died." Gwri looked suddenly pained, as if she were recalling something that had happened long ago. After a long pause, she spoke again. "Have you learned anything else?"

I hesitated, shifting my weight on the grass. "Well . . . that you must think carefully before bringing someone or something to a new place, since what you do could have unintended consequences. Serious ones."

"And why do you suppose that is so?"

Squeezing the knotted top of my staff, I thought hard. The wind whistled across the ridge, chafing my face. "Because, you see, one ac-tion is connected to another. Throwing a single pebble in the wrong place could start a rockslide. The truth is, *everything is connected to everything else.*"

Gwri burst into laughter just as my staff erupted in blue flames. A golden circle of light glowed in the air around her, even as the image of a star inside a circle appeared on the shaft. I let my fingers stroke it.

"You have learned well, Merlin. Everything plays a part in the great and glorious song of the stars."

Remembering the phrase from the walls of Arbassa, I nodded. "I only wish I knew enough to use the power of Leaping right now. For I must find my way, and quickly, to a dragon's lair, though I don't have any idea where to look."

Gwri turned to the east, her long hair shimmering. "The dragon you seek is the same one who was lulled into enchanted sleep ages ago by your grandfather, Tuatha. And yet even your grandfather's powers were not great enough to resist Balor, the guardian of the Otherworld Well. If you should survive the dragon and make your way there, do you really expect to fare any better?"

"No. I only hope to try."

For a long moment, she studied me. "The sleeping dragon's lair lies in the Lost Lands, just across the water from here. As it happens, it also lies not very far from the Otherworld Well—though that matters little to you, since you must still voyage all the way to the Forgotten Island before you go there."

With my finger, I traced the new marking on my staff. "Could you, perhaps, send us to the dragon's lair?"

Gwri's eyes shone a bit brighter. "I could, yes. But I prefer to let someone else do it. Someone you know, who can get you there almost as fast as I can."

Rhia and I traded perplexed glances.

The star motioned toward the dour jester, sprawled on the enormous brush pile. "Your sleeping friend over there."

"Bumbelwy? You can't be serious!"

Gwri's laughter rang out. "Not him, though I daresay he may yet show himself capable of some surprising leaps." Again she pointed. "I mean the sleeping friend beneath him."

Before I could ask what she meant, Gwri grew brighter and brighter, until she glowed so intensely that even my second sight could not bear to watch. Like Rhia, I turned away. A few seconds later, the light suddenly diminished. We turned back, only to find that Gwri of the Golden Hair had vanished.

At that instant, the brush pile itself stirred.

XXVII

ANOTHER CROSSING

The pile of brush lurched suddenly to the side, hurling the sleeping Bumbelwy into the air. His bells clanged like a blacksmith's hammer. And his shriek, easily heard above the rumbling from the valley below, joined with the surprised shouts of Rhia and me.

Spraying branches, leaves, and fern fronds across the grassy notch, the pile of leaves bent, twisted—and sat up. Two enormous arms stretched to either side, while a pair of hairy feet kicked free from the debris. A head lifted, showing wide pink eyes and a cavernous mouth that opened in a yawn. Just below the eyes, a gargantuan nose bulged like a swollen potato.

"Shim!" cried Rhia and I at once.

Finishing his yawn, the giant looked down on us in surprise. He rubbed his eyes, then looked again. "Is you a dream? Or is you real?"

"We're real," I declared.

Shim scrunched his nose doubtfully. "Really, truly, honestly?"

"Really, truly, honestly." Rhia stepped forward and patted one of his feet, which towered over her. "It's good to see you again, Shim."

With a great smile, the giant reached out with one arm and gently scooped us into the palm of his hand. "I thinks I is still dreaming! But it's you, the truly you." He brought his nose a little closer and took a sniff. "You smells like bread. Goodly bread."

I nodded. "Ambrosia. Like we had that night with Cairpré. Do you remember, good Shim? I wish we'd brought you some! But we're in a hurry, you see. A great hurry."

The immense nose scrunched again. "Is you still full of madness?"

"You could put it that way."

"Ever since that day we firstly meets, you is full of madness!" The giant rocked with a thunderous laugh, swaying on the grassy knoll, shaking loose some rocks that bounced down into the valley. "That day you almost gets us stingded by thousands of bees."

"And you were nothing but a blundering ball of honey."

Rhia, who had managed to rise to her knees in the fleshy palm, joined in. "You were so small I was sure you were a dwarf."

Shim's pink eyes glowed with pride. "I is small no more."

Another tumultuous crash from the valley filled the air, rocking the ridge. Even Shim's mighty arm swayed like a tree in a gale. Rhia and I clung to his thumb for support.

His expression turned serious. "They is workings hard down there. I is supposed to brings the branches, for cookings the supper." He looked suddenly sheepish. "I only wanted to rolls in the branches, then takes a little nap! A briefly little nap."

"We're glad you did," I replied. "We need your help."

A long, painful moan came from the loose branches at the far end of the notch. Before I could say anything, Shim reached over with his free hand and lifted out Bumbelwy by his heavy cloak. Draped with drooping ferns and broken branches, frowning with his whole face down to his layered chins, the gloomy jester looked half alive at best.

Rhia watched the dangling jester with concern. "Did you see him go flying when Shim woke up?"

I gave her a sardonic grin. "Maybe that was the leap that Gwri was talking about."

"Ohhh," groaned Bumbelwy, holding his head. "My head feels like a rock that just bounced down one of these cliffs! I must have rolled off that pile of—" All at once, he realized that he was being carried over the knoll by a giant. He struggled, swatting at the huge thumb that was hooked under his cloak. "Helllp! I'm about to be eaten!"

Shim grunted and shook his head at the bedraggled jester. "You isn't very tasty, that's easily to see. I wouldn't puts you in my mouth for anythings."

I waved at Bumbelwy. "Don't worry. This giant's a friend of ours."

Bumbelwy, swaying before Shim's nose, continued to flail wildly. "Such a tragedy!" he wailed. "All my humor and wisdom, lost forever down a giant's gullet."

Shim dropped him into the palm of his other hand. Bumbelwy landed in a heap beside Rhia and me. He struggled to stand, took a swing at Shim's nose, tripped, and fell flat on his face again.

An enormous grin spread across Shim's face. "At leastly he's funny."

Bumbelwy, who was trying to stand again, froze. "Do you mean that? Funny enough to make you laugh?"

"Not that funny," boomed Shim, his voice so powerful it almost blew us all over the edge of his palm. "Just enough to makes me grin."

The jester finally stood, trying to keep his balance while squaring his shoulders and straightening his cloak. "Good giant. You are more intelligent than I had thought at first." He bowed awkwardly. "I am Bumbelwy the Mirthful, jester to—"

"Nobody." I ignored his glare and spoke to Shim. "As I was saying, we need your help. We need to get to the lair of the sleeping dragon, the one Tuatha battled long ago. It's somewhere across the water."

The giant's grin faded, as the rising wind howled across the cliffs. "You must be kiddingly."

"I fear he's not," said Bumbelwy, his usual glumness returned. "You might as well eat us all now, before the dragon does."

"If it's really a sleeping dragon," asked Rhia, "just how dangerous can it be?"

"Verily," thundered Shim, his whole frame swaying like a great tree in a storm. "For starters, the dragon is still hungrily, even while it sleeps. For enders, it could wakes up anytime." He paused, tilting his huge head in thought. "Nobodies know when Tuatha's sleeping spell will wears off, and the dragon will wakes up. Although the legends say that it will happen on the darkest day in the life of Fincayra."

Bumbelwy sighed. "Sounds like a typical day for me."

"Hush!" I gazed up at Shim. "Will you take us there right away?"

"All rights. But it is madness! Certainly, definitely, absolutely." Scanning the knoll, strewn with brush, he bit his great lip. "But firstly I needs to brings these branches down to Varigal."

"Please, no," I begged. I scanned the afternoon sky, afraid to see the rising sliver of the moon. "Every minute counts now, Shim. I'm almost out of time."

"I supposes I is already late with these pokingly branches."

"Then you'll do it?"

Shim replied by standing and taking a single, enormous stride along the spine of the ridge. Rocked by the jolt, we fell together in a jumble on his palm. Untangling ourselves was made more difficult by the giant's bouncing gait, but we finally succeeded. Except for Bumbelwy, whose cloak had wrapped itself tightly around his head and shoulders. As he struggled to free himself, his bells were mercifully silent under the cloak.

Rhia and I, meanwhile, crawled to the edge of Shim's palm and peered through the gaps in his fingers. Wind rushed past our faces as we watched the landscape transform. So great were Shim's strides that the chanting of the giants, and the rumbling of their labors, soon faded away completely. He stepped over boulder fields as if they were mere clusters of pebbles, crushing rock ledges with his feet. Mountain passes that would have taken us days to scale he climbed in a few minutes. He traversed yawning crevasses with the ease of a rabbit hopping over a stick.

Before long, the terrain began to flatten. Hillsides of trees replaced the snow-draped ridges, while the valleys widened into broad meadows painted with purple and yellow flowers. Shim paused only once, to blow on the boughs of an apple tree, showering us with fruit. Unlike Bumbelwy, who hadn't yet regained his appetite, Rhia and I ate the apples avidly.

Shim sped along, so fast that I had only barely noticed the expanding sweep of blue ahead, when his heavy foot splashed into water. In another moment, he was wading through a channel, surrounded by a flock of screeching gulls. His voice boomed, frightening the birds. "I remembers when you carries me across a ragingly river."

"Right!" I shouted to be heard above the wind and screeching gulls. "The crossing was so rough I had to carry you on my shoulder."

"That would be hardly now! Certainly, definitely, absolutely."

Turning my second sight across the channel, I noticed a line of dark hills, as rugged as a row of jagged teeth, on the horizon. The Lost Lands. Well I remembered the words Cairpré had used to describe that territory. *Uncharted and unexplored.* With a deadly dragon sleeping somewhere in those hills, I didn't wonder why. Instinctively, I reached for the hilt of my sword.

Minutes later, Shim stepped out of the channel, his hairy feet slapping on the shore. He set us down on a wide bank of flat rock. No flowers, nor even grasses, sprouted here. Even the glowing light of approaching sunset brought no softer hues to the land. Only a shiny, black ash coated the rocks, stretching to the hillsides far inland. The air reeked of charcoal, like an abandoned fire pit.

I realized that this entire coastline, and everything that once grew on it, must have been scorched by powerful flames. Even the rocks themselves looked cracked and buckled, seared by repeated blasts of extreme heat. Then, scanning the rugged hills, I found the source: a thin curl of smoke rising from a hollow not far inland.

"That's where we're going," I declared.

Shim bent his worried face so low that his chin almost touched the top of my staff. "Is you certainly? Nobody goes to visit a dragon on purposely."

"I do."

"You is foolishly! You know that?"

"I know that. Too well, believe me."

The giant's moist eyes blinked. "Then good luck. I misses you. And you, too, sweetly Rhia. I hopes to makes another crossing with you one daily."

Bumbelwy's bells jangled as he wagged his head. "With the

dragon's lair just over there, we probably don't have another day."

With that, Shim straightened his back. He gazed down on us for another moment, then turned and strode straight into the channel. The setting sun, streaking the western sky with lavender and pink, outlined his massive shoulders and head. High above, a pale crescent moon lifted into the sky.

XXVIII

ELIMINATING

Rather than try to approach the lair of the dragon at night, I decided to wait until dawn. While the others slept fitfully on the blackened rocks, I sat awake, thinking. For the sixth lesson, the lesson of Eliminating, could mean only one thing.

I must slay the dragon.

My stomach knotted at the very thought. How could one boy, even a boy armed with a magical sword, possibly accomplish such a thing? Dragons, as I knew from my mother's stories, were incredibly powerful, astonishingly quick, and supremely clever. I recalled the night when, her face aglow from the fire in our earthen hut, she had described one dragon who destroyed a dozen giants with a single swipe of his tail, then roasted them for supper with his fiery breath.

How, then, was I to succeed? Unlike the wizard Tuatha, I knew none of the magic that might help. I knew only that, asleep or not, a dragon would be terrifying to approach, and nearly impossible to eliminate.

As the first rays of sunlight touched the charred shoreline, spreading like fire across the waves, I reluctantly stood. My hands felt cold, as did my heart. I pulled one of Shim's apples from the pocket of my tunic and took a bite. Crisp and flavorful though it was, I hardly tasted it. When nothing but the core remained, I tossed it aside.

Rhia sat up. "You didn't sleep at all, did you?"

I merely gazed at the jagged line of hills, now brushed with pink. "No. And I don't have even a hint of a plan to show for it. If you have any sense, stay here. If I survive, I'll come back for you."

She shook her head, so vigorously that some of the leaves enmeshed in her brown curls tumbled to the ground. "I thought we discussed that already. Back at the Lake of the Face."

"But this time the risks are too great. Rhia, you've been warning me ever since the Dark Hills that I could get lost. Well, the truth is there is more than one way to be lost. And that's how I feel right now." I blew a long, slow breath. "Don't you see? Only a wizard, a true wizard, can defeat a dragon! I don't know what it takes to be a wizard, really—strength, or skill, or spirit. Cairpré said it's all that and more. All I know is that whatever it takes, I don't have it."

Rhia's face pinched. "I don't believe it. And neither does your mother."

"For all your instincts, this time you're wrong." I glanced at Bumbelwy, huddled under his thick cloak. "Should I give him the same choice as I gave you?"

The lanky jester suddenly rolled over. "I'm coming, if that's what you mean." He stretched his long arms. "If ever you needed my wit and good humor, it's now, on the day of your certain death."

With an expression as somber as one of Bumbelwy's own, I turned toward the hills. From one of the wedgelike hollows between them rose a dark column of smoke. It twisted skyward, marring the sunrise. I took a step toward it. Then another. And another. At each step, the base of my staff clicked on the rocks like a door snapping shut.

Across the scorched land I marched, with Rhia by my side and Bumbelwy not far behind. Knowing that stealth was essential, we tried to tread as softly as foxes. No one spoke. I rested my staff on my shoulder to keep it from striking the rocks. The jester even clamped his hands over his hat to muffle his bells. As we drew nearer to the smoking hollow, my feeling of foreboding deepened. While the dragon might wait for Fincayra's darkest day to wake, my own darkest day had certainly arrived.

A low, roaring sound reached us across the blackened flats. Deep as the bass strings of a titanic harp. Regular as breathing. It was, I knew, the sound of the dragon snoring. It swelled steadily as we approached.

The air grew hot, uncomfortably hot, as the rocks lifted into the charred hills. Pace by pace, keeping quiet, we drew nearer to the column of smoke. Here the rocks had not just been seared by flames, but also pounded and trampled by enormous weight. Boulders had been crushed. Gulleys had been flattened. All living things had been destroyed. Eliminated.

Hardly daring to breathe, we crossed a pile of crushed stone. Suddenly Bumbelwy slipped and fell. Rocks skittered down the pile, smacking into the rubble at the bottom. That sound, however, was obscured by the clamorous banging of his bells. They rang out, echoing among the hills like a clap of thunder.

I glared at him, whispering, "Take off that cursed hat, you club-footed fool! You'll wake the dragon before we even get there!"

He scowled. Reluctantly, he pulled off his three-cornered hat and stuffed it under his cloak.

I led the way into the steep-walled hollow, wiping my brow from the heat. Even through my boots, the soles of my feet burned. The sweltering air rippled like water, vibrating with the snoring sound. Everything reeked of charcoal. With every step I took, the walls of rock drew closer together, submerging me in darkness.

Suddenly I halted. There, partly shrouded by shadows, lay the dragon. He was even larger than I had feared, as huge as a hillside himself. Coiled like a great serpent, his green and orange body, covered with armored scales, could have almost filled the Lake of the Face. His head, smoke pouring from the nostrils, lay across his left foreleg. Beneath his nose ran a row of scales, so blackened from smoke that they resembled a huge moustache. Every inhale revealed his rows of sharp-edged teeth; every exhale flexed his powerful shoulder muscles and shook the vast wings folded against his back. Claws, as sharp as the sword on my belt but ten times as long, glistened in the early morning light. Midway down one claw, like an oversized ring, sat a skull large enough to have belonged to Shim.

Beneath his scaled belly, treasures gleamed and sparkled. Crowns and necklaces, swords and shields, trumpets and flutes—all crafted of gold or silver, all studded with jewels. Rubies, amethysts, jades, emeralds, sapphires, and huge pearls lay strewn everywhere. Never in my life had I imagined that such a vast hoard existed. Yet I felt no desire whatsoever to comb through it, for scattered throughout were skulls of all sizes and shapes, some gleaming white, others scorched by fire.

I crept deeper into the hollow, with Rhia and Bumbelwy just behind. We cringed as one at the slow, roaring rhythm of the dragon's breathing. His enormous eyes were closed, though not completely, revealing slits of smoldering yellow. I couldn't shake the feeling that this beast was as much awake as asleep.

At that instant, the dragon's jaws opened a crack. A thin tongue of flame shot out, scorching the black rocks and some stray skulls. Bumbelwy jumped backward, dropping his bell-draped hat out of his cloak. It hit the rocks at his feet with a jarring clang.

The dragon suddenly snorted and shifted his gargantuan bulk. His eyelids quivered, opening a sliver more. Bumbelwy gasped in fright. His legs wobbled. Seeing that he looked about to faint, Rhia grabbed his arm.

Then, with gruesome slowness, the dragon raised the claw wearing the giant skull. Like someone about to eat a rare delicacy, he brought it to his nostrils, savoring its aroma. His eyelids trembled, but did not open, as he released a searing blast of flames. At last, the roasting completed, the dragon's purple lips grasped the skull and tore it from the claw. A loud crunching echoed in the hollow, the sound of enormous teeth reducing the morsel to splinters. With an immense puff of smoke, the dragon resumed snoring.

The three of us shuddered in unison. Glancing grimly at Rhia, I handed her my staff. At the same time, I lay my right hand on the silver hilt of my sword. Slowly, ever so slowly, I drew it from the scabbard. As it emerged, the blade rang faintly, like a distant chime. The sleeping dragon suddenly growled, releasing a puff of thick smoke from his nostrils. His pointed ears pricked forward, listening to the ringing sound. Meanwhile, his dream seemed to alter. He growled viciously, bared his teeth, and slashed at the air with his claws.

I stood as rigid as a statue. My arm began to ache from holding the heavy sword above my head, but I dared not lower it for fear it would make another sound. After several minutes, the dragon seemed to relax a little. The growling subsided, and the claws fell still.

Cautiously, I crept forward on the rocks, taking one small step at a time. The dragon towered over me, each of his scales as big as my entire body. Perspiration stung my eyes. *If I have only one blow, where to strike?* Those armored scales covered his chest, legs, back, tail, and even his orange ears. Perhaps, if I ran the sword through one of the closed eyes, that might do it.

Closer and closer I edged. The smoky air made me want to cough, but I did all I could to resist. My hand squeezed the hilt.

All at once, the tail lashed out like a monstrous whip. I had no time even to move, let alone to run. As the tail exploded to its full length, one of the barbs at the end coiled tightly around my chest, squeezing the air out of my lungs. In the same instant, the other barb wound around my arm holding the sword, preventing me from moving it at all.

I was totally helpless.

Rhia released a muffled shriek. I felt the dragon tense again, squeezing me all the harder. Yet the yellow slits of his eyes opened no wider. He seemed to be still asleep, or half asleep. And, judging from the curl of his lips, he seemed to be about to enjoy a thoroughly realistic dream about swallowing a boy with a sword.

At the edge of my second sight, I watched Rhia fall to her knees. Bumbelwy knelt awkwardly beside her. His head hung low on his paunchy chins. Then, unaccountably, he started to sing. It was, I soon realized, a funeral dirge, sung in low, moaning tones. As much as I squirmed in the dragon's grip, I squirmed still more at his words:

A dragon savors all he eats
But values best the living treats
Who squirm and squeal before they die,
The filling of a dragon's pie.

O dragon, 'tis my friend you eat!
Alas, how sweet the dragon's meat.

The dragon's loves the crunch of bones
And all the dying cries and groans
Of people gone without a trace,
Into deep digestive space.

O dragon, 'tis my friend you eat!
Alas, how sweet the dragon's meat.

My friend, in dragon's mouth interred,
Was even robbed his final word.
For down he went into that hole,
His parting sentence swallowed whole.

O dragon, 'tis my friend you eat!
Alas, how sweet the dragon's meat.

Even before Bumbelwy had finished, the dragon's jaws opened. I watched, aghast, as the rows of jagged teeth, charred by flames, revealed themselves. With all my strength, I struggled to escape. But the tail only squeezed harder. The jaws, meanwhile, opened wider.

Suddenly, out of the depths behind the open jaws came a gruff, hoarse sound that could be only one thing. A laugh. A deep, belching, hearty laugh. A billowing cloud of smoke came as well, blackening the air. The laugh continued, rolling right down the dragon's serpentine form, shaking first his head, then his neck, then his gigantic belly, then finally his tail. Before long, the entire beast quaked in raucous laughter, swaying on his hoard of treasures.

The tail released me. I dropped to the ground, breathless, dazed, but alive. Quickly, I crawled through the black cloud, dragging my sword. A moment later, Rhia ran to my side and helped me to my feet.

Coughing from the smoke, we stumbled out of the hollow. Behind us, the dragon's coarse laughter began to grow quieter. In a matter of seconds, his roaring snores had returned. I glanced back to see the thin slits of his eyes shining in the shadows. When at last we were well away from the dragon's lair, we collapsed on a bench of black rock. Rhia threw her arms around my neck. So different from the embrace of the dragon!

I squeezed her in return. Then I turned to Bumbelwy. In a hoarse voice I declared, "You did it, you know. You made the dragon laugh."

Bumbelwy's head drooped. "I know. A terrible, terrible thing. I am humiliated. Devastated."

"What do you mean?" I shook him by the shoulders. "You saved me!"

"Terrible," repeated the dour jester. "Just terrible. Once again I botched the delivery! I was singing one of my saddest, most sorrowful hymns. One that should break anyone's heart." He bit his lip. "But what did it do instead? Tickled him. Entertained him. When I try to amuse, I sadden, and when I try to grieve, I amuse! Oh, I'm a failure. A miserable failure."

He sighed morosely. "And to make matters worse, I've lost my hat. My jester's hat! So on top of not sounding like a jester, now I don't even look like one."

Rhia and I traded amused glances. Then, without further delay, I pulled off one of my boots.

Bumbelwy watched me gloomily. "Injure your foot, did you?"

"No. I have a promise to keep."

With that, I sunk my teeth into the leather tongue of the boot. I ripped a section loose and chewed vigorously. No amount of chewing could soften the leather, though it did fill my mouth with the flavors of dirt, grass, and perspiration. With great difficulty, I swallowed.

Bumbelwy suddenly caught his breath. He straightened his back slightly. His downturned chins lifted a notch. He was not smiling, nor even grinning. But, at least for a moment, he was no longer frowning.

As I began to take another bite, he laid his hand on my back. "Hold there. One bite is enough. You may need that boot for another purpose." An odd, muffled sound, almost like a smothered giggle, erupted from his throat. "I really did make him laugh, didn't I?"

"Indeed you did."

The frowns returned. "I doubt I could do it again, though. Just a fluke."

Slipping on my boot, I shook my head. "It was no fluke. You could do it again."

Thrusting out his chest, Bumbelwy stood before me. "Then when you go back into that smoking oven to try to slay that beast, I will go with you."

"As will I," declared Rhia.

I looked at their loyal faces for a moment, then slid my sword back into the scabbard. "You won't have to." I leaned closer on the scorched rock. "You see, I'm not going to slay the dragon."

Both of them stared at me. Raising the staff, Rhia asked, "You have to do it, don't you? How else can you learn the first lesson of Eliminating?"

I reached for the gnarled shaft of hemlock, spinning it slowly in my hand. "I think, perhaps, I already have."

"What?"

Fingering the staff's knotty top, I glanced toward the shadowed lair. "Something happened to me when the dragon laughed."

"Right," agreed Bumbelwy. "You broke free of his tail."

"No, I mean something else. Did you hear how full and hearty that laugh was? It made me feel that, well, as vicious and bloodthirsty as the dragon is, he couldn't be completely evil. Or else . . . he couldn't laugh like that."

Bumbelwy looked at me as if I had lost my mind. "I'll wager that dragon has laughed every time he has destroyed a village."

I nodded. "Perhaps so. But something about his laugh gave me the feeling that, somehow, he isn't so completely different from you and me. That he has some worth. Even if we don't comprehend it."

Rhia almost smiled.

Bumbelwy, though, furrowed his brow. "I don't understand what this has to do with Eliminating."

Lifting my right hand, smudged with charcoal, I touched the lids of my sightless eyes. "You see these eyes? Useless. Scarred forever, like my cheeks. And do you know why? Because I tried to destroy another boy's life! I don't know whether or not he survived, but I doubt it. I tried to eliminate him."

His brow wrinkled still more. "I still don't understand."

"The point is this. Eliminating is sometimes necessary. But it comes only at a price. It may be to your body. Or to your soul. But the price is always there. Because *every living thing is precious somehow.*"

The shaft of my staff sizzled with a blast of blue light. Where bare wood had been before, there was now the image of a dragon's tail.

"The sixth Song is done!" exclaimed Rhia. "Now you have only one left, the Song of Seeing."

Tapping the top of the staff, I examined the dragon's tail, etched not far from the glowing star within a circle. Shifting my gaze to the lifeless stretch of coastline, as blackened and burned as the inside of a fire pit, I viewed the deep blue channel and the distant peaks of Varigal beyond. "There may be only one Song left, but there are only a few days left, too."

Bumbelwy slumped lower. "No more than three, judging from the moon last night."

"And we need to get all the way to the Forgotten Island and back."

"Impossible," declared the jester. He shook his head for emphasis until he remembered that he no longer wore any bells. "Merlin, you have done well, impossibly well, to get this far. But you, like the rest of us, caught a glimpse of that place from the cliffs of the treelings. No one in living memory has ever gone to the Forgotten Island! How can you hope to find your way there and back in only three days?"

I tried to imagine the route we would need to travel—across water, over peaks, through forests, and past whatever barriers of enchantment shielded the Island. The entire breadth of Fincayra, full of untold dangers. Sadly, I turned to Rhia. "For once, I am afraid, Bumbelwy's right. This time, we don't have the wind, or a giant, to help us."

Rhia stomped her foot on the charred rock. "I'm not giving up. We've come too far! You have six of the seven Songs. And I even have the location of the Otherworld Well."

I jumped to my feet. "You have *what?*"

"The location of the stairwell. Where Balor stands guard." She ran a hand through her hair, twisting some curls in her fingers. "Gwri of the Golden Hair gave it to me—sent a vision of it right into my mind—when she told us the Otherworld Well wasn't far from the dragon's lair."

"Why didn't you tell me?"

"She told me not to! She thought you might be tempted to skip the Forgotten Island entirely."

Slowly, I sat down again on the bench of black rock. Putting my nose almost to hers, I spoke softly but firmly. "That is exactly what we're going to do."

"You can't!" she protested. "You'll need to find the soul of Seeing before you stand any chance at all against Balor. Don't you remember the words you found in Arbassa?

> *But lo! Do not attempt the Well*
> *Until the Songs are done.*
> *For dangers stalk your every step,*
> *With Balor's eye but one.*

"You'll die for sure if you try to fight Balor without all seven of the Songs."

My stomach knotted as I recalled Tuatha's own warning to me. *Heed well my words, young colt! Without all seven Songs, you shall lose more than your quest. You shall lose your very life.*

I cleared my throat. "But Rhia, if I don't drop the seventh Song, my mother will surely die! Don't you see? It's our only hope. Our only chance."

Her eyes narrowed. "There's something more, isn't there? I can feel it."

"No. You're wrong."

"I am not. You're afraid of something, aren't you?"

"Those instincts again!" My hands closed into fists. "Yes, I am afraid. Of the lesson on Seeing. It frightens me more than all the others combined. I don't know why, Rhia."

Shaking her head, she leaned back against the charred rock. "Then whatever awaits you on the Forgotten Island is important. You must go there, Merlin. For you as well as for Elen! And there's another reason, too."

"Another?"

"Gwri told me something else. She said that while you are on the Forgotten Island you must find a bough of mistletoe. Wear it, she said, when you enter the Otherworld Well. It will help you make your way safely to the realm of Dagda. Without it, your task will be much harder."

"My task could not be any harder as it is! Please, Rhia. No bough of mistletoe is going to make enough difference to justify using up what little time is left. You must help me. Show me the way to the Otherworld Well."

She scuffed her boot of woven bark on the blackened rock.

"Well . . . if I do, and you somehow survive, will you promise to do something?" Her eyes grew suddenly moist. "Even if I'm not around to hold you to your promise?"

I swallowed. "Of course I will. And why wouldn't you be around?"

"Never mind that." She blinked back her tears. "Promise me that, if you should survive, you will one day go to the Forgotten Island and learn whatever it is you're meant to learn there."

"I promise. And I'm going to take you with me."

She stood abruptly, scanning the bleak ridges. "Then let's go. We have some hard trekking ahead of us."

PART THREE

XXIX

THE FINAL TREK

Wordlessly, Rhia led us deeper into the wasteland of rubble. Somewhere on these ridges lay the entrance to the spirit world—and the deadly ogre who guarded it. Yet if Balor indeed lived here, he lived without the company of anything that breathed or sprouted or moved. For where the Dark Hills had seemed devoid of life, except for the occasional withered tree, these hills seemed utterly hostile to life. The dragon's fiery blasts had not left a single tree, nor shrub, nor clump of moss anywhere. Only charcoal. I wished that I still carried the Flowering Harp on my shoulder, and that I might use its magic to bring even a few blades of grass to these slopes.

No landscape could have been more different from Rhia's home in the lush glades of Druma Wood. Yet she moved with as much confidence and grace over the piles of scorched rocks as she would have moved through groves of scented ferns. She headed due east, never veering. If staying on course meant scrambling straight up a crumbling rock fall, or leaping over a deep crevasse, then that was where she led us. Hour after hour.

Still, as much as I admired her endurance, I admired some of her other qualities even more. She loved life, and all living things, true to her childhood in the boughs of a great oak tree. She carried with her a quiet, soulful wisdom, reminding me of the tales of the Greek goddess Athena. And, even more, of my own mother.

I felt a surge of gratitude that Rhia had allowed her life to entwine with my own, wrapping us together as tightly as the woodland vines of her garb. And I found myself appreciating as never before the virtues of her garb itself. The tight yet flexible weave around her elbows. The broad green leaves across her shoulders. The playful designs along her collar.

As we trekked over the desolate ridges, her suit of woven vines lifted my spirits, if only a little. Its very greenness somehow gave me hope that even the bleakest lands might be coaxed again to flower, that even the gravest fault might one day be forgiven. For, as Rhia herself knew well, those woven vines held a surprising truth. No wizard's magic, however impressive, could be greater than Nature's own magic. How else could a new sapling spring from lifeless soil? And was it possible that I, like every living thing, might actually share in some of that magic of renewal?

Because the ridges lay in parallel lines, running north and south, we couldn't turn down any of the valleys without changing direction. So we climbed up the steep slopes only to plunge immediately down the other sides. We reached the valley floors only to start climbing again. By the time the sun hung low in the sky at our backs, and long shadows fell from the blackened rocks, my knees and thighs wobbled from the strain. Even my staff hardly helped. It was clear from Bumbelwy's constant stumbling, often on the hem of his own cloak, that he felt no sturdier.

Still worse, we found not even a trickle of water. My own tongue felt like a dry sliver of wood inside my mouth. I might have been more thirsty than the others thanks to my bite of boot leather, but probably not much. The long day of trekking over the rubble had left us all parched.

Yet Rhia never slowed down. Though she said nothing, she seemed more grimly determined than ever. Perhaps it was simply the urgency of our quest. Or perhaps it was something else, something that only she knew. In any case, my own mood was no less grim. The voice of Tuatha still thundered in my ears, kindling my fears just as it had kindled the light in the blue stones surrounding his grave. Immensely wise and powerful though he was, he had still lost his life to Balor's deadly gaze. And why? Because of hubris. Wasn't I guilty of the same flaw, daring to confront Balor with only six of the Songs to my name?

Yes—and no. My hubris had spawned this whole mess to begin with. Yet now my actions were driven more by desperation. And also by fear. For Rhia had been right. I was relieved, truly relieved, to have avoided the Forgotten Island and whatever the Song of Seeing might have entailed. That Song haunted me like a terrible dream, as terrible as the one that had made me claw at my own face on that night in the Rusted Plains. I doubted that I could ever find the soul of Seeing, with my useless eyes and limited second sight. And I suspected that to see like a wizard could require something else entirely, something that I surely lacked.

And that was only the beginning of my fears. What if there were no truth to the prophecy that only a child of human blood could defeat Rhita Gawr or his servant Balor? Tuatha himself had hinted as much. *The prophecy may be true, and it may be false. Yet even if it is true, the truth often has more than one face.* Whatever the prophecy might have meant, I certainly couldn't rely on it. The sad truth was, I couldn't even rely on myself.

A loose rock clattered down the slope from above, barely missing the toe of my boot. I looked up to find Rhia disappearing over the top of an outcropping that jutted from the ridge like a chiseled nose. How odd, I thought. With so much of this ridge yet to climb, why had she chosen to go straight over such an outcropping rather than around it?

The answer struck me as I noticed a glint of moisture on the rocks ahead. Water! But from where? The higher I climbed up the outcropping, the more wet patches I discovered. Even a scraggly tuft of moss, alive and green, had rooted itself in the crack between two stones.

When, at last, I reached the top, I stopped short. For there, not ten paces away, bubbled a small spring, forming a clear pool of water. Rhia was already drinking from it. I ran to her side, plunging my whole face into the pool. With the first swallow, my tongue tingled ever so slightly. With the next, it sprang back to life, feeling the slap and sting of coldness. Like Rhia, I drank and drank, filling myself with liquid. Bumbelwy, too, collapsed beside the spring, his slurps and gasps joining with our own.

At last, when I could hold no more, I turned to Rhia. She was sitting with her knees drawn close to her chest, watching the setting sun paint streaks of red and purple across the western sky. Water dripped from her hair onto her shoulders.

I wiped the trickle from my chin and slid a little closer on the rocks. "Rhia, are you thinking about Balor?"

She nodded.

"I saw him in the Lake of the Face," I said. "He was . . . killing me. Making me look into his eye."

She swung her face my way. Though sunset pink glowed in her hair, her eyes looked somber. "I saw Balor in the Lake of the Face, too." She started to say something more, then caught herself.

My throat tightened. "Are we—are we close?"

"Very."

"Should we push on and get there tonight?"

Bumbelwy, who was arranging some rocks so that he could lie down beside the pool, jumped. "No!"

Rhia gave a sigh. "There's almost no moon left, and we need the sleep. We might as well camp here tonight." She felt the rough contours of the charred rocks, then reached for my hand, wrapping her forefinger around my own. "Merlin, I'm afraid."

"So am I." I followed her gaze to the horizon. Above the jagged hills, the sky now loomed as red as blood. "When I was little," I said quietly, "I sometimes felt so afraid that I couldn't sleep. And whenever that happened, my mother would always do the same thing to help me feel better. She would tell me a story."

Rhia's finger squeezed mine tighter. "Did she really? What a wonderful idea, telling a story just to ease someone's fears." She sighed. "Is that the sort of thing a mother does?"

"Yes," I answered softly. "At least a mother like her."

Her head, streaked with red from the sunset, drooped lower. "I wish that I had known . . . my own mother. And that I had heard some of her stories, stories I could remember right now."

"I'm sorry you didn't have that, Rhia." I tried to swallow, but couldn't. "But there is one thing almost as good as hearing stories from your mother."

"Yes?"

"Hearing stories from your friend."

She nearly smiled. "I would love that."

I glanced at the first star shimmering overhead. Then I cleared my throat and began. "Once, long ago, there lived a wise and powerful goddess by the name of Athena."

XXX

BALOR

Night fell cold and dark. Although after my story Rhia had seemed to drift off to sleep, I continued to lie awake, turning over and over on the rocks. For a while I watched the westernmost sky, recalling Gwri of the Golden Hair, but mostly I stared at the ghostly remnant of the waning crescent moon above our heads. In the morning, at most two days would remain.

Throughout the night, I shivered from the chill air of these treeless hills. And from the thought of that merciless eye, whose merest glance meant death. The vision that I had seen in the Lake of the Face stalked me. When I dozed, which wasn't much, I struggled and flailed.

I awoke as the first rays of light touched the rock-strewn slope. No chirping birds or scurrying beasts greeted this dawn. Only wind, howling in long, lonely gusts across the ridges. Stiffly, I stretched, the place between my shoulders throbbing painfully. I bent to the clear pool, which wore a delicate collar of ice, and took a last drink.

Cold, hungry, and grim, we set off. Rhia strode solemnly over the spiky rocks, her bark shoes blackened by charcoal. Wordlessly, she led us in the direction of the sunrise. Yet none of us paused to savor the rich bands of orange and pink that were spreading across the horizon. Absorbed in our own thoughts, we continued to trek in silence. Several times, the loose rocks gave way beneath my feet, sending me sliding backward. Once I fell over, slicing my knee on a rock.

Late that morning, as we reached the top of another slope, Rhia slowed her pace. She halted, casting me a worried glance. Without a word, she raised her arm, pointing to the next ridge. A great gouge split the crest, looking as if the jaws of a mythic beast had clamped down on it ages ago, ripping away the very rocks. Even as I stared at the gouge, it seemed to stare back.

I chewed my lip, certain that the Otherworld Well stood on that spot. Why hadn't the mighty Dagda simply descended from on high and struck Balor down? Surely, as the greatest warrior of all, he could have easily done so. Perhaps Dagda was fully occupied with battling Rhita Gawr himself. Or perhaps he didn't want mere mortals to enter the Otherworld, whatever their reasons.

I took the lead. Rhia stayed at my heels, so close that I could hear her anxious breathing behind me. As we dropped down into the next scorched valley, I found myself scanning the rubble for any sign at all of something green, something living. But no springs bubbled here, no moss filled the cracks. The rocks lay as bare as my own hopes.

Slowly, we climbed toward the great gouge. When at last we reached its very edge, Rhia grabbed the sleeve of my tunic. For several seconds, she probed me with her gaze. Then, her voice a whisper, she spoke her first words of the day.

"The eye. You mustn't look into the eye."

I clasped the hilt of my sword. "I'll do my best."

"Merlin, I wish we'd had a little more . . . time. For sharing days. And sharing secrets."

I furrowed my brow, unsure of what she meant. But there was no time now to find out. Setting my jaw, I handed her my staff. Then I marched into the gouge.

As I stepped between the dark cliffs that rose sharply to either side, I felt as if I were striding into the open mouth of a monster. Pinnacles, as jagged as the dragon's teeth, jutted from the rims of the cliffs. A frigid wind slapped my face, screaming in my ears. As I moved deeper into the gouge, the air quivered ominously, as if shaken by footsteps that I could neither see nor hear.

Yet I found nothing else. But for the jagged, black rocks, shining in the morning light, the place seemed utterly empty. No Balor. No stairwell. No sign of anything living—or dead.

Thinking I might have missed something, I started to turn, when all of a sudden the wind lashed me again. The air before me darkened, then quivered. This time, however, it parted like an invisible curtain. Out of the air itself stepped a huge, muscled warrior, standing at least twice my own size.

Balor! Towering above me, he seemed almost as broad as the cliffs themselves. His deep, wrathful growl echoed within the great gouge, as his heavy boots slammed down on the rocks. Slowly, he lifted his gleaming sword. I caught sight of the horns above his ears, and the dark brow over his one enormous eye, before turning my second sight aside.

I must look at something else. Not his head! The sword. I'll try the sword.

Barely had I focused on his broad, gleaming blade than it clashed against my own. My arm reeled from the powerful blow. To my surprise, the ogre grunted at the impact, as if the magic of my own sword had caught him off guard. Again he growled, then swung his weapon with even more force.

I leaped to the side just as his blade crashed against the rocks where I had stood only a split second before. Sparks flew into the air, singeing my tunic. As if the blurred edges of my second sight weren't enough of a disadvantage, I could not look directly at him for fear of glimpsing his eye. As the ogre raised his arm to strike again, I thrust at him. But he spun away in time. Pivoting with uncanny speed, he charged straight at me, his sword slashing the air.

Caught by surprise, I backed away. Suddenly my heel struck a rock. I hopped backward, trying desperately to keep my balance, but tumbled over in a heap. Balor released a vengeful snarl as he marched toward me, lifting his sword high. It was all I could do to avoid looking into his face, his eye.

At that instant, Rhia sprinted out of the shadows and threw herself at the ogre. She lunged at his leg, holding tight to his thigh. He tried to kick free, but she continued to cling to him. This distracted him just long enough for me to roll to the side and leap to my feet.

Before I could renew the attack, however, Balor roared angrily at Rhia. He seized her by the arm, ripping her loose. Then, roaring again, he whipped her around and hurled her headlong at the cliff wall. Face first, she slammed into the rocks. She staggered backward, then slumped motionless on the ground.

My heart split in two at the sight. Just then Bumbelwy emerged from hiding and ran to her side, waving his arms wildly. Seething with rage, I charged straight at the ogre, swinging my sword while still averting my gaze. Yet Balor sidestepped me with ease. His fist smashed into my shoulder, sending me sprawling. The sword flew out of my hand and clattered on the rocks. I crawled madly after it.

A huge boot kicked me in the chest. I flew through the air and landed with a thud on my back. My ribs screamed with pain. The pinnacles of the cliffs seemed to wobble and whirl above me.

Before I could try to sit up, Balor's immense hand closed around my throat. He squeezed until I gagged. Then, with a sharp jerk, he lifted me into the air. My head swam. I flailed my arms and legs, swaying helplessly. But he only squeezed tighter, throttling me. I pounded on his arm, trying desperately to breathe.

Slowly, he lowered me, until our faces almost touched. His grip tightened. His snarl tore at my ears. Then, pulled by a spell I no longer had the strength to resist, I looked into his dark eye. Like a pit of quicksand, it drew me in.

With all my remaining power, I fought to break free. But I couldn't resist the eye. It pulled me deeper, deeper, sucking out my strength. Darkness shrouded my vision. I felt myself go limp. *I should just give in. Just let go.* I stopped trying to fight, stopped trying to breathe.

Suddenly, I heard Balor roar in agony. He released my throat. I fell onto the rocks, coughing and gasping. Air filled my lungs again. The darkness clung to me for another moment, then faded away.

Weakly, I raised myself up on one elbow, just in time to see Balor collapse on the rocks. He fell with the force of a toppled tree. From his back protruded a sword. My sword. And standing behind him was Rhia, half her face bloody. Her neck bent strangely, as if she couldn't straighten it. Then her own legs gave out and she crumpled next to the fallen ogre.

"Rhia!" I called hoarsely, crawling to her side.

Bumbelwy appeared, looking grimmer than grim. He lifted me by the arm so that I could stand. As I stumbled over to Rhia, I heard him moan, "I told her she'd kill herself if she moved, but she wouldn't listen."

I knelt by her side. Gently lifting her head with my hands, I tried to straighten her neck. Above one ear I found a deep gash. It bled profusely, staining her suit of woven vines, as well as the rocks. Carefully, I sprinkled some of the herbs from my satchel on the wound.

"Rhia. I'll help you."

Her blue-gray eyes opened halfway. "Merlin," she whispered. "This time . . . there's nothing . . . you can do."

"No." I shook my head vigorously. "You're going to be all right."

With difficulty, she swallowed. "It's my time . . . to die. I'm sure. When I looked . . . in the Lake of the Face . . . I saw you fighting Balor . . . and losing. But I . . . also saw . . . one of us dying. It wasn't . . . you. It was . . . me."

Holding her, I tried to pour strength into her head and neck. I tore off the bottom of my sleeve and pressed it against her skin, willing the gash to heal as I had willed her bone to knit itself together in Eagles' Canyon. Yet I knew that these injuries were far more severe than a broken arm. Even the torn vines of her garb seemed to be fading a little with each passing second, their vibrant green showing hints of shadows.

"It doesn't have to be that way, Rhia."

"Oh yes . . . it does. I never told you . . . but I was told . . . a long time ago . . . that my life would be lost . . . to spare yours. That staying with you . . . would mean my own death. I wasn't sure whether to believe it . . . until now."

"What nonsense!" I concentrated harder on the wounds, but the blood continued to flow, soaking the cloth and seeping through my fingers. "What fool ever told you such a thing?"

"No fool. Arb . . . assa. That's why . . . you were never welcome . . . inside the door."

I winced. "You can't die now! Not because of some foolish prophecy!" I bent lower. "Listen to me, Rhia. These prophecies are worthless. Worthless! A prophecy said that only a child of human blood could kill Balor, right? Well, you saw what happened. Balor had me in his death grip. I was helpless—I, the child of human blood! It was you, not me, who killed him."

"That's because . . . I too . . . have human blood."

"What? You're a Fincayran! You're—"

"Merlin." Rhia's eyelids quivered, as the wind wailed beneath the cliffs. "I am . . . your sister."

I felt as if Balor's boot had once again slammed into my ribs. "My what?"

"Your sister." She drew a difficult breath. "Elen is . . . my mother, too. That's another reason . . . I had to come."

I pounded the black rocks with my fist. "It can't be true."

"It is true," declared Bumbelwy. He bent his lanky frame to kneel beside me. "When Elen of the Sapphire Eyes gave birth to you in a wrecked ship somewhere on our shores, she also gave birth, a few minutes later, to a daughter. She named the boy Emrys, and the girl Rhiannon. The bards of Fincayra all know that story."

His glum sigh melted into the wind. "And also the story of how that daughter was lost as an infant. Her parents were traveling through Druma Wood when they were attacked by a band of warrior goblins, the soldiers of Rhita Gawr. A fierce battle ensued. The goblins finally scattered. But in the turmoil one of Elen's twins, the girl, was lost. Hundreds of people searched for weeks, without success, until at long last even Elen stopped looking. Heartbroken, all she could do was pray to Dagda that her daughter might someday be found."

Rhia nodded weakly. "And she was. By . . . a treeling. Cwen. It was she . . . who brought me . . . to Arbassa."

"My sister!" Tears welled in my sightless eyes. "You are my sister."

"Yes . . . Merlin."

If the towering cliffs had caved in and crushed me just then, I would have felt no greater pain. I had found my only sibling. And yet, as had happened so many times before, I was about to lose what I had only just found.

Tuatha, I remembered now, had warned me that the prophecy about a child of human blood could have an unexpected meaning. *It may be true, and it may be false. Yet even if it is true, the truth often has more than one face.* How could I possibly have known that it would be the face of Rhia?

"Why," I asked in a quavering voice, "didn't you tell me before?"

"I didn't want . . . you to change . . . your course to try . . . to protect me. What you do . . . with your life . . . is important."

"Your life is just as important!"

I threw away the bloody rag and tore a new piece off my sleeve. Even as I tried to mop the gash, I recalled a night long ago in Cairpré's room full of books. So this was why he had hesitated so strangely in telling me the story of my birth! I had suspected then, and knew now, that he was on the verge of telling me something more. That a sister had been born on that same night.

I cradled Rhia's head in my lap, feeling her warm breath on my arm. Her eyelids had nearly closed. The shadows on her garb deepened. As a tear slid down my cheek, I said, "If only I could have seen."

Her eyelids fluttered. "Seen? Are you talking about . . . your eyes?"

"No, no." I watched the blood dripping from her brown curls. "This isn't about my eyes. It's about something else, something my heart has known all along. That you are, well, more than someone I just happened to meet that day in Druma Wood. My heart knew that from the very start."

She made a slight movement with her lips that could have been a grin. "Even when I . . . hung you up . . . in that tree?"

"Even then! Rhia, my heart could see it, but my head just didn't understand. I should have paid more attention to my heart, I'm telling you! *The heart can see things invisible to the eye.*"

A blue flash erupted from the rocks where Rhia had left my staff. Without even looking, I knew that it bore a new marking, in the shape of an eye. For I had discovered, somehow, the soul of Seeing. Yet my gain paled in comparison to my loss.

In that same instant, the air began to shimmer near the out-stretched arm of the fallen ogre. The invisible curtain parted, re-vealing a low circle of polished white stones. A well. Not a stairwell leading up, but a deep well leading down.

I could see it! And I also understood, for the first time, that the pathway to the Otherworld—to Heaven and also to Hell—meant going down, not up. Down into the very deepest places, not up to somewhere in the universe far removed from myself.

The bitter wind swept over us, howling. Rhia spoke so faintly that I could hardly hear her. "You will be . . . a wizard, Merlin. A . . . good . . . one."

I lifted her head to my chest. "Don't die, Rhia. Don't die."

She shuddered. Her eyes closed at last.

I held her tight, sobbing quietly.

Then, as if the dawn were breaking within my very arms, I sensed the presence of something that I had not noticed before. Something within Rhia's body, yet apart from it as well. Passing through my fingers like a breeze of light. Her spirit. Leaving her body on its way to the realm beyond. In a flash, an idea seized me.

I called to her spirit. *Please, Rhia. Don't leave me. Not yet.* I pulled her head close to my heart. *Come with me. Stay with me. Just for a while.*

I glanced toward the circle of white stones, the entry to the Otherworld. The pathway to Dagda. Even if it were too late for him to save Elen, maybe—just maybe—he could still save Rhia. And, if not, at least we might be together for a little while longer.

Come with me. Please.

I inhaled deeply, drawing far more than air. And with that breath, a powerful new feeling flooded into me. It was vibrant. It was robust. It was Rhia.

I turned to Bumbelwy, whose drooping cheeks showed the streaks of his own tears. "Help me up, will you?"

Solemnly, he eyed me. "She is dead."

"Dead." I felt the new life force within me. "But not gone, my good jester."

With difficulty, Bumbelwy helped me to my feet. In my arms I bore the empty body of Rhia, her head dangling. "Now bring me my sword. And my staff."

Shaking his head, the dour jester pulled the sword out of Balor. He used his boots to wipe the blade clean. Then he gathered up my staff from the rocks. Returning to me, he slid my sword into its scabbard and the staff into my blood-soaked belt.

He studied me somberly. "Where are you going with her?"

"To the Otherworld."

His eyebrows lifted. "Then I will wait here for you. Even though you won't ever return."

I started toward the ring of white stones, then stopped and faced him again. "Bumbelwy, in case I don't return, I want you to know something."

He gave me a many-layered frown. "What is that?"

"You are a terrible jester. But a loyal friend."

With that I turned toward the Well. I strode across the rocks, my arms as heavy as my heart.

XXXI

INTO
THE MIST

A gust of warm air struck my face as I looked into the Other-world Well. A spiraling stairway, made from the same polished white stones as the entrance, dropped down from the center of the circle. I couldn't tell how far down the stairs went, though I suspected it was far indeed.

Holding Rhia's limp body in my arms, I stepped carefully onto the first step. With a deep breath, perhaps my last, of Fincayran air, I started down the spiral. Downward I plunged, taking care not to stumble. As much as my ribs, throat, and shoulders ached from my battle with Balor, my heart ached still more to be bearing the body of my friend. My sister.

After descending more than a hundred steps, I noticed two surprising things. First, the Well never grew any darker. Unlike it would in a drinking well or tunnel hollowed out of the ground, the light did not diminish at deeper levels. In fact, it seemed to grow stronger somehow. Soon the white stones of the stairs glowed with the luster of pearls.

Second, the spiraling pathway did not need any walls. Only mist, curling and shifting, surrounded the stairs. The deeper I went, the more intricate and tangled the fingers of mist became. Sometimes they would twirl around my legs, or the curls of Rhia's hair. Other times they would condense and twist themselves into strange shapes I could not identify.

The mist of this Well reminded me of the mist surrounding Fincayra's shores. Not so much a boundary, or a barrier, as a living substance possessing its own mysterious rhythms and patterns. Elen had often spoken about *in between* places like Mount Olympus, Y Wyddfa, or Fincayra. Places not quite our world and not quite the Otherworld, but truly *in between*. In the same way that this mist was not really air and not really water, but something of both.

And I thought of the day when, on the dirt floor of our hut in Gwynedd, she had described Fincayra to me for the first time. *A place of many wonders*, she had called it. *Neither wholly of Earth nor wholly of Heaven, but a bridge connecting both.*

As I dropped deeper into the mists, drawing nearer to the Otherworld with every step, I wondered what kind of world it might be. If Fincayra were indeed the bridge, where then did the bridge lead? Spirits lived there, I knew that much. Powerful ones, like Dagda and Rhita Gawr. But what of the simpler, quieter spirits, like my brave friend Trouble? Did they share the same terrain, or did they live elsewhere?

Turning endlessly on itself, the spiral stairway led me downward. It struck me that there might be no difference between day and night in this world. Without the sunrise or sunset, or the moon sailing overhead, it would be difficult to tell time. There might not even *be* any time, or what I would call time. I vaguely remembered Elen saying something about two kinds of time: historical time, which runs in a line, where mortal beings march out their lives, and sacred time, which flows in a circle. Could the Otherworld be a place of sacred time? And if so, did that mean that time there turned in on itself, turning in circles like this spiraling stairway?

I stopped, tapping my boot on one of the steps. If there was a different kind of time in this world, I could return to the surface—if I ever did return—too late to save Elen! I might easily spend my two remaining days, and months besides, without even knowing it. I arched my back, lifting Rhia higher on my arms. Her weight, like the weight of my quest, felt heavier than ever.

All I could do was try to find Dagda as soon as possible. Let nothing delay me or throw me off course. I started again down the stairs.

As I followed the Well deeper, something about the mist began to change. Instead of hovering close to the stairs, as it had near the entrance, the mist pulled farther away, opening into pockets of ever-changing shapes. Before long the pockets expanded into chambers, and the chambers widened into hollows. With each step downward the misty vistas broadened, until I found myself in the middle of an immensely varied, constantly shifting landscape.

A landscape of mist.

In wispy traces and billowing hills, wide expanses and sharp pinnacles, the mist swirled about me. At some points I encountered canyons, cutting into the cloudlike terrain, running farther and deeper than I could guess. At other points I glimpsed mountains, towering in the distance, moving higher or lower or both ways at once. I found misty valleys, slopes, cliffs, and caverns. Scattered throughout, though I couldn't be sure, moved shapes, or half shapes, crawling or striding or floating. And through it all, the mist curled and billowed, always changing, always the same.

In time I discovered that the stairs themselves had changed. No longer stiff and solid like stone, they rippled and flowed with everything around me. Although they remained firm enough to stand on, they were made from the same elusive fiber as the landscape.

An uneasy feeling swelled in me. That what surrounded me was not really mist at all. That it was not even something physical, made from air or water, but something . . . else. Made from light, or ideas, or feelings. This mist revealed more than it obscured. It would take many lifetimes to comprehend even a little of its true nature.

So this was what the Otherworld was like! Layers upon layers of shifting, wandering worlds. I could plunge endlessly deeper on the stairs, move endlessly outward among the billows, or travel endlessly inward in the mist itself. Timeless. Limitless. Endless.

Then, out of the flowing landscape, a shape appeared.

XXXII

A GOLDEN
BOUGH

Small and gray, the shape rose aloft from a burgeoning hill. As I watched, it spread two misty wings. It sailed toward me, floating on a current, then suddenly changed direction, climbing so steeply that I almost lost sight of it. Abruptly, it veered and plunged straight downward, until it spun into a series of loops and turns that seemed to have no other purpose than the sheer joy of flight.

Trouble!

My heart leaped to watch the hawk fly again. Although my arms were wrapped around Rhia, I could still feel the leather satchel against my hip. Within it, along with my mother's herbs, rested a banded brown feather from one of Trouble's wings. Nothing more had remained of him after his battle with Rhita Gawr. Nothing, that is, save his spirit.

Out of the billowing mists he came soaring to me. I heard his screech, as full of spunk and vigor as ever. I watched his final flying swoop as he approached. Then, with a rush of warm air, I felt his talons grab hold of my left shoulder. He folded his wings upon his back, prancing up and down my shoulder. Though his misty feathers had changed from brown to silver gray, streaked with white, a touch of yellow still rimmed his eyes. He cocked his head toward me and gave a satisfied chirp.

"Yes, Trouble! I'm happy to see you, too." Then my moment of gladness vanished as I hefted the limp, bloodstained body in my arms. "If only Rhia could, as well."

The hawk fluttered down to the leaf-draped girl's knee. He studied her for a moment, then piped a low, somber whistle. With a shake of his head, he leaped back up to my shoulder.

"I carry her spirit within me, Trouble. I'm hoping that Dagda might still be able to save her." I swallowed. "And also my mother."

Suddenly, Trouble gave a loud shriek. His talons squeezed my shoulder, even as the mist before me billowed strangely.

"Ahhh," said a slow, almost lazy voice from somewhere in the mist. "How nice, how terribly nice, of you to come."

Trouble whistled anxiously.

"Who are you?" I called into the clouds. "Show yourself."

"I intend to do just that, young man, in a moment's time." The mist before me swirled like soup in a gently stirred bowl. "And I also have a gift for you, a terribly precious gift. Ahhh, yes."

Something about the voice's slow, relaxed tones made me feel a bit more at ease. Yet a vague sensation, from someplace within me, made me feel more cautious than ever. Better, I decided, to err on the side of caution.

I adjusted Rhia's weight in my arms. "I haven't time for manners right now. If you have something to give me, then show yourself."

"Ahhh, young man. So impatient, so terribly impatient." The mist churned. "But you needn't worry. I shall heed your request, in just a moment's time. You see, I'd like to be your friend."

At that, Trouble gave a shrill whistle. With a powerful flap of his wings, he lifted off from his perch. He whistled again, circled me once, and flew off, disappearing in a cloud of mist.

"You have no need to fear me," murmured the voice. "Even though your hawk friend certainly seems to."

"Trouble doesn't fear anything."

"Ahhh, then I must be mistaken. Why do you think he flew away?"

I swallowed, peering into the flowing mist. "I don't know. He must have had a good reason." I turned back to the spot from which the voice seemed to come. "If you'd like to be my friend, then show me who you are. Quickly. I need to keep going."

The mist bubbled slowly. "Ahhh, so you have an important meeting, have you?"

"Very."

"Well then, that is what you must do. Ahhh, yes." The voice sounded so relaxed as to be sleepy. "I'm sure you know how to get wherever you're going."

Instead of answering, I searched the billowing mist for Trouble. Where had he gone? We had only just met again! And I'd hoped that he might be able to lead me to Dagda.

"Because if you don't," continued the soothing voice, "my gift may be useful to you. Terribly useful. Ahhh, I offer you the gift of serving as your guide."

That feeling of caution, from whatever source, rose in me again. Yet . . . perhaps this person, when he finally revealed himself, could really show me the way through the swirling clouds. It could save precious time.

I shifted my weight on the misty step. "Before I can accept your offer, I need to know who you are."

"In a moment's time, young man. In a moment's time." The voice yawned, then spoke as gently as the wisps of mist that brushed against my cheek. "Young people are in such a hurry, such a great hurry."

Despite my doubts, something about the voice made me feel increasingly relaxed. Almost . . . comfortable. Or maybe I was just feeling tired. My back ached. I wished I could set Rhia down somewhere. Just for a moment.

"Ahhh, you bear a heavy burden, young man." Another agonizingly slow yawn. "Would you allow me to lighten your load just a little?"

Against my will, I too yawned. "I'm fine, thank you. But if you'd like to guide me to Dagda, I will let you." I caught myself. "First, though, show me who you are."

"To Dagda, is it? Ahhh, the great and glorious Dagda. Warrior of warriors. He lives far, terribly far, from here. Still, I would be pleased to guide you."

I straightened my stiff back. "Can we go now? I'm running out of time."

"Ahhh, in a moment's time." Curling arms of mist swayed before my face. "It's a pity, though, you can't take a little rest. You look as if you could use one."

Still holding Rhia, I crouched down, resting her on my thighs. "I wish I could. But I must get going."

"Whatever you say. Ahhh, yes." The voice gave the longest, sleepiest yawn yet. "We shall leave directly. In a moment's time."

I shook my head, which felt strangely clouded. "Good. Now . . . you were going to do something first. What was it? Oh, yes. Show yourself. Before I follow you."

"Why, of course, young man. I am almost ready." The voice heaved a slow, relaxed sigh. "It will be pleasing, terribly pleasing, to help you."

The feeling of caution nudged me again, but I ignored it. I moved the arm that had supported Rhia's thighs, resting my hand on a damp step. I wondered how it might feel to sit down, if only briefly. Surely a little rest couldn't hurt.

"That's right, young man," purred the voice in its most soothing tone. "Just let yourself relax."

Relax, I thought dreamily. *Just let myself relax.*

"Ahhh, yes." The voice sighed sleepily. "You are a wise young man. So much wiser than your father."

I nodded, feeling half dazed. *My father. Wiser than . . .*

The feeling of caution surged through me. How did he know my father?

I yawned again. Why worry about my father now? He wasn't anywhere near the Otherworld. My head felt foggy, as if the mist surrounding me had somehow flowed into my ears. What was I in such a hurry about, anyway? A little rest would help me remember. Crouching on the stairs, I lowered my head against my chest.

Once again, so weakly that I could barely detect it, the feeling of caution pricked me. *Wake up, Merlin! He's not your friend. Wake up.* I tried to ignore it, but couldn't quite do so. *Trust in your instincts, Merlin.*

I stirred, raising my head slightly. There was something familiar about that feeling, that voice inside me. As if I had heard it somewhere before.

Trust in your instincts, Merlin. Trust in the berries.

With a sudden jolt, I awoke. It was Rhia's voice! Rhia's wisdom! Her spirit was sensing what I was not. I shook the fog from my head.

Taking my hand from the step, I wrapped it tightly around Rhia's legs. With a grunt, I slowly stood up again.

"Ahhh, young man." An edge of concern had crept into the sleepy voice. "I thought you might rest a little while."

Clutching Rhia firmly in my arms, the leaves drying but still soft against my hands, I drew a deep breath. "I am not going to rest. I am not going to let you lull me into enchanted sleep. For I know who you are."

"Ahhh, you do?"

"Yes I do, Rhita Gawr!"

The mist started to froth like a boiling pot. It bubbled and whirled before me. Out of the swirling vapors stepped a man, as tall and broad as Balor, wearing a flowing white tunic and a thin necklace of gleaming red stones. His hair, as black as my own, lay perfectly combed on his head. Even his eyebrows looked exquisitely groomed. It was his eyes, though, that caught my attention. They seemed utterly hollow, as vacant as the void. As much as the memory of Balor's deadly eye made me shudder, these eyes frightened me more.

Rhita Gawr lifted one hand to his lips and licked the tips of his fingers. "I could have taken any number of forms." His voice, harsh and snapping, held none of the lazy tones I had heard before. "The wild boar is one of my favorites, complete with the scarred foreleg. We all carry scars, you know."

He stroked one eyebrow with his wet fingers. "But you have seen the wild boar before, haven't you? Once on the shore of that rock pile you call Gwynedd. And once again, in a dream."

"How . . . " Perspiration formed on my brow as I recalled the dream, and the feeling of daggerlike tusks growing into my very eyes. "How do you know about that?"

"Oh, come now. Surely a would-be sorcerer has learned at least a little about Leaping." He licked his fingertips, as his lips curled in a smirk. "Sending dreams to people is one of my few amusements, a brief distraction from my many labors." The smirk expanded. "Though there is something I enjoy even more. Sending the death shadow."

I tensed, squeezing Rhia's lifeless form. "What gave you the right to strike down my mother?"

Rhita Gawr's vacant eyes fixed on me. "What gave you the right to bring her to Fincayra?"

"I didn't mean . . . "

"A little touch of hubris." He ran his hand over his scalp, patting the hairs into place. "That was your father's fatal flaw, and your grandfather's as well. Did you really expect to be any different?"

I straightened up. "I am different."

"Hubris again! I thought you would have learned by now." The white tunic fluttered as he took a step toward me. "Hubris will bring your death, that is certain. It has already brought your mother's."

I reeled, staggering on the misty step. "That's why you delayed me all this time!"

"But of course." He licked his fingertips with care, one at a time. "And now that you know you have failed to prevent her death—the death that you yourself brought on—I shall relieve you of any further misery. I shall kill you, here and now."

I backed up one step, trying not to stumble.

Rhita Gawr laughed, while he stroked his other eyebrow. "Your hero, Dagda, isn't here to save you this time, as he did on Gwynedd. Nor is that fool bird, whose rashness prevented me from finishing you off at the Shrouded Castle. This time, I have you."

He took another step through the mist toward me. His enormous hands flexed, as if they were preparing to crush my skull. "Just so you know the extent of your folly, your hubris, let me explain something to you. If only you hadn't tried to avoid your lessons, you might know that if only you had worn a mantle of mistletoe, that cursed golden bough, you could have traveled straight to Dagda's lair. I could not have waylaid you as I have."

I blanched, remembering Rhia's plea to take a bough of mistletoe with me to the Otherworld. And I had dismissed her advice out of hand!

Once again Rhita Gawr smirked. Arms of mist, sprouting out of his head, clawed at me. "I do so love arrogance. One of humanity's most endearing qualities."

His hollow eyes narrowed. "So much for your lessons. Now you shall die."

At that instant, a winged shape shot out of the clouds. A screech echoed across the shifting landscape of mist, even as Trouble soared straight at me. Behind him he trailed a loose, flowing bough of gold. Mistletoe. Rhita Gawr roared with rage and leaped at me.

Only a fraction of a second before he could seize me, the golden bough fell over my shoulders like a cape. I felt his powerful hands closing on my throat. Suddenly, I became vapor, dissolving into the mist. The last thing I felt was a pair of talons grasping my shoulder. And the last thing I heard was the wrathful cry of Rhita Gawr.

"You have escaped me once again, you runt of a wizard! You will not be so fortunate next time."

XXXIII

WONDROUS
THINGS

Skin, bone, and muscles dissolved. Instead, I consisted of air, water, and light. Plus something more. For now I belonged to the mist.

Rolling like a cloud of vapor, I stretched my limitless arms before me. As the golden bough of mistletoe propelled me along the hidden pathways to Dagda's home, I swirled and swayed, melting into the air even as I moved beyond it. Through the spiraling tunnels and twisting corridors of mist I flew. And while I couldn't see them, I could sense that Trouble and Rhia, in whatever form, traveled with me.

Too many times to count, I glimpsed other landscapes and creatures within the vapors. Boundless variety seemed to inhabit each and every particle of mist. Worlds within worlds, levels within levels, lives within lives! The Otherworld, in all its vastness and complexity, beckoned.

Yet I had no time now to explore. Elen's life, and Rhia's as well, hung in the balance. I might have lost my chance to help one or both of them, thanks to my own supreme folly. Even so, as Rhia herself had declared when my staff vanished in Slantos, *as long as you still have hope, you still have a chance.* And hope remained with me, though it seemed no more substantial than the shifting clouds.

My thoughts, rolling like the very mist, turned to Dagda. I felt a deep pang of fear at the prospect of facing the greatest of all the spirits. While I expected that he would judge me harshly for my many mistakes, would he also refuse to help? Perhaps saving my mother's life would disturb some delicate cosmic balance that only he understood. Perhaps he would simply not have time to see me. Perhaps he would not be in his realm at all when I arrived, and instead be somewhere far away, in this misty world or another, battling the forces of Rhita Gawr.

I wondered what so powerful a spirit would look like. Surely, like Rhita Gawr, he could assume any form he chose. When he had appeared on the day I washed ashore on the coast of Gwynedd, he had come as a stag. Immense, powerful, with a great rack of antlers. What had struck me the most, though, were his eyes. Those brown, unblinking pools had seemed as deep and mysterious as the ocean itself.

Whatever form he might take, I knew it would be as strong and imposing as Dagda himself. A stag in human form, perhaps. What had Rhita Gawr called him? *The great and glorious Dagda. Warrior of warriors.*

Like a cloud flowing into a hollow in the hills, my forward motion slowed, little by little, until finally it stopped. Then, imperceptibly at first, the mist around me started to dissipate. Slowly, very slowly, it thinned and shredded, pulling apart like a wispy veil. Gradually, I could discern the outline of a tall, towering form behind the veil. Dark and brooding, it hovered before me.

All at once, the remaining mist melted away. The towering form, I realized, was actually an enormous, dew-coated tree. As tall and mighty as Arbassa it stood, with one prominent difference.

This tree stood upside down. Its massive roots reached upward, disappearing into the tangled threads of mist. They curled majestically around the clouds, as if they embraced the entire world above. From these soaring roots hung countless boughs of golden mistletoe, swaying gracefully. Down below, at the base of the trunk, burly branches stretched across a wide plain of steaming mist. And the entire tree, covered with thousands upon thousands of dewdrops, sparkled like the surface of a dancing stream.

So captivated was I by the sight of the tree that it took me a moment to realize that I, too, stood on the misty plain. My body had returned! Rhia slumped in my arms, while Trouble made soft, gurgling sounds in my ear. A bough of mistletoe, just like the ones dangling above me, draped over my shoulders. My sword hung at my side, while the staff still rode under my belt.

I looked into Trouble's yellow-rimmed eyes. "Thanks, my friend. You saved me once again."

The hawk released a high, almost embarrassed whistle and fluttered his gray wings.

"Welcome to the Tree of Soul."

I spun to face the source of the weak, unsteady voice. It came from a frail, old man, whose right arm dangled uselessly at his side. Although he sat on the floor of mist, leaning against the branches, he was so small and slight that I had not noticed him at all before. His silver hair glistened like the dew-covered bark around him.

"Thank you. Very much." I spoke stiffly, not wanting to be fooled again. Still, with time so scarce, I had no choice but to be direct. "I am looking for Dagda."

Trouble's talons pinched my shoulder. He squawked at me reproachfully.

The old man smiled gently, soft lines crinkling his face. Laying his withered arm across his lap, he studied me intently.

Suddenly I noticed his eyes. Deep, brown pools, full of compassion, wisdom, and sadness. I had seen them before. On the great stag.

"Dagda." I bit my lip, gazing at the frail, little man. "I am sorry I didn't recognize you."

The elder's smile faded. "You did, in time. Just as you may, in time, come to know the true source of my power. Or do you already?"

I hesitated, unsure how to respond. "I know nothing, I'm afraid, about your power's true source. But I believe that you use it to help living things take their own course, whatever that may be. That's why you helped me on the day I washed ashore."

"Very good, Merlin, very good." His brown eyes sparkled with satisfaction—and a touch of annoyance. "Even if you did try to avoid one of the Songs."

I shifted uncomfortably.

He examined me, as if he could see into my deepest heart of hearts. "You carry a great load, in addition to the friend in your arms. Here. Lay her down beside me."

"Can you—can you help her?"

"We shall see." His brow, already webbed with wrinkles, creased some more. "Tell me of the Songs, Merlin. Where does the soul of each lie?"

"And my mother? If she has any time left, it isn't much."

"She, too, must wait."

Stooping on the vaporous ground, I gently laid the body of my sister beside Dagda. Curls of mist flowed over her shoulders and across her chest, covering her like a wispy blanket. He glanced at her, looking profoundly sad, then returned his gaze to me.

"First. Show me your staff."

Trouble clucked with admiration as I drew the staff out of my belt. I held the knotted top toward Dagda, twirling the shaft slowly. All of the markings, as deep blue as the dusk, gleamed before us. The butterfly, symbol of transformation. The pair of hawks, bound together in flight. The cracked stone, reminding me of the folly of trying to cage the light flyer. The sword, whose name I knew well. The star inside a circle, calling back the luminous laughter of Gwri of the Golden Hair. The dragon's tail, which somehow reminded my tongue of the taste of soiled leather. And, last of all, the eye, so different from Balor's, yet in its own way just as terrifying.

Dagda nodded. "You carry a sword now, I see."

I patted the silver hilt.

"Guard it well, for the destiny of that sword is to serve you until the time comes for you to place it into a scabbard of stone. Then it shall pass to a boy, no older than you are now. A boy born to be king, whose reign shall thrive in the heart long after it has withered on the land."

"I will guard it well."

"Tell me now, my son. What melodies have you heard within the Seven Songs? Start with the first one, Changing."

I cleared my throat. "I learned from a butterfly—and from a traitor, a treeling, who redeemed herself—that all of us, all living things, have the potential to change."

The old man studied me intently. "It is no accident that this was your first Song, Merlin. I believe you have been hearing its strains for some time."

"Yes." I looked into the dewy boughs for a moment. "I see now why the Greek words for butterfly and soul are the same."

"Good. Now tell me about Binding."

I glanced at Rhia's face, pale and still. "The strongest bonds are of the heart. I learned it from watching a pair of hawks soaring together."

Trouble pranced proudly across my shoulder, preening his wings.

"And from a trickster, perhaps?"

I sighed. "That, too."

A shred of mist passed over Dagda's left hand. With a deft twirl of his fingers, he wove the mist into a complex knot. Then, with a pensive nod, he let it drift away.

His gaze returned to me. "Next you found your way into the underground realm of my old friend Urnalda. She is wiser than she appears, I can assure you! No doubt she enjoyed the chance to be your teacher."

I shook my head. "I'm not sure how much. I was a rather slow learner. Eventually, though, with the help of a light flyer, I finally found the soul of that Song."

"Which is?"

I pointed to the image of the cracked stone. "The best way to protect something is to set it free."

Dagda leaned back, gazing upward into the burly roots of the Tree of Soul. As he raised an eyebrow, a curl of mist spiraled up the trunk. "The next lesson, I believe, came as a surprise for you."

"Naming. It took awhile—and a broken bread knife—to teach me that a true name holds true power." I paused, thinking. "Is my true name Merlin?"

The elder shook his silvery head.

"Then would you, perhaps, know my true name?"

"I know it."

"Would you tell me?"

Dagda considered my request for a while. "No. Not yet. But I will do this. If we should meet again at a happier time, when you have won over the most powerful enemy of all, then I will tell you your true name."

I blanched. "The most powerful enemy of all? You must mean Rhita Gawr."

"Perhaps." He pointed to the star within a circle. "Now Leaping."

"That's an amazing skill. The Grand Elusa used it to send us all the way to the land of the treelings. Gwri of the Golden Hair used it, too—to give Rhia a vision of the Otherworld Well." My voice lowered. "And Rhita Gawr used it to send the death shadow to my mother."

The silver eyebrows lifted. "To your mother?"

My boots shifted uneasily on the misty ground. "Well, no. To me. But it felled my mother instead."

"So what is the soul of the art of Leaping?"

My attention turned to the flowing mist that surrounded us. Gracefully, it wound its way around Dagda and myself, touching both of us as it touched the upside-down tree, embracing the great roots that themselves embraced the world above. "Everything," I declared, "is connected to everything else."

"Good, my son, good. Now what of Eliminating?"

"That one I learned from a sleeping dragon. And from . . . a jester." I grinned slightly. "They showed me that every living thing is precious somehow."

Dagda leaned toward me. "Even a dragon?"

"Even a dragon."

He stroked his chin thoughtfully. "You will meet that dragon again, I believe. When it awakens."

I caught my breath. Before I could ask anything, however, he spoke again.

"Seeing. Tell me, now, about Seeing."

My tongue worked against my cheek before any words came. At last, in a voice not much louder than a whisper, I said, "The heart can see things invisible to the eye."

"Hmmm. What else?"

I thought for a moment. "Well, now that I know a little about seeing with the heart, I can, perhaps, see better into myself."

Dagda's deep brown eyes regarded me. "And when you look into that place, my son, what do you see?"

I cleared my throat, started to speak, then stopped myself. Searching for the right words, I paused before starting again. "It's . . . well, it's like going down into the Otherworld Well. The deeper I go, the more I discover." Turning away, I said under my breath, "And what I discover can be truly frightening."

The old man watched me with compassion. "What else do you see?"

I heaved a sigh. "How little I really do know."

Dagda reached toward me, taking my hand in his own. "Then, Merlin, you have learned something invaluable." He drew me nearer on the floor of mist. Shreds of vapor curled about us both. "Truly invaluable! Until now, you have been searching for the souls of the

Songs. But knowing how little you really know—having humility—that, my son, is the soul of wizardry itself."

Puzzled, I cocked my head.

"In time, I believe, you will fully understand. For humility is nothing more than genuine respect for the wondrous, surprising ways of the world."

Slowly, I nodded. "That sounds like something Rhia would say." Looking again at her lifeless form, I asked anxiously, "Can you still save her?"

Dagda gave no answer.

"Can you?"

For an extended moment, he watched me in silence. "I know not, my son."

My throat constricted as if Balor still held me in his grasp. "I've been such a fool! I've caused so much harm."

Dagda pointed a finger at a rolling ribbon of mist, which instantly straightened. At the same time, he glanced at another wispy line, which suddenly changed into a tight little ball. Then, turning back to me, he smiled sadly. "So you have come to see both the dark and the light within yourself. The dragon as well as the star. The serpent as well as the dove."

I swallowed. "When you first greeted me, you said I might come to know the true source of your power. Well, I'm not sure, but I think your power is quieter, subtler than other kinds. It is guided by your head and your hand, but it springs from your heart. Really, your power is about the seventh Song. Seeing not with the eyes, but with the heart."

His eyebrows lifted ever so slightly.

"There was a time," I continued, my voice a mere whisper, "when

I would have given anything to see again with my own eyes. I still want to see that way again. Very much. But now I know there are other ways to see."

Lightly, Dagda squeezed my hand. "You see well, Merlin."

He released his grip, then observed me for a long moment. "And I will tell you this. As much pain as you have known and are yet to know, wondrous things await you, young man. Truly wondrous things."

XXXIV

ELIXIR

Dagda's deep eyes turned to the trunk of the tree, sparkling with diamonds of dew. He followed the column higher and higher, to the gnarled roots that melted into the mist far above. His gaze lingered there momentarily, as if he could see through the mist into the lands beyond. At last he spoke. "Now for your friend, bound to you by love as well as by blood."

He reached for Rhia, lying on the vaporous ground, with his un-injured arm. She seemed so still, so silent, the color drained from her skin as well as her garb of leaves. My stomach churned in anguish, for I suspected that her body had grown too cold for even the great-est of the spirits to revive. Hadn't Gwri told me that Dagda, for all his power, could not bring back to life someone who had died?

Ever so gently, he lifted her limp hand, closing his eyes as he did so. He seemed to be listening for something far away. Then, with-out opening his eyes, he gave me a command. "You may release her, Merlin."

I hesitated, suddenly fearing that this would surely mean her death. Once her spirit had left me, once it had flown, I could never hope to see her live again. As much as I yearned to hear her laugh again, still more I feared that by letting her go I would lose her forever.

"Merlin," repeated Dagda. "It is time."

At last, I released her. Deep within, I could feel her spirit stirring subtly. Then it began to flow out of me, at first like a trickle of water, gathering strength, until finally it felt like a river bursting through a dam. My sightless eyes brimmed with tears, for I knew that whether or not Rhia survived in mortal form, she and I would never be so utterly close again.

Slowly, very slowly, I exhaled. Shreds of mist knitted themselves in the air between us, creating a shimmering bridge linking my chest and hers. The bridge hovered, glowing, for barely an instant, before fading away completely.

Just then I noticed the gash on the side of her head. It started closing, healing from within. As the skin pulled together, the bloodstains, now more brown than red, evaporated from her curly hair, her neck, and her suit of woven vines. Color began to flow into her cheeks. Her garb softened, as the green vitality returned to every leaf and stem.

Rhia's forefinger trembled. Her neck straightened. Then, at last, her gray-blue eyes opened, along with Dagda's. Gazing up into the roots draped with mistletoe, she drew a halting breath of her own. Turning her face toward Dagda, she smiled, even as she burst into speech. "You live with a tree, just like I do!"

Her bell-like laughter rang out. I joined her, while Dagda erupted with a full, resonant laugh of his own. As he shook with mirth, the great tree, too, began to sway on the misty plain. Droplets of dew fell from above, spinning and shining in the air. Even Trouble, perched on my shoulder, piped a joyous whistle. It seemed to me that the universe itself had joined in our laughter.

Her eyes alight, Rhia sat up and swung her head toward me. "Merlin, you did it. You saved me."

"No. Dagda saved you."

"Not without your help, young man." The elder pushed a few silver hairs off his brow. "By holding so lovingly her spirit as well as her body, you kept her from truly dying, long enough that I could still revive her."

His gaze moved to Rhia. "And you helped, too."

"I did?"

The old man nodded slowly. "Your spirit is a radiant one, Rhiannon. Exceptionally radiant. You possess a force of life that is as powerful as the one I placed in one of the Treasures of Fincayra, the Orb of Fire."

Rhia's cheeks flushed.

I recalled the glittering orange sphere that I had rescued from the ruins of the Shrouded Castle. "It has something to do with healing, doesn't it?"

"Healing, yes. But of the soul, not the body. For the Orb of Fire, in the hands of someone wise, can rekindle hope and joy, even the will to live."

Dagda turned to me. "You, Merlin, know more than anyone how bright the spirit of your sister shines."

I realized that I could still feel, deep within me, a touch of Rhia's spirit. A bit of my sister had remained with me. And, I knew, always would.

"Yes," declared the frail, silver-haired man. "Your training as a wizard has only begun. Yet embracing the wisdom, as well as the spirit, of your sister has been part of it. An important part."

"My eighth Song, you could say."

"Yes."

I looked at Rhia. "Aylah tried to tell me, but I didn't understand. Now, though, I think I have a glimmer."

She touched her amulet. "Or you could say . . . an instinct."

Trouble made a clucking sound that resembled a laugh.

Passing my hand through the mist rising from beneath us, I searched the face of Dagda. "I have an instinct that Fincayra is my true home. And yet . . . I have another instinct that it's not. Which one is right?"

The old man gave a sad smile. "Ah, you are learning! Just as true love often melds both joy and grief, true instinct often mixes contrary feelings. In this case, though, I can help you. Humans are not meant to live long on Fincayra. As much as you have come to feel at home there, you must one day return to Earth. You may stay a while longer, for you still have work left to do, but ultimately you must leave."

I bit my lip. "Can't you just allow me to stay?"

Compassion in his eyes, Dagda shook his head. "I could, but I will not. The worlds must remain apart, for each has its own fabric, its own spirit, that must be honored." He sighed gravely. "That is why I am forced to wrestle with Rhita Gawr on so many fronts. He would pull apart the fabrics of Otherworld, Earth, and Fincayra—in order to weave them into his own twisted design. He wants only to rule them all, as his kingdom."

"Is that why the Fincayrans lost their wings?" asked Rhia, glancing at the swirling clouds. "They forgot how to honor the fabric?"

"Your instincts are indeed strong, Rhiannon. You are on the right track, but the rest you must discover for yourself."

"Dagda, may I ask you something?" I hesitated, searching for the right words. "There's a prophecy. It says that only a child of human blood can defeat Rhita Gawr or his servants. Is that true? And if it is, is the human child one of us?"

The elder ran his hand over a sprig of mistletoe hanging nearby. "Though I cannot tell you all you wish to know, I can say this. The prophecy carries much weight. Yet while it was your sister who vanquished Balor, the only person who can stop Rhita Gawr in Fincayra is you."

I tried to swallow, but my throat had tightened again. Suddenly I remembered the death shadow, plunging down the throat of Elen. When I spoke, it was in a whisper. "If I must die fighting Rhita Gawr, you must tell me this. Is there any way—any way at all—that our mother can still live?"

Rhia turned anxiously from me to Dagda. Trouble paced across my shoulder, fluttering his wings.

The old man drew a long breath. "You still have time, though not much. Only a few hours remain before the moon's fourth quarter expires. And when it does, so will your mother."

"The Elixir," I pleaded. "Can you give it to us?"

Dagda reached down to a burly branch. Carefully, he touched one of the dewdrops with the end of his finger. As it came free, it covered his fingertip with a thin, glistening cup. Using his other fingers, he removed the cup. It sat upright in the palm of his hand, like a tiny, crystalline vial.

He winced slightly. At the same instant, the little vial filled with a single drop of red fluid. Dagda's own blood. When the vial brimmed full, its mouth sealed tight.

"There now." He spoke thickly, as if he had been weakened by his act. Quivering slightly, he handed the vial to me. "Take it."

Even as I opened my leather pouch and placed the Elixir inside, I felt Trouble's talons digging into my shoulder. The hawk nuzzled his soft feathers against my neck.

Dagda knew my question before I could ask. "No, Merlin, he cannot join you. Your friend Trouble gave his mortal life at the Shrouded Castle to spare yours. He belongs here now."

The hawk whistled faintly. As the mist billowed around us, the gaze from his yellow-rimmed eyes met my own. We looked at each other for the last time.

"I'll miss you, Trouble."

The bird nuzzled my neck again, then slowly moved away.

Dagda's expression, too, showed pain. "It may not lighten your heart now, Merlin, but I believe that one day, in another land, you will feel the grip of a different bird's talons on your shoulder."

"I don't want a different bird."

"I understand." The elder stretched his one able hand toward me, brushing my cheek. "You must take separate paths now, I am afraid. Though no one knows all the turns those paths may take."

"Not even you?"

"Not even me." Dagda lifted the mantle of mistletoe from my shoulder. "Go now, my children, and be brave."

Trouble's final screech sounded in my ear, even as the swirling mist swept over me like a wave, swallowing everything.

XXXV

A WIZARD'S STAFF

The flash faded into darkness. The only light came from the sprinkling of stars overhead. I found myself still kneeling, with Rhia still sitting by my side. Yet jagged rocks and steep cliffs replaced the steaming mist; a circle of polished stones replaced the Tree of Soul. Not far away, the corpse of a huge warrior lay still and silent.

I took Rhia's hand. "We're back at the Well."

"Too true, too true, too true." The hunched figure of Bumbelwy approached in the near-darkness. "I never thought you'd return. And I see you've brought back the body of—"

"Rhia," she interrupted. "Alive and well."

Bumbelwy froze midstep. Even in the dim light, I could see his eyes grow wider. Then, for a brief instant, his mouth and multiple chins turned upward ever so slightly. It lasted only a fraction of a second. Yet I felt certain that he had actually smiled.

I turned my gaze toward the sky, searching for any sign at all of the moon. Yet I could find nothing. Nothing at all. I bit my lip. If only I hadn't wasted those precious minutes with Rhita Gawr.

Rhia suddenly pointed to a faint glimmer of light that had just emerged from behind a cloud. "Oh, Merlin! That's all that's left of the moon. It will be gone before dawn!"

I leaped to my feet. "So will our mother, unless we can get to her first."

"But how?" Rhia stood, facing the southern sky. "Arbassa is so far away."

As if in answer, the entire ridge shook with a sudden tremor. Then came another, still stronger. Another. Another. Rocks tumbled down from the cliffs on both sides of us. I pulled my walking stick out of my belt and leaned on it for balance. Then my second sight perceived a new shape rising on the horizon. Like a swiftly growing hill, it blocked out the stars behind. Yet I knew at once that this was no hill.

"Shim!" I shouted. "We're over here!"

A moment later, the giant's immense form towered above the three of us. As his feet crushed against the loose rocks, he lowered a great hand. Quickly, Rhia and I climbed into his palm, followed reluctantly by Bumbelwy.

Beneath his bulbous nose, Shim grinned crookedly. "I is gladly to sees you."

"Seize us," moaned Bumbelwy, his hands wringing his cape. "He's come to seize us."

"And we're glad to see you!" I replied, ignoring the jester.

"How did you know we needed you?" asked Rhia. "And where to find us?"

Shim lifted his hand as he straightened himself. Though I tried to keep on my feet, I tumbled into the fleshy palm, barely missing the huddled form of Bumbelwy. Rhia, for her part, sat down beside us with the grace of a landing swan.

"I is asleepily, dreamings of . . . " The giant paused, pursing his enormous lips. "I can't remembers! Anyways, the dream changes into a bird. A hawk, like the one who once rides on your shoulder, except he is all whitely gray instead of brown."

I cringed. I could feel the old pain between my shoulder blades, and another one besides.

"Then this hawk screeches at me, so loudly I wakes up." Shim scrunched his nose. "With the powerfully feeling that I needs to find you! And, most strangestly, a picture in my mind of where to go."

Rhia smiled. "Your dream was sent by Dagda."

The giant's bushy eyebrows lifted.

"You are a loyal friend, Shim! Now take us to Arbassa." I glanced at the trace of the remaining moon. It seemed even fainter than just a moment before.

A bracing wind swept over us, blowing against my tunic as if it were a sail, as Shim turned and started lumbering back across the hills of the Lost Lands. In three or four strides he scaled slopes that had taken us hours to climb, his hairy feet crunching on the rubble. No sooner had he reached a valley floor than he had nearly gained the next ridge. In minutes, a hint of smoke scented the air and I knew we had reached the hollow of the sleeping dragon.

As Shim veered south to cross the channel, sea fog swirled around us. His pink eyes gleamed. "Didn't I tells you I hopes to make another crossing with you one daily?" His laughter rolled across the waves that slapped against his legs. "Certainly, definitely, absolutely!"

Yet none of us joined in his mirth. Bumbelwy hugged his belly, muttering about the demise of a great jester. Rhia and I, meanwhile, studied the night sky, trying to keep track of the swiftly fading moon.

By the sounds and smells that moved through the darkness, as well as the shifts in Shim's strides, I could sense some of the changes in terrain. After emerging from the channel, he marched over the rising coastal plane and swiftly mounted the hills. Soon his steps shortened as the grade steepened. We moved higher into the snowy ridges near the city of Varigal. At one point I thought I heard deep voices chanting in the distance, though the sound quickly died away.

The alpine air grew misty and damp as we descended into a maze of hills and swamps. Somewhere near, I knew, lay the crystal cave of the Grand Elusa. Was the great spider there herself, curled up among the Treasures of Fincayra? Or was she out prowling for wraiths and goblins to satisfy her limitless appetite?

The crashing and snapping of limbs below announced our entry into Druma Wood. Rich, resiny smells tickled my nostrils. Immense shadows, some nearly as tall as the giant who bore us, pushed skyward. I couldn't help but recall Shim's ardent wish that he had confided in me so long ago. *To be big, as big as the highlyest tree.*

His wish had been granted, to be sure. Sitting in the great palm, I stared all the harder at the dying moon, glimmering high above us. And I felt increasingly sure that my own deepest wish would not be granted.

Just when I began to wonder whether I could still detect the moon at all, or whether I was only imagining its pale glow, a new shadow loomed before us. Taller and fuller than the rest, it stood with all the grandeur of Dagda's Tree of Soul. Here, at last, rose Arbassa. In its immense branches, glowing like a star, sat the aerial cottage that held Elen of the Sapphire Eyes.

Shim bent low, placing his hand on the oak tree's burly roots. I grabbed my staff and leaped to the ground, followed closely by Rhia and a stumbling Bumbelwy. With a shout of thanks, I turned to Arbassa, hoping that this time the tree would not resist allowing me to enter.

At that instant the enormous trunk made a low, grinding sound. The bark creased, cracked, and opened. I plunged through the doorway. Taking the stairs two at a time, I bounded upward, not even bothering to glance at the runes carved on the walls. As I burst through the curtain of leaves at the top of the stairwell, Ixtma, the large-eyed squirrel, shrieked. He whirled around, dropping a bowl of water on the floor. Then, seeing Rhia come in just behind me, he scampered over to her, chattering noisily.

Elen, her eyes closed, lay on the floor just where we had left her. The same pine-scented pillow supported her head, while the same shimmering blanket covered her chest. Yet, as I set down my staff and knelt by her side, I could tell that much had changed. Her once-creamy cheeks looked whiter than dried bones; her brow showed the furrows of prolonged suffering. She seemed much thinner, as wispy as the vanishing moon. I lay my head upon her chest, hoping to hear the beating of her heart, but heard nothing. I touched her cracked lips, hoping to feel the slightest breath of air, but felt nothing.

Rhia crouched beside me, her face nearly as pale as our mother's. She watched, motionless, as I reached into my satchel and removed the vial containing the Elixir. Touched by the light from the hearth, it flashed with brilliant red, the color of Dagda's own blood. The whole room flooded with scarlet hues.

Barely able to breathe myself, I dropped the Elixir into my mother's mouth. *Please, Dagda, I beg of you. Don't let it be too late. Don't let her die.*

I barely noticed when Ixtma whimpered, wrapping his bushy tail around Rhia's leg. Or when Bumbelwy entered the room, shaking his head morosely. Or when the first faint rays of dawn touched the leaves draping the eastern windows. Yet I noticed with every particle of my being when my mother opened her eyes.

Seeing Rhia and me, she cried out in surprise. Rosy hues flared in her cheeks. Drawing a tentative breath, she weakly lifted a hand toward each of us. We clasped her hands in our own, squeezing the living flesh. Tears brimmed in my eyes, while Rhia sobbed quietly.

"My children."

Rhia smiled through her tears. "We're here now . . . Mother."

Elen's brow creased slightly. "Forgive me, child, for not telling you before you left. I thought that, if I died, your pain would be too great."

"You didn't have to tell me." Rhia touched the amulet of oak, ash, and thorn upon her chest. "I already knew."

I nudged her and grinned. "Whatever this girl knows about instincts, she learned from me."

We laughed, mother and daughter and son, as if all our years of separation had never occurred. For even if someday hence we might be forced to part again, right now a single, unalterable truth filled our hearts. On this dawning day, in the boughs of this great tree, we sat together. Reunited at last.

Only after much more laughter and much more talk did we pause to eat a hearty breakfast of Ixtma's honey-soaked nuts and rosemary tea with plenty of mint. And only after my fifth helping did I catch sight of the glittering object resting by the hearth. The Flowering Harp, its magical strings aglow, leaned against the wall of living wood. Suddenly I caught my breath. Behind the Harp, several more objects lay stacked. Staring at them with amazement, I licked the honey from my fingers, pushed myself up from the floor, and stepped closer.

I couldn't believe it, yet I knew it was true. All of the Treasures of Fincayra were here! Right here in Rhia's cottage.

There, gleaming darkly, sat the Caller of Dreams, the graceful horn that Cairpré had once told me could stir any dream into life. Beside it rested the double-edged sword Deepercut. When I reached to touch its hilt, the powerful blade hanging on my belt rang softly, reminding me that my sword, too, had been wrought to fulfill a remarkable destiny. Next to the twining branches of the wall rested the fabled plow that could till its own field. Beside it stood the hoe that nurtures its own seeds, the saw that cuts only as much wood as is needed, and the rest of the Wise Tools, except of course the one that had been lost. I wondered, for an instant, what sort of tool it was— and where it might be now. Then my attention turned to the last of the objects, the Orb of Fire. The orange sphere glowed like a radiant torch. Or, as Dagda had said, like a radiant spirit.

"The Treasures," I said aloud, unable to turn away from them.

Rhia, who had silently joined me, took my arm. "Ixtma told me the Grand Elusa brought them here, not long before we arrived." Hearing the squirrel chatter angrily, she grinned. "He reminds me that she only brought them to the clearing outside Arbassa. Since she was far too big to carry them inside herself, she asked—well, commanded—Ixtma and his family to do the rest."

Perplexed, I ran my finger over the Harp's oaken sound box. "Dagda must have sent the Grand Elusa a message, as he did Shim.

But why? The Treasures were safe enough where they were, in her crystal cave. She had agreed to guard them for all time."

"Not for all time. Only until she could find someone wise enough to choose the right guardians to take care of them. The Treasures, before Stangmar, belonged to all Fincayrans. The Grand Elusa believes it should be that way again. And I agree."

More confused than ever, I shook my head. "But who is wise enough to choose the guardians? Surely the Grand Elusa herself could do that better than anyone else."

Rhia observed me thoughtfully. "That's not what she thinks."

"You don't mean . . . "

"Yes, Merlin. She wants you to do it. As she told Ixtma, *The isle of Fincayra holds a wizard once more.*"

I swallowed, glancing again at the objects stacked by the wall. Each of them, regardless of shape or size or materials, possessed a magic that could enrich all the inhabitants of Fincayra.

Rhia grinned at me. "So what are you going to do?"

"I really don't know."

"You must have some ideas."

Bending down to the floor, I retrieved my staff. A wizard's staff. "Well . . . I think the Caller of Dreams should go to Cairpré, wisest of the bards." I indicated Bumbelwy, still stuffing himself with nuts and honey. "And I think a certain humorless jester deserves the honor of delivering it to him."

Her grin broadened into a smile.

Warming to my task, I grasped the handle of the plow that tills its own field. "I'm not sure just yet about most of the Wise Tools. But this plow is different. I know a man named Honn who will use it well. And share it gladly."

Then I bent to retrieve the glowing Orb of Fire. I hefted it, feeling its pulsing warmth. Without a word, I handed it to Rhia, whose leafy garb danced with the orange light.

Surprise filled her face. "For me?"

"For you."

She started to protest, but I spoke first. "Remember what Dagda told us? The Orb of Fire can rekindle hope, joy, and even the will to live. It belongs in the care of someone whose spirit shines as bright as it does."

Her eyes glistened as she studied the sphere. "You've given me something even more precious than this."

For a long moment, we held each other's gaze. At last, she pointed to the Flowering Harp. "Now what about that?"

I grinned. "I think it ought to go to two people with a garden. A garden that flourished even in the middle of the Rusted Plains, when everything around it lay dying."

"T'eilean and Garlatha?"

I nodded. "And this time, when I carry the Harp to their home, I'll expect nothing more than to be welcomed as their friend." Again I touched the oaken sound box. "First, though, I will take the Harp myself for a while. I have some unfinished work to do in the Dark Hills."

As she lifted her gaze to Arbassa's arching boughs, Rhia's face glowed. "Well, as it happens, so do I."

"Really?" I raised an eyebrow. "What work do you have there?"

"Guiding. I have a brother, you see, who gets lost easily."